Never Home

The Otherness of Immigrants

Norma Armon

Table of Contents

Dedication

To displaced persons who become immigrants: may your dream of belonging come true.

Prologue

So, you want to hear the family lore: you keep asking where our ancestors came from, why they left their birthplace, and how they ended up where they did. You get that from your mother who, years ago, also begged to hear our stories. One day, if I keep up writing, you'll learn about your grandparents' and their parent's adventures; to glean who they were through their memorable actions; to better understand what made them tick by listening to their tales and what they lived through.

The massive, weather-beaten, locked-up trunk kept in one of the empty rooms next to the garage at the back of the house at Campeones #37, fascinated your mother. Whenever I spring-cleaned, she hovered around hoping I'd let her look inside the once-black trunk I dusted carefully: maybe she could talk me into telling an anecdote prompted by the sepia photographs and yellowing letters with the thin, black, spidery handwriting it contained.

You've interviewed me and asked myriad questions so as to clarify relationships and family connections. You've done it gingerly, without emphasis, almost off-handedly, afraid to show too much interest, hoping to delay my inevitable "Why do you want to hear such *bobe maises*?"[1] when you pressed too much.

Because you never came up with a good enough reply, my question cut off the conversation. Now I can tell you the answer: so those who come after us can know; to recognize the elder from whom that particular character trait derived or understand the source of a peculiar emotional tic. To identify roots and connect to the past.

Don't be disappointed if others in the family dismiss these stories. I expect that every character in the cast will have an objection to some part of it. Unconditional love is an ideal that most of us do not easily achieve. And having one's "dirty laundry hung in public" is never pleasant. But, no story is worth telling unless the characters are true to life, warts and all.

I've always been reluctant to speak about the past, leading everyone to think the topic was almost forbidden. Although the Torah commands "Recall the days of old, consider the years of many generations: ask thy elders, and they will tell thee." (Deut. 32-7), your grandfather and I chose not to. We ignored *l'dor va dor* – the biblical injunction to maintain a link from one generation to the next.

When I die, you'll inherit those photo albums and can become the custodian of our past. The albums contain pictures that have often served to prompt my memories. They were all I saved in the fire that destroyed my home.

To tell is one thing, to commit to paper is another. I haven't been very successful at it. I've been piecing together scraps of notes with anecdotes grudgingly surrendered by some of the protagonists, years after the events took place. Those tidbits were

---

[1] This book contains several words and phrases that are in Yiddish. A glossary of terms can be found at the end of the book.

but kernels of the tales. I'm trying to weave them together into a novel that flows.

Clearly, even the "facts" come through each narrator's prism, colored by emotion, selected to make their point, to meet a particular agenda. After all, much of what I've gathered is based on siblings assessing siblings, and you know how hairy that can be. Certainly, some of their judgments are biased, and of course, there will be unwitting distortions of my own. Keep in mind that some of the stories are based on hearsay, pieced together through deduction and conjecture, and many are inconclusive.

It's taken much of my life to become willing to share my past, particularly with family. I didn't want anyone to know my failings: the many times I dodged being caught flaunting rules or regulations or avoided showing love to my dear ones. Most of the time, I didn't have empathy for others' lesser capabilities or fewer advantages to deal with the ups and downs of life. Decades of experiences have served as a process of healing. I never thought I could love you or my children so much or just enjoy playing with Rover in the yard or delight in inviting everyone in our extended family to come here to celebrate holidays and reunions.

Life didn't use to be this way. I was much more driven when I was young, proud to be considered a never-satisfied, unbending taskmaster. My purpose in life was to be a truthteller, no matter how hurtful; to be perceived by others as the model of meeting goals I set; and above all, to have those around me meet those goals even when they wouldn't or couldn't. My expectations allowed me no understanding of human nature or the ability to enjoy the learning derived from being supportive instead of dismissive, the pleasure of giving and receiving. I am forever grateful for the lessons derived and for being older yet happier, healthier, surrounded by people I admire and love, and feeling loved as well.

I'm the only one who can pass these stories on, and I'm beginning to forget them. They should be made available to the next generation, and inspire you to become the keeper of memories for those who come after. Our ancestors bequeath us our past; without it, we belong to no one.

G. G.

New York
1978

BREADWINNER

Krasnoe

1.

In the fading afternoon light, Binyamin Gesheftman strained to make out the Hebrew characters in the musty book. Behind the glasses, his brown eyes narrowed to discern the dots and slashes on the page. He intoned the passages he had to memorize, pondering on the significance of his impending *bar mitzvah*. *Baruch ata Adonai, Eloheinu melech ha olam…*Binyamin shuddered; once those blessings were uttered, he'd be bound to the commandments, now held accountable before God and counted one of the *minyan*. Binyamin cringed. It was an awesome responsibility, indeed!

Earlier in the day, the crack that rippled along the ceiling allowed in a shaft of light; by now, with the sun sinking into the horizon, the central room of the tiny house was almost dark. Binyamin hesitated before lighting the candle. He got one a week on Shabbat and it had only been two days ago. He remained seated in the now dark corner; hugged by dusky shadows that helped conceal him from his siblings. Although slight of build, Binyamin was quick and sometimes able to evade corpulent Menashe's physical attacks. With his sharp wit, he easily parried Esther's and Raisl's taunts. However, Binyamin preferred to avoid conflict altogether. He thought fighting was a waste of time, so he hid to avoid his tormentors.

Tatte was his sole ally in the household, providing the only encouragement he received. Binyamin remembered watching Yosef sternly hush the others and place a candle next to him, saying, "Leave the boy alone, he's done his chores, let him read in peace."

Menashe had become the oldest male child when Isaiah, the firstborn, was killed. Isaiah had been drafted into the Tzar's army during the build-up after the Russo-Japanese War. Menashe wielded the rights of the eldest imperiously. Just 13 with the defiant attitude of one much older, the short, stocky youth demanded—and received—what few advantages were available in the Gesheftman household. Right after his *bar mitzvah*, Menashe was apprenticed to Shuster, the village shoemaker. A year later, Yosef brought from Vinnytsia a machine to cut the holes to thread the shoelaces.

Soon, Menashe had his own thriving business making shoe toppers for Shuster. Hearing the *ping* and *thwap* of the hole puncher brought visions of clinking coins to Binyamin's mind. His was the personality of an entrepreneur who chafed at having to follow anyone's orders. Binyamin raged inwardly at the order of birth succession which kept him from being the boss.

Once Yosef left for America, Menashe would become the breadwinner— which meant the younger children would painstakingly produce the shoe toppers while Menashe ordered them around, collected and stashed the profits, and occasionally gave Mama a few *groschen* to feed the family.

Binyamin was certain his work days would grow longer once Yosef left. Beatings would be more frequent and school forbidden with Menashe in unsupervised charge. Within the traditional Jewish pecking order, Binyamin had few prerogatives as the youngest son. Only his sisters, being girls, suffered more abuse than he.

The thought of his father's departure was enough to twist Binyamin's stomach into knots. In an effort to quell his fear, Binyamin chanted the *bar mitzvah* lesson over and over determined to memorize the Hebrew texts to avoid dwelling on what was sure to be Menashe's unbridled reign of terror. *I need to come up with a scheme to get rid of that mamzer!* Like Jacob in the Bible, he needed to overturn the accident of birth that favored his Esau-like brother.

As if thinking about him materialized Menashe, Binyamin heard him call out, "You there, Binyamin! You'll be in the White

Army against us, the Red Army." He was playing war games with his friends and was intent on dragging his younger brother into the fray.

Binyamin didn't respond, but he could hear the stomp of Menashe's feet and the whoosh of the rope that he used as a whip to emphasize his pronouncements.

"You'll be in the opposing army against me," Menashe thundered, his beady, brown eyes flashing dangerously. "For a real battle, they need another soldier, so drop the books and get yourself (whoosh) outside (whoosh)."

"I'm no soldier. I don't fight," Binyamin protested. "Fighting is stupid and make-believe fighting is even more stupid."

"You fight if I say so," roared Menashe, his fury mounting. He flung Binyamin's book to the ground, dragged him up from his corner, and shoved him toward the door.

"You'll have to catch me first," countered Binyamin as he raced out, knowing full well that Menashe couldn't catch up to him. When he was out of sight, Binyamin doubled back, avoiding his brother's wrath.

While Menashe and other boys excitedly recreated war encounters, Binyamin stayed away. Of course, he'd heard the rumors that filtered into the village about new armies being gathered and men once again being taken from their families. He knew his father was leaving to avoid being drafted. The new battles being fought were among various factions with strange-sounding names: White Russians, Bolsheviks, and Communists.

Binyamin had only been nine years old when his eldest brother, Isaiah, was taken away to serve in the Tzar's army. Four years later, he hardly remembered Isaiah. But he would never forget his father's piercing wail as he read the note informing them Isaiah had been killed in action in the Russo-Japanese War.

The seven days that followed Isaiah's death compounded Binyamin's belief that war was the worst of horrors and to be avoided at all costs. The house was shuttered down, the mirror covered by a sheet, and his somber-faced, silent parents sat on cushions on the ground while neighbors filed in to mouth hushed condolences.

Binyamin salivated at the mountainous platters of *gefilte* fish and *cholent* and *kishkah* that visitors brought, catering to the Jewish belief that events were made happier—or less sorrowful— on a full stomach. But the pain and sorrow displayed, as Isaiah's death was mourned during the *shivah,* made it crystal clear to Binyamin: *I will never serve in any Army; I will do everything I can to avoid fighting of any kind.*

In spite of his pacifist tendencies, now and then Binyamin yearned for one of those armies to reach Krasnoe. He wondered whether they ever would—and what that would mean for him. He was 13 and too young to be drafted, but Menashe, ah yes! Menashe was older, as Binyamin was never allowed to forget. *Maybe, just maybe, Menashe would be taken away*, Binyamin thought with relish. Binyamin dreamed of being in charge, certain he would do a much better job of it than his tyrannical brother. Sooner than he imagined, he too would have occasion to recall his father's oft-repeated warning, "Be careful what you wish for—you never know when God will grant it as punishment!"

"Soon, there'll be no hiding," Binyamin murmured. "What will happen when *Tatte* goes to America? Who'll protect me from that bastard—that *mamzer*? *Tatte* leaves when I become *bar mitzvah*!" His shoulders sagged and he massaged his Adam's apple to ease the knot in his throat. Without Yosef's presence to restrain Menashe, Binyamin feared for his life. He had seen his brother's bad temper turn to fury and knew firsthand the consequences of his attacks. Would he be able to continue finding ways to avoid his brother's violent outbursts and aggressions?

2.

Not that his father was much protection; Yosef Gesheftman never came back home before the sun set. And two days a week he was on the road from their village, Krasnoe, to Vinnytsia, the market town to the North, only to return home even later. Binyamin once asked Yosef why the family didn't just move to Vinnytsia so he wouldn't have to travel so much.

"Jews aren't allowed to live in Vinnytsia," his father replied. "The year Yankl was born, the Tzar granted the Cossacks the right to kill any Jew they found closer than 35 kilometers from a town. We have to live in villages at the proper distance from the town."

"So we're forced to live in a Jewish ghetto," Binyamin said.

"No, my son, think of it as *undzere shtetl*, our village," Yosef corrected kindly.

Yosef bought, sold, and bartered the goods of the *shtetl* among the villagers. On Mondays and Thursdays, he traveled the 35 kilometers to Vinnytsia to sell the remaining wares and purchase staples ordered by his neighbors: flour for the widow Sopher who was cooking for her entire family for Rosh Hashanah; a new wheel for Mendel's cart; a feather to brighten up little Hannah's wedding dress.

The rest of the week, Binyamin's father, the rag peddler, could be seen ambling along the dirt roads of the *shtetl* coaxing Beheime, their mangy-looking mare, to keep pulling the cart. To the village housewives, Yosef was a familiar sight in his worn dark blue jacket and carefully mended white shirt, more suited for sitting behind a desk than collecting and delivering odds and ends. He sported a faded fedora precariously perched on his abundant curly black hair in an attempt to keep the dust off.

Leaving the cart on the side of the dirt road, Yosef walked slowly between rows of dilapidated houses, tinkling a bell to announce his coming. The housewives flocked out to pick up the supplies he bought for them, display their cast-offs, or bargain for someone else's. The women kept up a volley of chatter with the rag peddler while they picked up and placed their orders or showed what they wanted to trade. Yosie's broad smile was almost completely hidden behind a massive beard and whiskers; but the facial hair couldn't hide his twinkling hazel eyes.

"So, Yosele, what's new?" "Did you know that…" "Have you heard who Yente is seeing in Mintz?" "What's wrong with Moishe? They brought the doctor from Chelm to look at him!" Yosef's customers all called out in unison, wanting to be the first to provide the most recent gossip and Yosef seldom needed to respond—he knew it was more about letting them have their say.

Yosef selected his occupation with unerring instinct. It provided a seemly living for his family, allowed him to indulge his delight in exchanging jokes, spreading gossip, and to enjoy the only spotlight available to an ignorant, un-bookish Jewish man. Above all, it offered a much-needed respite from Malkah—his strait-laced, domineering, nit-picking, somber wife and the continuous bickering among their five children. In the evenings, after a grueling day, Yosef was forced to listen to Malkah's constant daily grousing.

In an attempt to forestall his wife's barrage of complaints, Yosef told her a little about his day. "Today, Frau Melamed said they might soon be having Yente's wedding…"

Bent over, tending the wood fire in the same position he'd left her in the morning, Malkah grumbled without looking up, "Why on earth waste time talking to those harpies?"

"Sha, sha, Malkah, you should be nicer to the neighbors," Yosef replied. "Just today, Rifka, the tailor's wife, asked after you."

"Maybe you should talk less and work more," Malkah muttered, wiping her brow with a corner of the ever-present black shawl draped around her shoulders. "You run around making nice to those fishwives, enjoying yourself, while I have to add more and more water to the soup to feed your children."

Your children… the harbinger of the complaint contained in the daily litany of the sibling's squabbles: today, Menashe had pulled the pins out of the dress his sister Esther was altering, then used them as bars between cardboard rounds to cage flies whose wings he had pulled off. Then, he'd hidden Binyamin's glasses or doodled on his books, or erased the cheating marks on his brother Yankl's playing cards. Raisl, the youngest, whimpered incessantly about the bloodied nose Menashe had given her when she tattled that he had unraveled Esther's knitting, while Esther moaned about having lost her hard-earned *kopeks* playing cards with Yankl.

As Yosef listened to Malkah drone on the recitation of the day's frustrations, he hung his head in guilt. *Soon I'll be free of her complaints for a few years…and if all goes well, I can bring the family over and if life gets better in America, maybe Malkah will stop with the kvetching.* Why is Malkah angry all the time? The matchmaker described Malkah Seltzer as a quiet girl from a well-to-do family from Kishinev. She wasn't like this when we first married. She didn't smile much, but she didn't complain like now. Of course, marriage meant moving to a *shtetl* from her fancy home in Kishinev, and having so many children and so little money, and having to work hard when she wouldn't have lifted a finger before.

The decision to go to America after Binyamin's *bar mitzvah* had been prompted by the rumblings of new wars and fear of the draft. The last war against the Japanese had taken his first son away, and now there were increasing rumors of other wars and escalating prohibitions against Jews. By emigrating now—with hard work and a little luck—Yosef could get the family over to America before the *pogroms*—which generally started at the same time as wars—began, looking for Jews to be blamed. His hands became clammy with fear of what he—and the family—would have to face before they were reunited in New York. He understood Malkah's current source of upset: remaining alone with five children to feed and little income until he started sending money from America.

In his secluded corner, Binyamin tried to drown out his mother's accusatory recital of the day's events as he intoned what he believed must be at least the hundredth repetition of the second Torah blessing. The scent of chicken soup wafting up to his nostrils made him salivate. He closed his eyes and visualized Yosef, dressed in the long white robe and embroidered head cover, responding with the prayer traditionally murmured by the *bar mitzvah's* father: *Baruch she-petarani me-onsho shel zeh.* "Blessed is He who has freed me of the obligation of my son."

<h1 style="text-align:center">3.</h1>

Binyamin's *bar mitzvah* took place. He'd recited his portion of the Torah not too haltingly, didn't falter much or make too many mistakes, and thought his father looked at him with a proud gleam in his eyes. He felt like a man when he managed to swallow his sobs and pretended not to notice his father's tears as they hugged goodbye, but now *Tatte* was leaving. He promised it would only be for a few years until he could save up to buy the visas and passages to bring the whole family to America.

America! Binyamin savored the sound of the word and smiled at the images conjured in his mind. It was the closest thing to heaven he could imagine: a place where one could make dreams come true. A place where he could live without fear that the Cossacks might turn up at the door, drag him out, strip him naked on the street and shoot him just for being a Jew. America was a land where one could study and learn everything there was to know about making money. Above all, he'd heard it was the place where the only limit to success was your skill in figuring out the system, and the willingness to work that system to your advantage. *Ach! How I would bloom in such a place!*

A few months later, like an answer to Binyamin's prayers, the Army descended upon Krasnoe. The pounding hooves and the thudding boots created a deafening roar, a man-made tempest of dust and noise. The regiment halted by the *shtetl's* well and 10 gaunt, bedraggled officers dismounted with alacrity, barking orders that could be overheard in the cacophony that filled the air.

"записки…Papers!" they demanded.

The townspeople cowered, shrinking away from the soldiers, their faces pinched, peering out behind eyes widened with shock and fear. The air was thick with the stench of horse manure and urine mixed with the dust, sweat, and grime clinging to the soldiers' ragged uniforms. The palpable scent of the villagers' terror hung over everything.

Against a wall, Binyamin hung back and watched the soldiers methodically tramp through dwelling after dwelling, shoving the residents aside, shouting at the women to move, signaling every male that looked old enough to draft to gather beside the horses drinking from the well. Those who hesitated were prodded with a rifle butt, those who protested silenced with a clout.

The process was hurried, yet efficient. Within an hour, the soldiers and their new recruits departed, leaving behind a gaggle of blank-faced old men, their shoulders slumped in defeat, women with tears streaming down their faces, wailing their thanks to God that the Cossacks were gone, while hugging those who had been blessedly judged too young or too old to take.

Among those who were swept away was Menashe, his defiance quashed with a crack of the soldiers' whip. Binyamin heard Menashe hurl curses at next-in-line Yankl, in an attempt to call him back as he fled into the forest at the first sound of the soldiers' horses' hooves. Since Yankl didn't stop, Menashe was unable to dictate instructions to him on how to keep the business running in his absence. Binyamin watched the squadron disappear into the distance and sweep his nemesis away. He rubbed the grin off his face and went in search of Yankl.

Seizing the opportunity presented by Menashe's departure, Binyamin intended to manipulate his older brother into relinquishing his succession to boss. Binyamin would take over the business if Yankl consented to move to Vinnytsia.

Binyamin cornered Yankl for an intense heart-to-heart. "I know how much you'd love to live on your own in Vinnytsia," Binyamin said. "I've heard you say over and over you wanted to get away from here to do whatever you want."

"So how am I going to do that… did the Tzar all of a sudden give permission for Jews to live in cities?" Yankl asked, his glass eye almost popping out in frustration. "Besides, where am I going to get money to move?"

"I'll give you money from my *bar mitzvah* presents: enough to rent a room in town. And I'll help move your things. You'll have to find yourself a job there," Binyamin said.

Yankl hesitated at first—but only for a moment. He thought about the dangers he'd face by breaking the Tzar's laws of residence, but he knew some of the villagers had done it. He'd dreamed of being on his own for as long as he could remember. To be able to do what he pleased. *Phah! To be away from the constant bickering at home!* Yet without Binyamin's money and prodding, he knew he would never actually have the courage to attempt it.

"So you'll support me until I'm working, right?" asked Yankl. "And help me out if I get caught?"

"No. I'd help you move and pay a landlord for your room and board for a month or so. You'll have to find your own funds to gamble with," said Binyamin.

"A month or so! As if jobs were that easy to find!" Yankl complained. "You don't even care if I starve and have to live on the street…"

"You won't, if you work, which I'm sure you would prefer not to. Oh, all right. I'll pay your room and board through the winter. Then you'll be on your own," Binyamin said, ending the discussion. "But you'll have to go right away."

Yankl accepted his brother's offer without further discussion, delighted at the chance to move away, to lead the quiet life of a gambling bachelor in "the big town." His leaving left Binyamin free to run the shoe shop. Thus, not long after his father left and against all tradition, Binyamin, the youngest son, became the breadwinner in the Gesheftman family.

<h1 style="text-align:center">4.</h1>

At first, Malkah was oblivious to the ways her husband's migration to America, her oldest son's deployment to the wars, and the younger son's move to Vinnytsia would affect the family's circumstances. To her, it simply meant fewer demands: three fewer mouths to feed, less bickering and disruption, and with "Beheime" sold, no more manure to clean up!

Moreover, she would gain status, be counted among the "elite" of the village, accorded respect for being *grenitza* — having family members living away: a husband in America and a son who was "passing" in Vinnytsia, despite the risk of punishment for flouting the residence decree.

That Menashe had been conscripted added no prestige. Few Jews were patriots to the Tzarist regime that had long oppressed them. Nor did Malkah—or any other Jew—harbor any hope that the forces that opposed the Tzar—whichever one ended up in charge—would stop oppressing them. It was simply the way things were, and no one questioned it.

The villagers went to great lengths to avoid military service. When children were born, the year on the birth certificate was left blank, which allowed the parents to fill in the date as required to prove the person was older or younger than the current conscription age. Most Jewish families kept a box into which they stashed spare *kopeks* to bribe military officials for exemptions from active duty, if the need arose.

Although Malkah didn't mind a smaller household, there was now less money to put enough food on the table, even for fewer mouths. Though clever and hardworking, Binyamin was still just a boy, and it took months to assert himself and stop Shuster from shortchanging him. Yosef had sold the old nag to help pay for his passage, so there was no income from the rag trade or staple deliveries. Esther's sewing helped a little, but there never seemed to be enough. The family anxiously awaited the remittances that Yosef had promised would come from the land of plenty, but as the months passed and they had no word from him, despair set in.

Bewailing her fate, Malkah put the empty barn to use by selling home-brewed beer and offering a place for customers to play cards. It was a desperate solution for desperate times and brought opprobrium upon them all. The very men who patronized the makeshift tavern joined their wives in looking down upon Malkah and her two single daughters who served the beer—and who knew what else—at the back of their house.

As they drew water from the well, the villagers murmured: A *harpe un a shande*—a disgrace and a shame.

"Yosef Gesheftman would turn in his grave if he's dead," said Mendl's wife.

"Pheh! Pheh!" spat Mendl. "Don't tempt Adonai talking about death!"

The widow Sopher added, "Malkah's stinky drinks will kill you and your card-playing friends!"

"If not, your wives will," recently married Hannah pointedly piped in, "for making eyes at those scrawny girls!"

"Who says anyone makes eyes at them?" Chaim asked. "The men just play cards without having you all around us, chattering."

"It's also a *mitzvah*, helping the widow and her family stay alive," said Saul, smirking at having come up with an excuse that placed him in a charitable light while also salving his guilt that he joined in on the gossip and helped spread the ugly rumors about Malkah and her daughters.

5.

Shame provided the impetus that propelled Binyamin into his business age. Almost five years had passed since Yosef's departure so Binyamin gave up expecting his father's letter to rescue them from their precarious situation. As the only male in the household, it was his responsibility to provide for the family. After all, he had schemed to become the breadwinner. It was up to him to figure out a solution. After careful consideration, Binyamin made his decision—he would first sort things out with the shoemaker.

On the following Friday as the sun started to sink in the horizon and the villagers passed by hurrying home to prepare for Shabbat, Binyamin knocked on Shuster's door. He waited a few minutes before knocking again, harder this time. He knew Shuster was inside, reluctant to open. It was difficult to get Shuster to come to the door when it was time to settle accounts.

"So, what's so important that you have to knock the door down?" said Shuster, patting his generous belly.

"I knock until you open," Binyamin answered. "You owe us for 30 toppers. Pay up."

"I'll pay when the shoes are sold," Shuster said, pushing to close the door. "And you only brought 22! Now go home and light your candles!"

Binyamin leaned his slight frame against the door, digging his heels in. He raised his voice to make sure the passersby heard every word of the full-throated argument. "I'm not leaving until you pay me for 30 toppers," he insisted.

The villagers knew Binyamin was as good as his word. They had seen him sit for days outside someone's door, determined to collect old debts owed to his father; Yosef had always had a hard time charging those he thought less fortunate than himself.

Shuster knew that continuing to argue in full view of everyone would be bad for business. "*Beseider*! Okay, go home now and I'll settle for 30 toppers when the shoes are sold," Shuster said, trying to negotiate.

"No. Pay me now, or it'll be on your head that I break the sanctity of Shabbat, because I'm not leaving until you pay what you owe," replied Binyamin, unwavering.

Shuster slammed the door shut. Binyamin knew Shuster was behind the door, ruminating, hoping to stand his ground and expecting Binyamin to leave to uphold the sanctity of the Sabbath. But Binyamin continued banging loudly on the door. Shuster could hear loud voices as villagers congregated to see what was going on. A few minutes later he returned to the door with the money.

Within a year, Binyamin was able to bring in enough for Malkah to keep the back door closed during the week and open the tavern only for a couple of hours after Shabbat. He organized his sisters' work at the shop so Esther had time to sew; Binyamin let her keep what she earned from alterations, requiring only that she contribute to the rent. And he ensured his youngest sister, Raisl, had an hour or two in the afternoons to play outside. Their whining dwindled and the girls' performance improved. Binyamin was now accorded full respect as the man of the house.

Binyamin had been under the impression that, as boss, Menashe merely gave orders while he and the others labored to produce the shoe tops. He never realized how much more was involved in running a business. He'd believed that—liberated from the harsh rule of his tyrant brother—he'd have more time to study.

On the contrary. Since Menashe's departure, Binyamin worked incessantly: cutting out shoe tops and managing the girls' work, delivering the tops to the shoemaker, collecting payments, and keeping accounts. He no longer had a chance to even glance at his books, much less attend classes at *cheder*.

Tears welled up in his eyes as he recalled his father's words. After all, he *had* wished to be on his own without being ordered around by Menashe. Mostly, he cried for the abrupt end of his childhood. But not for very long; the maturing Binyamin took hold. "At least I don't have to put up with Menashe's yelling and beatings or argue about what to do with Shuster or how long to cure the leather. Learning can wait."

The little shop flourished. Shuster, the shoemaker, was unable to keep up with the Gesheftmans' increased production. Binyamin experimented until he figured out how to construct the soles. He was then able to manufacture both toppers and soles and talked Shuster into simply joining them together to make the final product. Now, there was no production backlog, and the shoes were completed more quickly. The shortened turnaround time to finished product allowed Binyamin to begin "exporting" to the big town.

"Now that I'm delivering shoes regularly to Vinnytsia, I could again shop for the neighbors," Binyamin told Malkah. "If I have to travel, I might as well have the cart full both ways."

"So now you want me to feed, house, and clean up after a horse again?" Malkah spat out. "I don't know when you'll stop with the plans … always thinking about more and more money, never about how much work you make for me."

"Sha, sha Mama. I'll use Itzhok the builder's horse—it's cheaper to rent one for a few days a month, and it's less trouble."

Binyamin's neighbors had been struggling to obtain staples after Yosef left, and were forced to personally slip into the "big town" for supplies. When Binyamin announced he was reopening the delivery service, the villagers were eager to pay whatever he charged. The "market on wheels" as he called it, quickly became profitable.

Although Binyamin considered "rag peddling" beneath him and refused to deal in secondhand goods, he did take on consignment what gold and jewelry the residents of Krasnoe had. He sold it in Vinnytsia, taking a percentage of the sale as a commission, and thus creating another source of income.

Worried about keeping these more expensive items safe from pilfering, Binyamin thought of getting a dog to protect the house while he was gone. He had always loved dogs and pleaded for one since he was a child, but his mother refused to allow it, adamant that he was not to bring an animal into the house. When he was young, his father had consoled him, telling him he would have to wait until he had his own home to keep a dog.

Thinking about his father reminded Binyamin that Yosef would never have allowed him to deal in gold, because Jews were forbidden by the Tzarist regime to do so. But, who would suspect a boy of daring to defy an order that could get him killed? Binyamin mentally countered his father's opposition. *I've got to do what I can to care for the family, Tatte, I'm the breadwinner now.*

6.

By the time Menashe returned from military service, Malkah had permanently closed the tavern in the back room. Since Yosef left for America five years earlier, they hadn't heard a word from him. He was presumed dead. His children were no longer children: the Gesheftman family was now living entirely from what Binyamin and the girls produced and Binyamin sold.

Menashe strutted into Krasnoe wearing a threadbare khaki uniform, filthy stormtrooper boots, and brandishing his pistol. A cat lay lounging at the entrance to the village, sunning itself in the middle of the main road. Village children played near the tabby, careful not to disturb it. The cat's contented purring was joyous background to the children's giggles and outright hoots of laughter.

Menashe stomped directly towards the reclining cat, viciously kicked it awake, and as it raced off, aimed a shot at it, causing the wide-eyed children nearby to flee, wailing in terror. When the injured animal appeared to somersault and crash to the ground, Menashe smiled his crooked smile with barely parted lips, then emitted a grunt of pleasure as he raised his arm and emptied the pistol's chamber into the sky. Seven blasts announced the return of the eldest Gesheftman; the years in the Army had simply hardened his notorious ill temper into sadistic cruelty.

At home, Menashe's face turned ashen and he sputtered taking in the changes instituted by Binyamin. The one-room structure seemed to reverberate with his screaming invective. The women absconded to the barn, hoping to evade the brunt of Menashe's anger. He became more incensed when he asked where Yankl was hiding and learned that Yankl, who would have been much more compliant, was now living in Vinnytsia. "How did he manage to afford that?" Menashe demanded to know, his face splotched with red spots. "What do you mean you helped him? You bribed him, Binyamin, so you could take over the shop, you no good *gonef*."

"*Gonef*? I am not a thief! Yankl wanted to go," Binyamin said, "I just loaned him the money so he could."

Menashe exploded. "How much money have you stashed away, Binyamin?" He waved his pistol and pushed his brother—who was trembling with fear—outside to sit on a tree stump. The tyrant towered over him and continued to point the pistol at Binyamin while demanding a minutely detailed accounting.

Much as Binyamin had matured in the years during his brother's absence—successfully running three businesses, supporting the entire family, and saving for their exodus to America—he was no more able to stand up to Menashe at eighteen than he had been as a youngster.

"So, you're back," said Binyamin, making himself smaller. "You want what you had when you went away…sure, you can have it—it's yours!"

Menashe raised his shoulders up with a sneer. "Of course, I want it back! And the accounts including all profits! And the pure gold you've kept hidden away;" pointing with the pistol at Binyamin's foot, "or maybe you like hopping around!"

Binyamin continued to try to derail Menashe's fury, "You know, we kept your machine in perfect order. And I'll tell Shuster you are now the boss."

"I keep talking about profits and you keep pretending to be deaf. You think you can just return what was already mine…you owe me for all the years you had it and the stupid changes you made…What about the profits you've hidden away," growled Menashe, walking behind his brother and pushing the pistol into Binyamin's neck

"Where do you hide it? And when are you turning it over?" Menashe spat into Binyamin's face as he pulled his head back by the hair. "And you will turn over the entire haul. Unless you want to die…"

"I can't speak unless you let go…" Binyamin was able to sputter out. Menashe let go.

"Put the gun down and maybe you can hear that I've been saying 'yes' to what you've asked. We can talk about the details once you give the gun to Mama for safe keeping," Binyamin said. "Then I'll sell it for you when I go into town. That business I will keep for myself."

Menashe lowered the pistol, paced back and forth, then put it inside its holster. He turned away and followed Binyamin into the barn. Malkah was distraught about their quarreling. Binyamin imagined his mother must be pleased to be spared from sitting *shivah* for another son lost to war. Yet he wondered, if she also wished Menashe hadn't come back.

Binyamin told Malkah and his sisters that he decided to return the shoemaking business to Menashe and asked his mother to hold the gun until he took it to Vinnytsia. Worried that Menashe might eventually hurt someone and bring tragedy onto the family, Malkah agreed to keep the gun if the bullets were removed. It was a way to stop the escalating confrontation between her sons.

Without a word, Menashe reluctantly handed the gun to his mother then spoke to Esther. "I'm told you're busy sewing so you don't work with the shoes. You'll turn over to me what you earn."

Esther ignored him.

Menashe stood crowding her with his arms akimbo, "You heard me: hand over your week's earnings."

Esther pushed him away and said, "Binyamin let me keep what I make. I just pay rent."

"Binyamin's not in charge anymore," he growled. "I am." He slapped her hard and knocked her down. She wailed, more in anger than in pain.

Malkah cried out loud, addressing Menashe: "I will not stand by while you hurt your sister. You'll help Esther move to Vinnytsia so she'll be safe from you."

7.

The American Jewish Joint Distribution Committee was established during the Great War of 1914 with the purpose of aiding, providing relief, and rescuing Jews from war zones. Its mission was to fulfill the commitment to the precept that Jews are responsible for one another. But it wasn't until months after Menashe came back, once the Bolshevik Revolution was over, that the JDC was able expand its services into Russia.

Abraham Levinsky, a former neighbor of the Gesheftmans, who had emigrated at the start of the war now worked at the JDC in New York and traveled regularly to Russia. The JDC sent packages and letters from relatives in America to inhabitants of the *shtetls* throughout the Pale, the region where Jews were settled, from its central office in the capital city, Kiev. But Levinsky wanted to visit relatives who still lived in Krasnoe so he delivered the package for the Gesheftmans in person.

The whole family, even Yankl from Vinnytsia, came to hear about Yosef's whereabouts—the first news they'd had from husband and father since he'd left for America.

"I'm happy to bring good news: not only a package from Gesheftman, but also to tell you what happened to him all these years when he couldn't get a word to you. With the Revolution going on, it was impossible for the JDC to deliver letters or information," Levinsky said.

"You're saying you know my father?" asked Menashe.

"Is he well? Have you seen him?" Binyamin jumped in.

"Open the package!" said Esther.

"What did he send us?" added Raisl.

"Please, one at a time, I can't answer everyone at once. Sit down and I'll tell you what I know; you can ask your questions later. When we first got to America, my mother got a job translating for the newcomers from the old country. I was very young, but I started out by volunteering for the JDC. When she learned there was an old neighbor of ours in the hospital, I went with her to visit him," he explained

"In the hospital?" Yankl interrupted, "What happened to him? Is he healthy now?"

"Yes, he's alright now. He was run over by a truck the day he arrived. Yosef remained in a coma at Beth Israel Hospital for months until he recovered from his injuries. After he regained consciousness, we visited often and became friends; he would tell us how worried he was about you, Levinsky continued.

"Poor *Tatte*. I wonder…How did things go for him in America? Where did he live? How did he earn a living? Did he miss us…" Binyamin asked.

"When he was released from the hospital, he came to live with us. Once he was strong enough to work, Yosef followed the advice of other recently-landed *lantzmen*. He took a pushcart like many others until they could establish themselves in business; they were nomads until they could afford to rent a space. When he was able to pay, he became our boarder and he still lives with us.

"At least it's good that he found a job like he had here…" Yankl said.

"He likes what he does; he enjoys peddling from door to door, meeting and chatting with people. Instead of buying the visa and passage for one of you, he could have rented a space and stopped selling from the pushcart. But he thought only of saving up for visas for all of you. He was pained that you might think he had abandoned you. Above all, he feared Krasnoe's inhabitants would be in danger of *pogroms*, official or unofficial, as it always plays out. Whenever there is trouble—be it a war, famine, plague or Revolution—the scapegoats are always the Jews; so when he heard I was coming, he sent the one passage and visa he was able to save for." Levinsky added as he rose to leave, "When I report back, I can imagine he'll be overjoyed to hear you are all well and that the *shtetl* survived the Revolution."

<h1 style="text-align:center">8.</h1>

Malkah listened to Levinsky's report with her head tilted. Her lips puckered in a perpetual frown, she muttered, "So Yosef's not dead after all. Just when we were used to his being gone, he turns up and wants to change everything. The family will be more torn apart again…I won't leave until we all go. Decide who wants to go to America now."

Having recently returned from the wars and with a bustling business to manage, Menashe refused to even consider moving to a strange new place.

"They don't even speak Russian, those barbarians," he scoffed, "What am I supposed to do, learn English? *Meshugeneh*—crazy!" Ship her out," Menashe spat, pointing at Esther. "You were already expecting me to pay to move her to Vinnytsia."

Malkah agreed. "With the visa, it makes more sense for her to go to America than trying to make a living where she has to hide from the authorities. She has a trade: what she earns by sewing would speed up getting passages and visas for the rest of us. More than that, Esther has no prospects here at her age. Soon, no one will even look at her; marriage options in America will be greater even than in Vinnytsia."

Esther took the visa. The rest of the family members would wait until there was enough money to secure four passages and visas: one each for Malkah, Yankl, Binyamin, and Raisl. Menashe remained obstinate in his refusal to go. "I'm not afraid of *pogroms*: I served in the army."

Menashe's determination to remain in Russia intensified when Binyamin mentioned he had run across Shoshanna in Vinnytsia. "I wonder what happened? Strange that she returned home after only a year at University in Odessa," Menashe mused. "Did she say why?"

"She just said she was back and asked after you"

"What did you tell her?" Menashe asked. "What exactly did you say?"

"I told her you were back and as difficult as ever."

"So, what else did she say?"

"Nothing else, we just stopped to say 'hello' on the street."

"So it was special, huh? She didn't ask after anyone else in the family? I wonder why she came back…she had turned every suitor down, as she wanted to become a doctor before even thinking of marriage. I will go to see her tomorrow."

"I know you chased her before you were drafted…she never showed any interest in you. Why would such a beautiful and lovely girl ever want anything to do with someone like you? How could Shoshana possibly want a husband as bad-tempered and coarse as you are? She was just being polite."

The following day, Menashe took the train into Vinnytsia. He returned from visiting Shoshanna to announce that, to everyone's surprise, she had accepted his offer of marriage. They were to have the ceremony as soon as it could be arranged. With the exodus plans of the rest of the family, they hoped to be settled before everyone left.

Menashe felt even safer now. Shoshanna could help with the shoe shop and his soon to be father-in-law, as principal of the gymnasium in Vinnytsia, ranked among the intelligentsia who still had some power under Lenin. *Of course, my wife and I will be safe from possible political repercussions.*

ENTREPRENEUR

Vinnytsia

1.

*H*aving turned over the shoe shop to Menashe, Binyamin now focused his attention on the staple delivery service and the gold trade in Vinnytsia. He employed his brother Yankl, who enjoyed shopping and welcomed a salary to fill the villagers' requests for essentials and other items, while Binyamin concentrated on his dealings in gold.

In a matter of months, Binyamin was able to afford to take the train the 35 kilometers into the big city instead of driving the horse and cart. It was a faster, cleaner way to travel, and riding through the bleak countryside with someone else driving allowed him the freedom to immerse himself in his thoughts and plan his next move. Visualizing his next endeavor was what Binyamin liked best, so he relished the trips as an opportunity to concentrate on his vision of the future.

During the train rides, it dawned on him with increasing clarity that his hopes and dreams of becoming wealthy would no more materialize within the confines of a post-1917 Socialist state than in a pre-1917 Imperial one. He recognized that to pursue his dreams, he had to find a way to leave Russia. For months, Binyamin explored emigration options. As he had no papers, he knew he would need to pay to be smuggled out, and he would need to have the wherewithal to survive wherever he ended up. Realizing that smelted gold held a more objective and universally recognized value than jewelry, and coins could be easier to smelt and more efficient to stack and hide, he hoarded gold coins for the next few years.

Binyamin contributed to the household expenses and insisted a percentage be regularly added to the "escape" fund, but kept the family in the dark about the added resources he was stashing, and with which he intended to start a business in America.

He was obsessed and determined to fulfill the destiny of the family name: *geschäftsman* means "shopkeeper" or "business-man" in German and Yiddish. Of Yosef's children, Binyamin was the one who best embodied their surname.

Traveling by train was certainly more convenient, but it was also more public, where more eyes could see what he was up to. Although Binyamin feared it could invite trouble, he was careful not to attract attention and had outfitted his coat in ways that were as discreet as possible. *Life is full of risks, after all, and thank God, so far I've been lucky enough.*

On a cold Thursday afternoon in 1922, as Binyamin made his way back home, he arrived panting to the Vinnytsia train station, trying to evade the *goy* hoodlums who, emboldened by tacit approval from the Bolshevik authorities, had graduated from taunting Jewish schoolboys to harassing Jews of any age.

Although he kept himself in good physical shape, Binyamin had a hard time eluding his chasers, weighted down with the heavy stash hidden along the inside of his arm in the leather roll he had specially constructed for the purpose. He had just scored big, trading a brooch studded with miniature diamonds for gold coins to add to his growing collection. He dropped the bags of items for the villagers and diverted his pursuers.

Binyamin jumped on the train as it pulled out of the station, accidentally bumping into an *apparatchik*, a minor official in the administration, as he clambered on. Grabbing Binyamin by the arm, the apparatchik felt the hardness of the gold strapped inside his armband.

"Show me," the *apparatchik* demanded, fingering his handgun.

Feeling sweat trickling down his clothes, Binyamin waved a hand, motioning the official to move towards a more secluded corner. The official shoved the muzzle of the gun into Binyamin's back and pushed him against the wall in the boarding alcove. The official held the pointed gun while growling, "Papers!" Shivering,

Binyamin dug around in his coat pocket. He slipped off one of the coat's sleeves to reveal the bulging armband. "Your papers!" the *apparatchik* barked again. Binyamin handed over his documents, then slowly unknotted the contraption's straps, uncoiled them and pointedly removed the pouch inside.

The official questioned him and scrutinizing the permits, grimaced when he realized he was dealing with a Jew. The official licked his lips, glanced up, and announced, "It's jail for you, you know…for being in town…" His hands shaking, Binyamin unwrapped the pouch's contents and watched his persecutor's eyes light up at the sight. The official's eyes glinted as much as the coins did. "We should keep this between ourselves," wheedled Binyamin. *Perhaps I can still avoid imprisonment.* He wrapped the pouch again, deliberately showing the *apparatchik* how to wrap it within the contraption.

"You're in luck, you filthy Jew!" the *apparatchik* whispered. "Just hand it over and make sure I don't ever see you again," placing the leather roll of coins under his fur hat.

Binyamin let out an explosive breath as he skulked away. For the moment, he was safe: the official would confiscate and keep the gold rather than report the incident. Binyamin's heart thumped and his ears rang. He was distraught; partly with anxiety at such a narrow escape, partly over the loss of his gold coins, but mostly over the inescapable realization that, his cover blown, it would no longer be safe to continue this lucrative business.

Unfortunately, in showing the official his documents, he had called attention not only to himself but inadvertently to all the inhabitants of the *shtetl,* who had until then, fallen through the cracks within the newly-formed administrative structure of the Soviets. There was no alternative now. Binyamin had to make the move he had been contemplating for four long years, ever since they had received the package from the American Jewish Joint Distribution Committee.

After his encounter with the *apparatchik* on the train, Binyamin knew arrangements to leave Russia had to be made immediately. He could no longer continue to wait for the whole family to emigrate together to America. It was only a matter of time before the official would come looking for more gold. He would slowly chew over his thoughts about the bonanza and eventually conclude that there must have been other occasions when the Jew had traded in gold. He'd come searching for it, and no hiding place would be safe. Binyamin was not ashamed of being cowardly. He knew he would certainly succumb to threats of conscription and give the *apparatchik* the payment in gold that he would surely demand to issue an exemption from military service. Binyamin had to leave before he lost his little fortune and his freedom.

On the rest of the train ride back to Krasnoe, Binyamin mulled over all possible options and, methodically discarding what he thought wouldn't work, mapped out his plan of action. He had to leave within days; he could no longer stay in Russia. To travel outside the guberniya, a regional permit was required, and there was no way he—or any Jew in the Russian Pale, where the Jews had been forced to move generations ago—could obtain a permit. The only option was to contact the Jewish organizations known to smuggle people across the border to Rumania.

At Shabbat dinner the following night, Binyamin made his announcement: he would start his voyage to America as soon as he could get smuggled out.

After a long few minutes, Menashe growled, "So, what's the rush, all of a sudden?" scowling the words into his soup plate.

Malkah, Yankl, and Raisl looked up to listen to Binyamin's response with wide-eyed attention. They all wondered what prompted the urgency of the departure, but didn't dare speak up until Menashe did.

"It's time," Binyamin replied, not wanting to explain the reason for his abrupt decision. "It's getting more and more dangerous to be Jews here. As you all know, we have enough saved up to pay for four of us to be smuggled out somewhere safer. With what I earned this week, I can pay for my own passage. We should all wait for the visas from *Tatte* wherever the JDC can host us, possibly Rumania."

"I'm not going. I'm going nowhere, not America, not Rumania. I'm staying right here," Menashe retorted. "Haven't you heard? I'm getting married and I am the man of the house, so they can all stay, and we'll wish you well."

"You can all do what you like. I can arrange for the JDC to smuggle out whomever decides to go. I'm leaving as soon as possible; the JDC instructed that those of us who are ready to leave will do so the day after tomorrow."

2.

Yankl wished he hadn't come back home for Shabbat dinner. There was always tension around the table, but Binyamin's announcement had just turned it into a shouting match, creating even more anguish than usual. Yankl wasn't particularly competitive, so he couldn't understand Menashe's and Binyamin's constant struggle for the upper hand. He was perplexed by Binyamin's insatiable need to be involved in business dealings—all of which were way over Yankl's head. And he simply couldn't fathom why Menashe was always so angry and ready to fight.

To make business deals is hard work. I like winning money, but working for it is no fun. It was infinitely more entertaining to sleep the day away and win at cards at night. Throughout his life, Yankl tried to make a living at cards. Only in his bachelor days in

Vinnytsia was he able to come close to it: when he got away with cheating a lot and spending very little.

Yankl lived a pretty decent life in Vinnytsia: being a boarder was wonderfully liberating. *No worry about meals or the cleaning. It's quiet. Don't have to share a room or listen to my sisters squabbling or put up with Menashe's constant picking on me.*

No one cared if he played cards all night and didn't have a real job during the day. He had no chores and very few concerns. He played for money, and as long as he came out ahead, he could make the rent which included all food except the Shabbat meals, which he ate at home in Krasnoe. During the week, he ate with the landlord's family, so he had company at meals. Since he wasn't family, they didn't pick on or taunt him. He didn't feel lonely or henpecked.

In Vinnytsia, Yankl didn't have to endure Malkah's constant harping that he should "do something useful" or Binyamin's goading to be more enterprising or the girls' eternal whining and bickering. He wasn't forced to tolerate Menashe's ruturn from war and the row that ensued as Menashe retook his rightful place. He didn't have to take sides when Menashe threw Esther out, other than put her up for a couple of weeks when she came through on her way to Odesa to ship out to America.

Yankl wasn't eager for the visas Yosef promised to send. He certainly felt no desire to move to America. As he knew almost no Russian and never studied Yiddish, he was convinced he would have trouble learning to speak English. He wasn't even sure whether anyone played cards for money in America. *What else could I possibly do to earn a living?*

Binyamin's hurried move to be smuggled out of the country worried Yankl. He felt insecure remaining in Russia. Even though the Tzarist regime was gone, things were not good economically and were even getting worse; soon, someone would need to be blamed. As always, who would it be, if not the Jews? The Jews, of course; it had always been so.

Now Binyamin was adding urgency to the process with his rushed exit to Rumania. Yankl was puzzled: what had prompted the sudden decision? Had his brother been the victim of some anti-Semitic incident too horrible to recount, or had it been over some business misdeed—not repaying a debt, or not having the proper permit? If it had something to do with the staple delivery business, Yankl would be connected to it. If whatever happened made Binyamin run away almost without notice with just the clothes on his back, abandoning the business…*certainly my turn can't be far behind*. Binyamin's plans became a catalyst, but still he demurred. The final straw that turned Yankl's indecision into effective action was his mother's announcement, "Going with you means at least part of the family will be together with *Tatte* again. That's as it should be. Go ahead, Binyamin, and arrange for Raisl's and my going."

Yankl had neither the money nor any idea how to make arrangements to leave. He said to Binyamin, "When the women go on that dangerous trip to join you, a man should go along. I'll go too, so I can protect them."

Kyiv
Lviv
Ternopil
Vinnytsia
UKRAINE
Ivano-Frankivsk
Uman
Kosice
Carpathian Mountains
Chernivtsi
Prut
Debrecen
MOLDOVA
Oradea
Chisinau
Cluj-Napoca
Odesa
ROMANIA
Brasov
Danube R.
Galati
Black Sea
Craiova
Bucharest
Constanta

3.

"So you're all leaving me here? Mama, you too?" Malkah lowered her head and said nothing. Menashe approached, lifted her face up, and asked, "Mama, you don't want to be at my wedding? To be around the grandchildren I'll give you and watch them grow?"

Malkah held his hand. "You and your bride could come with us. I'd wait here with you."

Menashe's face contorted as he pulled his hand away. "You don't understand...none of you see that we are in for better times now. You are wrong to leave. But—harrumph—you be the stupid ones and leave. Yes, you should all—all of you—go as soon as possible. I don't need you. You won't be eating at my table anymore. Good!" Menashe grimaced with his semblance of a smile. "Now I can marry Shoshana right away as she insisted. She can move in now to learn to help me and with you gone, we will have room in the house to start my own family."

4.

Rumania

A few days after the family agreed to undertake the exodus to America, Binyamin sat in used farmer's clothing next to the driver of a cart loaded with produce, in the pitch black of the hour before the sunrise.

The JDC provided two outfits that would help Benyamin blend into his mode of travel. "The first leg of the trip is in a cart," the JDC representative explained. "You are to take only a rucksack with a blanket, a towel, a bottle of water, and food to sustain you for a couple of days. Wear these and keep the hat on—it will cover you from the blazing sun and hide your face so you can pass unnoticed among the many government representatives that might want to stop you. Pretend you're a farmer. Keep the suit in your rucksack and change clothes to board the trains. Good luck!"

The rest of the family would follow as soon as the JDC could make arrangements, which was more difficult, as there were three of them. They would travel together and meet Binyamin in Bucharest. The JDC selected Rumania as a transition point because it was ruled by a liberal constitutional monarch who accepted Jews as long as they had steady employment within six months of having immigrated.

Binyamin smiled from ear to ear. He was finally on his way to the land of his dreams. He had no idea what route the JDC would be sending him on or how long it would take. He started up a conversation with the driver. "It's a good day to start out, don't you think?"

"Mmph!" said the Ukrainian peasant hired by the JDC to take his passenger as far as he was going.

"How far am I going with you?"

"To Umań."

"How long will it take?"

"Until the sun's straight above us, God willing."

"And what happens after that?"

"I deliver the produce and come home."

"No, I mean, what do *I* do then?"

"I only know what I do—leave you at the school in Umań. If you don't know what you are doing, why do you expect me to?"

It makes sense that the JDC doesn't disclose its plans or reasons to those they hire. And the driver was right…I should have asked a lot more questions of the JDC representative that I didn't dare. But he seemed so harried shepherding the many trying to leave…I just turned up where I was told to go, got on the cart, and assumed the driver had all the instructions.

The driver was reluctant to speak, so Binyamin settled into his perch and let excitement take over as he admired the full expanse of the view before him. This was further than he had ever been into the rest of the world. The landscape was already changing from waving plumes of corn to isolated trees among clumps of stumps as they clip-clopped along a road that lead into the once heavily-forested areas of the Kiev region. The briskness of a new day melted into the morning warmth, bringing with it a deafening buzz of insects. As the heat intensified with the sun straight above them, Binyamin saw structures dotting the side of the road, the outskirts of the large city.

The cart stopped at a building with a playground and the driver announced, "This is where you get off."

Feeling disconcerted at the emptiness of the schoolyard and the road, Binyamin descended and thanked the driver, then watched the hay cart lumber off. He peered up and down the deserted road in both directions. He walked to the locked school gate, and saw no other living things. He decided to wait under the shade of a tree next to the entrance, and figured someone would eventually come along.

For several hours, Binyamin was on his own, other than a cart traveling in each direction, their drivers ignoring him. He was tired of standing, so he followed the shade to the other side of the tree, sat down, and soon fell asleep, with his head nestled on top of his rucksack.

The ringing of the school bell and the bustle of the students leaving for the day woke him and he stood up. As the schoolyard emptied, a man came out of the gate towards him.

"Gesheftman?" the bespectacled man asked, glancing right and left to make sure they were alone. Binyamin nodded, and the man ushered him to a shed inside the playground, and closed the door behind them. "You don't have a permit to be in this *guverniya,* and if you get caught, you're not the only one that suffers. I'm just a volunteer helping the JDC. Many emigrating Jews leave through Rumania, and this is just one of the many ways to get to Bucharest that the JDC has marked."

"You're with the JDC?" Binyamin asked. "I was dropped here and not given instructions, so I don't know what to do."

"Well, you should have been taken to the other end of town. There, my friend Podolski is waiting to lend you a bicycle. You ride a bicycle?"

Binyamin shook his head. "So what can I do?"

"The JDC is sending unprepared migrants every day, which makes it more difficult to hide our underground connections," the volunteer groused. "You'll have to walk across town to the bike and then learn to ride or walk to the next leg. You'll get the hang of it quickly, and it's only 10 minutes to the bus stop in Yuzhnoukrainsk, where you'll leave the bike. The bus runs one more time today to Odesa. That's the big town where you will get on the train that goes to the border. You'll probably get there too late to catch it tomorrow. You'll have to find someplace to hide in Odesa."

Binyamin expected to follow a circuitous route to avoid being caught without papers, but he certainly didn't plan on different types of conveyances to make the trip to Bucharest. He cursed himself for not having prepared better—or at least to have asked for more information—but he was on his way already, so it was a moment for action, not for regrets.

"Be careful," the JDC volunteer insisted, "because the government is determined not to let young healthy recruits who should be in the Army, escape. Particularly Jews. The train from Odesa to the Moldavian border at Galati, stops in Tellodor, Novoroskiya, and Bothrad, and passengers' papers are checked at one or more of those stations."

Binyamin's face paled, realizing the arduousness of the journey ahead. He swallowed hard and tried to keep his objective in mind. He was on his way and that much closer to America. Surely that was a good thing!

"If you are on the lookout," the JDC volunteer continued, "you can see the *apparatchiks* climb aboard; there are usually two or three officers. You leave the train and leave the station. You can try again the next day. There are always local JDC representatives there, you'll just have to let them come to you. They'll recognize the suit."

"What happens then?" Binyamin asked.

"When you travel an underground route, you never know. Everywhere you can be stopped and get all the volunteers into serious trouble. Sometimes the officials can be bought off. I assume you've come prepared for that."

"I have some money, Binyamin said haltingly, but I thought the entire trip was all arranged."

"Even when you get to Moldavia or Rumania, the borders change practically every day and we don't know whether the border guards we bribed to look the other way on the route we arranged will be there tomorrow. Today, Galati is Rumania, but tomorrow it might be Moldovian or Polish or whatever country is successful in signing the latest treaty. Here is some bread and salami—don't know whether the other volunteers will be able to provide you with more food, so make it and your water last."

"Thank you. I'd better get going," Binyamin said. "I have a bus to catch."

Although it took him much longer than planned to walk across Umañ to pick up the bicycle, Podolski waited for him. Seeing how worn out Binyamin was and hearing he didn't know how to ride, the volunteer offered him a night's rest in his shed and a ride to the bus stop the next morning.

Binyamin's luck continued to hold. He caught an early bus that got him to the Odesa station with hours to spare. He washed up and changed into the suit the JDC representative had provided and boarded the train.

It took Binyamin four days to reach Galati at the border with Rumania, as he was forced to change trains several times to avoid the *apparatchiks*. Without local currency, he had been unable to buy food without calling attention to himself; he finally arrived in Bucharest scared, disheveled, and starving. Barely able to stand, he opened the door to the JDC offices.

"Welcome. Your name?" the man behind the desk said.

"Gesheftman."

The man looked down at his register and said, "Ah. Yes. We were somewhat concerned about you; we thought you'd be here two days ago. Looks like you need to eat and clean up. Come, I'll take you to the building complex where you'll be housed. You can get food in the dining room. Here's your paperwork; fill it out and bring it in tomorrow so we can discuss the next steps."

Binyamin was given paperwork to obtain his temporary Rumanian residence papers and a week's worth of meal tickets, then walked a few steps to the housing complex where he would hopefully be joined by the rest of the family members later. He wolfed down the meal while struggling to keep his eyes open. Binyamin thought of Yankl, Malkah, and Raisl. Would they survive a trip like the one he just lived through? Perhaps the women would be spared such a circuitous route. He was glad none of them had any idea what to expect. *Maybe that's why the JDC gives no instructions ahead of time—how many would balk if they knew what the trip was like?*

As soon as he finished eating, Binyamin went to his assigned room. He had been told that when the family got to Bucharest, Yankl would share this room in the communal apartment, while the women would be lodged in another room next to the tiny communal kitchen. This would be his home for the time it took to obtain the visas from America. *It's still a long time and a long way from the Promised Land, but the first part is done!*

Binyamin fell into a dreamless sleep until he was startled awake by the JDC representative banging on the door. "You didn't come back with your papers yesterday, so we figured you had slept through the whole day. But today we were worried about you. You'd best be up to get your residence papers together. Fill in your name as Ben, which is what your permit will say."

"That will be my name from now on. It's easier for finding a job," Ben said, while rubbing his eyes and pulling his glasses on.

5.

With residence papers now in his pocket, Ben set out to familiarize himself with his new environment and to look for opportunities for employment. Although he had enough gold to convert into currency to last him for a bit, he was anxious to find a source of income to avoid depleting his hoard. He still hoped to arrive in the *Goldeneh Medina* with some of the stash. Bucharest was a cosmopolitan city, not a backward Jewish village, and looked enormous to Ben. Its bustling port was often the departing point for Jews to America and other destinations, so the Jewish population had swelled. As the seat of banking, industry, and political power, the city created a social and economic openness that made post-1918 Rumania feel comparatively liberal.

As other fortress cities, Bucharest was built on seven hills. Ambling up and down throughout Bucharest, Ben discovered its circular shape adorned by a shimmering water necklace created by two tributaries of the Danube, joined to each other by natural lakes in the northern neighborhoods of the city.

Standing on bridges along the rivers—some ornate and some rudimentary—Binyamin created detailed mental maps that always included connections to the exits and marked the quickest escape route in case the temper of the town changed and a scapegoat was sought. Ben was on a mission to figure out the most effective way to maneuver his environment; he called it "painting my geography." He also needed to discover the venues that offered opportunity and to prepare resources that might protect him and his family from certain-to-come dangers; which he called "designing my history." The purpose of this daily circuit was not only to situate himself in the physical space, but also to make connections. He had to learn how to communicate with Rumanians—first by engaging with the locals through signs and gestures; then adding to his collection of nouns and verbs by pointing and miming the question and, finally, practicing those words with locals and foreigners alike, to a chorus of chortles at his mispronunciation and often misuse.

6.

A few weeks later, the family arrived at the JDC housing complex as exhausted as Ben had been, and slept for two days before filling out their paperwork and thinking about what came next. No one mentioned the voyage or the perils they overcame. They had no desire to recount the rigors of their trip, and Ben was grateful he didn't have to relive his in the retelling. Now they were all here in safety, and needed to adapt to the circumstances.

In Bucharest, the reunited Gesheftmans simply recreated their disjointed family routines: silences alternated with the ebb and flow of testy responses provoked on cue by well-rehearsed triggers. Little was said about the fact that they had forever left their birthplace behind, or that a suitcase now contained all they possessed. No mention was ever made of the strong emotions any such uprooting provoked. It was as if only the background had changed.

The family was among the undocumented Jews fortunate to have immigrated in the period when Rumania held an open door to those escaping from discrimination in the Pale. Even though they were Jews, they were allowed to become residents of the capital city as long as they could pay their way and ply a trade within six months' time. When they settled in Bucharest, it seemed a halcyon time for people escaping from the turmoil and *pogroms* in Russia. Waiting for their visas to America to come through, each Gesheftman simply continued to do what they did back in the *shtetl*.

Malkah complained as bitterly and constantly as ever as she prepared meals for the four of them in the diminutive kitchen of the communal apartment. Yankl earned some cash helping other Jewish refugees move and doing odd jobs in the building. He tracked down the local card sharks and spent his spare time among them, learning new games and tricks and losing most of his money. Raisl learned how to embroider Rumanian patterns and, being 15, discovered boys and her capacity to attract them. Determined to learn English, Ben ran errands for the JDC in exchange for attending evening English classes without cost while he kept his eyes and ears open to find a paying position; he just needed to remain alert enough to notice an opportunity.

"The opportunities are out there, we just have to notice them," Ben tried to cheer Yankl up.

"How come all the opportunities—the *mazal*—comes to you?" Yankl asked.

"*Mazal*? Luck? You believe I'm lucky? You think Madam Luck just comes by herself?" Ben asked, the croak in his voice trumpeting his irritation. "Success isn't only hard work or dumb luck. For example, the Binyamin in the Torah for whom I was named, shouldn't even have been born; Yacov, his father, was already 100 years old when he married his mother Rachel, the love of his life. And yet, he was born."

"So just being born…that's luck?"

"No, *dumbkof*. Being named after someone who was lucky to be born isn't what sends luck my way. The Torah tells us 'As a man's name is, so is he.' If you hadn't stayed away from Hebrew school, you would know that Rachel named the child they conceived Ben-oni (the child of my sorrow) because she was to die in childbirth. Yacov, his father, changed the name to Binyamin, the son of my right hand, the symbol of strength. I am named after that child. See, not luck!"

"So, you who know everything, what does 'Yankl' mean?"

"You were named Jacob, like the Patriarch who became Israel 'he who prevails with God.' But you preferred the nickname Yankl, which means both 'deceiver' and 'yokel.' Which is what you are! Enough jabbering! *lah reh-veh-DEH-reh*."

"What does that mean?" Yankl said, his face scrunched in frustration. "Is it Rumanian? For what?"

"It means 'see you later' or 'Bye' in Rumanian."

"Where do you go? And what do you do there?" Yankl shouted out to Ben's fast disappearing back. "What is it you do all day?" he yelled out into the narrow passageway that had swallowed his brother up. The response was an echo of his words.

Ben walked most of Bucharest's 226 square kilometers, taking note of structures that sparked his interest. He was tireless in finding out what the building, bridge, or neighborhood was named, its purpose, how long it had been there, and how the locals felt about it. Ben was ecstatic to learn that the enormous, yet simple, brown-patinaed Art Deco building on Doamnei St.—towards which he felt an uncommon attraction—housed the Bursa de Valori București, a stock exchange. He particularly liked the building because of its passageway and the light that filtered through the skylights which gave the inner walls a golden hue. But it was when he understood what took place inside the Bursa that Ben found the channel for his passion: a place where making deals was not only permitted, but was the sole purpose of its existence.

Every morning, Binyamin studied the Bursa's huge, ornate entrance for an hour before the doors creaked and swung open for the trading session. A few men in suits, some threadbare, others sporting expensive brand names, and a few clearly bespoke, sauntered up to stand in line behind him. Bantering away, they waited for the opening of the trading day. Ben listened to the chatter intently, pretending to concentrate on the carvings that decorated the massive panels, training his ears to the sounds of the language which was totally different from Russian, Ukrainian, or Yiddish. When the doors opened, he moved aside to let the brokers pass and then left on his morning walk to map another neighborhood.

After a couple of weeks, he invested in a cheap, three-piece suit and became as much a fixture at the Bursa as the *bas relief* sculptures and pictures on the doors. Binyamin was able to distinguish the voices of the men in line behind him and to pair the sound of each voice with the individual. The traders also began to recognize him and some acknowledged his greeting; one day, one of them even responded. Ben smiled and followed him inside as far as the barrier through which the trader was allowed in, but where Ben was denied passage and dismissively waved away towards the front row of benches.

Ben sat down and soon other onlookers drifted in to sit behind the barrier that separated visitors from the activity on the stock trade floor. From then on, he entered with the traders and claimed his seat in the front row. He spent hours, elbows on the railing, watching intently with pupils widened in excitement, listening with a cocked ear until he began to follow what was going on and could decipher how gains and losses were accounted for and reported to the public. Not long after, he realized he could understand much of what the traders were saying.

When he knew he had mastered enough of the language to express himself, Ben buttonholed the broker who responded to his greeting. In his rudimentary Rumanian splattered with Yiddish phrases, he told of his overwhelming interest in processing trades.

"I could work for you, Domnul Janacek. I can help and stay out of your way. I've been watching how you do things, and I can learn from that. It's just about knowing how to make money for clients, right? Happy clients pay you for choosing the right stock; that's what a commission is, no?" Ben asked.

"I wish! There is much more to learn about trading on the primary market, which is how companies finance their creation or expansion. The shares are first purchased by investors directly from the investment bank which sets the beginning price range for a given security. Then, of course, there's the secondary market, where investors buy the stock from other investors and the company is not involved. That's what we do here, and the basic force of supply and demand determines the price of the stock," said the broker. "Do you know about supply and demand?"

"I guess it's that the stock is worth what someone is willing to pay for it, no? So it's up to you to convince someone to buy it at a price where they can ask more for it when they sell. But where do you make your money on the deal?"

"*Beseider!* Good! You know the only question to ask: 'What's in it for me?' From our commission, which is added to the cost of the stock itself." Amused at the young man's intensity, the rotund, florid-faced Mr. Janacek took Ben on at first as his "boy Friday." He eventually became Ben's mentor, and was delighted to have found such a willing and enthusiastic protégé.

Ben picked up the intricacies of dealing in stocks quickly and was soon explaining to everyone who would listen why they, too, should be trading in stocks. "Even if you only have a few *lei* to invest," he said. "I can help you do that. We'll grow your investment into big money. Even I bought some of the shares. Can't miss on this one…you'll regret it when you see how much money I made with such a small risk. No way you can refuse…I just won't let you…we'll make out big on this one!"

Ben's intensity frightened some potential clients, but inspired others. With each success, word-of-mouth spread and his clientele grew exponentially. Once again, his capacity to make deals provided for the family's basic needs. Thus, Yosef and Esther's earnings in New York could be used in their entirety to save for the four steerage passages to America. By the time their visas arrived two years later, Janacek had awarded Ben a small percentage of the income his own roster of clients' stock trades brought in.

"Maybe I should forget America. I could sell the visa and passage for a lot more than what *Tatte* paid and grow the difference easily," Ben said to Yankl. "Want to do that as well? Think Mama and Raisl would stay?"

"My luck hasn't liked Rumania, but who knows whether it would behave better in New York? And Mama and Raisl are used to doing whatever you say," Yankl said. "But what about *Tatte*? And Esther? Family should be together!"

"Already, the family split. Don't forget that *mamzer,* Menashe the pig, who refused to come. He showed us it was OK to go our own separate ways."

"Yes, but do you want to be a pig like him?"

"My success tempts me to ignore all that and stay here… yet everything I've done has been to prepare for the move to America…I guess I really should go. If I remain in Rumania, I might attract your rotten luck."

7.

Manhattan

It took a week's train journey from Bucharest to Riga, the port in Latvia where Malkah, Yankl, Ben, and Raisl boarded the Estonia in the Baltic. Through the North Sea, they crossed to the Atlantic Ocean, finally arriving, four weeks later, at Ellis Island on July 23rd.

Ben was to remember the crossing as the worst experience of his life. He was constantly seasick, not only from the ship's rocky motion but primarily from the smell of stale vomit and excrement which surrounded him in the cramped quarters below deck. Too sick to attempt to reach the one latrine they shared or the upper decks to throw up, many of Ben's 1,054 shipmates in steerage simply lay inert in puddles of filth, which increased the stench as the days went by.

The cries of "There she is!" "Look at the enormous figure!" and "America! America!" brought many of the passengers to the rails to look out at the long-awaited view.

In spite of the weakness in his legs from the many days of overwhelming retching, Ben crawled up to the top deck as the Estonia sailed into New York Harbor. He had to have a look at the Statue he had heard so much about. He wanted to feel personally welcomed by Lady Liberty.

Ben never forgot the moment he first saw the statue as the boat approached the harbor, a huge woman with a lifted arm lighting the way, rising up from the black water, blocking the sun. *She's even larger than my dreams, promising to make them come true. She's an omen of good things…*

The reality of the arrival in America contrasted dramatically with what Ben imagined. Once the Estonia docked, the interminable formalities began: being quarantined and doused with chemicals, waiting in long lines, standing before officious men with tired, sulking faces who spoke with vertiginous speed, being shunted from desk to desk in the cavernous shed where new immigrants were processed.

For almost a week, they lived in the courtyard, where they slept on the ground under the open skies. After days of waiting to hear their surname first mispronounced, and then shortened, Malkah, Yankl, Ben, and Raisl were finally processed and given their American names. Marsha, Jacob, Ben, and Ruth were permitted to climb aboard the ferry boat that would take them from Ellis Island to Manhattan. The now-Geshefts had finally made it to America.

Yosef, now Joseph, was waiting at the ferry terminal. Seeing his father after all those years brought home to Ben how much time had passed, and how much he had gone through during that time. They had both changed. Papa was now an aged parent, a wizened old man; and the child who dreaded his *bar mitzvah* and all it symbolized was long gone.

New York was much larger than Bucharest, and infinitely harder to break into. There was a Stock Exchange there as well, but no matter how hard he tried, Ben was unable to discover a way to even slip inside the doors to look. No choice but to find a job. Having no other option, he turned to the only trade he knew. He made the rounds of shoemakers and eventually managed to place himself and his brother Yankl—now Jake—in a shoemaking shop owned by a Jewish acquaintance of his father. Though far from being automated, the factory was organized into production lines, which dictated repetitive, mechanized actions from the operators.

"Day after day after day, I punch in the second hole on the left flap of hundreds of shoe toppers," Ben muttered, the despair in his voice palpable. His burning desire was to "make deals," not sell his time to make a living. He would hold a job only until he could strike out on his own, and then, "I will never again work for someone else," he swore.

Evenings he went to night school to improve his English, knowing that "to do business" he had to have more than his rudimentary language skills. Between long hours at the shoe shop, classes, and studying for lessons, Ben had time for little else, even though at 24, he felt that he should have already begun the process of starting his own family. *I should be going to places to meet girls.*

The situation at home was as unpleasant as ever. With the six of them sharing two rooms, it was also more crowded. His mother's disposition had, if anything, worsened. She refused to answer to the Americanized name or even try to learn English, so she had no contact with anyone outside her family. Joseph retreated into silence, as absent as he had been before they were all reunited. Even with the larger pool of options, Esther had not found a husband; she became more surly by the day, constantly picking on her brother Jake and sister, Ruth. Nobody liked living there. Ben was anxious to leave home as well; but not until he could earn enough to support a household.

Ben had been at his job for just a few months when he developed and implemented an idea to reduce the steps in the production line. When the supervisor noticed the improvement, he asked the foreman to bring Ben to his office. "I think you're industrious and seem to have brains enough to perhaps become a line leader. Meanwhile, you merit a salary increase for reducing cost, how much bonus do you think you deserve?"

Ben furrowed his brow, remembering his stock exchange lessons, answered, "I think the bonus should be connected to a percentage of how much money I saved the company in the process. I have an idea how we can figure that out, but until we get the measurements in place, I'd just like a change in my clock-in time for a few days. Maybe I could try running a second shift—the regular one from 9 to 5 and a second shorter shift from 5 to 9. Let me try being the leader in the short shift from 5 to 9 for a few days and you'll decide if it's working."

"I was thinking of doing just that…ready to start today?" the supervisor asked. Ben was happy to accept and asked Jake to let the family know he would be getting home late.

When Ben got off work at 9:00 p.m., he was tired and hungry; he hurried home, and hoped his mother would not be too upset at having to serve another meal. It had been a good day, Ben could see that the future looked better than the present.

Outside the subway exit, a large sleeping dog attracted Ben's attention. He really liked dogs, so he stopped to allow the animal to smell his hand, then petted it. He'd never had a pet because his parents refused to let him keep one. The dog wagged its tail as it rose up, stretched, and began to follow Ben. *It doesn't have a collar, I wonder whose it is.* The day had been propitious: in getting his supervisor to agree, he not only increased his take-home pay, but perhaps his new hours and pay could allow him to keep a pet. "Come on, pooch, I'll at least give you a meal and then we can go look for your owner," Ben said to the dog as it followed him home.

THE HEART HAS EYES

1.

Tergovitche

Vast expanses of the Tzar's forests surrounded Umań, an important city at the crossroads between the port of Odesa and Kiev. Tergovitche, the small village where the Kaminskis and 400 other Jewish families resided, was on the outskirts of those lush woods.

Moishe Kaminski was one of the most respected neighbors in that small Jewish *shtetl*, an enclave in the Pale of Settlement where Jews were allowed to live. Three generations of Kaminskis had lived in the village, and both his father and grandfather had been the local *melamed*—the teachers—in a culture that highly respected learning.

Moishe ran a small *cheder* in their home, tutoring his neighbors' and his own children. When Velvl, his son, walked into the schoolroom on his first day of class, he tripped on his own feet, distracted by the occupants of the front row. *Am I seeing things, or am I in a class with two angels of the Lord?* Still bemused, he sat behind them.

Velvl's father called him out, "Seems like my son forgot his brain today, didn't you, Velvl?"

"Yes, *melamed*,"

"How did you manage to remove it?"

The entire room burst into laughter as Velvl's red face showed he realized he must have answered the wrong question.

"I'm sorry, *Tatte*, I didn't hear the question…" Velvl said, lowering his gaze.

"And why do you think that was?"

"I've never read in the Book that double *malachim* exist," Velvl answered.

"Oh, you mean Miriam and Tema Gorodetsky? They are not angels, they're twins." The teacher addressed the whole classroom. "You better get used to two girls who look alike in the front row."

Yes, they looked very much like each other, but Velvl never mistook who was who. Tema was the love of his life and Miriam was her older sister by a few minutes. Tema adored him in return. For years they studied together and were inseparable after class: playing together, now and then inviting Miriam to join in. She would reluctantly leave her painting to play with them. Their favorite pastime was House.

"In our house, you can hear the children laughing," Tema said with a sweet smile on her face.

"So, you plan us to have a lot of children?" Velvl asked.

"God willing, there'll be many little children, ours and Miriam's," Tema said, and turning to her sister, "You'll come and visit us with your children, won't you?"

Miriam roared with laughter, "You two can have all the babies—artists don't have time for children. Of course I'll visit, silly, after I'm famous! I'll even paint a portrait of you two lovebirds and the entire brood."

2.

Right after Velvl's *bar mitzvah*, his father took him to the Gorodetsky's home, and on the way, let him know they were going to sign his betrothal contract.

Velvl stopped in his tracks. "Why, *Tatte*, what a wonderful *bar mitzvah* present! There is nothing more I want than to be betrothed to the love of my life, Tema."

"You are to be betrothed to Miriam, the elder Gorodetsky sister," his father corrected him. "Because the older sister is expected to marry first, following Jewish tradition."

Velvl grimaced, holding back tears. "You can't do that, *Tatte*! You know Tema and I love each other and have planned our life together. I don't want to marry Miriam—and she doesn't want to marry me. She wants to move to town to take painting and sculpting lessons."

"There is to be no discussion. Their father and I have agreed that the twin who came into the world first will marry first."

Velvl and Tema consoled themselves with the fact that the wedding was years away.

But nothing had changed four years later once Velvl had a job and could support a wife. Velvl and Miriam reluctantly obeyed their parent's wishes, respecting traditional 19th century strictures for arranged marriages. Tema put on a brave face and announced she would remain a spinster, as she would have no one but Velvl for a husband. The three tried to make the best of a situation in which they were all unhappy. Following their parents' insistence, Velvl and Miriam tried to make a success of their marriage, while Tema made efforts to accept the role of spinster aunt to the children her sister would give birth to.

Although divorce is discouraged by many aspects of Jewish law and frowned upon by social mores, "no-fault" divorce is accepted among Jews as an unfortunate fact of life. Armed with arguments based on rabbinical commentary that effectively recognizes companionship, love, and intimacy as the primary purposes of marriage, Velvl and Miriam repeatedly appealed to their respective parents to sanction their divorce.

At first, the parents counseled them saying, well-being in marriage comes from years of daily living together. After two years, when Velvl and Miriam both continued to request their permission to separate, the parents said everything would change when they became parents. A year later, Miriam gave birth to a little girl, Tzipah.

After months of the in-laws continuing to refuse to listen to Velvl and Miriam's appeals, Tema offered to accompany them the next time they brought the subject up. The couple hadn't included her during the previous entreaties, concerned that the touchy subject would embarrass her. Tema convinced her sister that perhaps they would be more successful if she added her pleas to increase the pressure for the elders to agree.

The following Shabbat, they all walked back from evening prayers to dinner at the younger couple's house and put Tzipah to bed. Once she was asleep, they stood around the table as the older men chanted the blessing of the bread and wine. Then they sat down. Miriam signaled Velvl to stand up again to address the elders, before she brought the food in, "We've called you here to discuss a serious matter," he said.

"Before eating?" said one mother-in-law. "That's strange," added the other.

"I'll be back with the food in a minute, and you can think about what we're proposing while we eat," said Miriam.

Velvl cleared his throat and said, "We all know how Miriam and I have tried hard for years to live with tradition and respect your direction."

Miriam came in with food platters and interrupted him, asking whether he would help bring out the rest of the meal. She then continued presenting their case as Velvl walked out. "Tema and Velvl have always loved each other, and suffered greatly when you insisted I marry before she did."

Tema jumped in. "And as long as I could eventually marry Velvl, we would have waited until Miriam found a husband. But you wanted her to marry Velvl and they just couldn't defy you," Tema said. "It's been a very unhappy situation for all three of us—I will never marry anyone but Velvl. And Miriam wants to go to the big city to study sculpture under a famous artist."

"Happiness, pha! Other things are more important!" said Miriam and Tema's father.

"Sha, sha, Tatte, you've told me how sorry you are that Velvl can tell us apart," Tema said. "Otherwise he could have been fooled like Jacob was in the Bible."

"The heart has eyes," one mother-in-law said while the other nodded to emphasize.

Taking Miriam's hand in his, Velvl said, "Yes it does. Now, the three of us have agreed to fix this unhappy situation, if only you will bless our separation and allow me to marry Tema."

<h1 style="text-align:center">3.</h1>

After years of repeated entreaties, the in-laws finally gave their consent and the divorce was sealed. Miriam moved to St. Petersburg to follow her dreams of an artistic career. She entrusted Tzipah to her father and his new wife—her sister Tema. Miriam never returned to the *shtetl* and Tzipah didn't learn who her birth mother really was until she grew up.

Tema and Velvl were as compatible as they had believed they would be, and in the *shtetl,* their household was held up as an example of the success of love marriages. Two years' later Tzipah was part of a growing family, but she was disappointed that the babies she had so eagerly awaited had both been boys.

"I'm bored. No one to play with," Tzipah often complained, twirling the ends of her hair.

"Why don't you play with Isrulik and Nochum?" Tema asked.

"They're my brothers. I want sisters to play with," pouted Tzipah, underlining the disdain for the boys with an emphatic stomp of her foot.

Tzipah did eventually get the sisters she wanted, as in succession, Tema gave birth to three girls with different personalities. Sheine, the oldest, was quite contrary. She chafed against authority and shirked her chores, often claiming she was tired. She tried to fob her tasks on her sisters or blame a stomach upset for not doing them. Bruche was obedient and quiet, preferring to "be good" rather than face parental disapproval. Feigue was adventurous, and often got herself into trouble.

Much as she loved all her children, Tema couldn't help but develop a special spot in her heart for Nochum. When Isrulik, her first-born, was killed serving in the Tzar's army during the war against Japan, her only son became particularly dear. Five years later, Tema learned she was pregnant and hoped for another boy but gave birth to a girl, whom Velvl insisted be named Goldah.

Although Goldah was the youngest among the siblings in the Kaminski family, she was first in her father's heart. The year she was born, Tzar Nicholas extended his official protection to the woodlands of elm and ash, maple, and linden that grew so lushly in the environs of the little village. Velvl was appointed administrator of the Tzar's forests in the region. "When Goldah came into the world, she was true to her name—she made my luck shine like gold," he said. "She took away the pain of losing Isrulik, my eldest son, to the Tzar's wars. And she not only brought me a job, but my job created the mills where Nochum, my only son, now works!"

4.

Velvl spent six days a week away from Tergovitche, supervising early attempts at forest conservation, protecting the trees from poachers, and harvesting those to be sold for lumber or fuel. His salary was paid from the profits of those sales. Known as *Velvl fun der Veldt*, "Velvl of the Woods," his was the last word about which trunks were mature enough to be cut down. Velvl was highly respected by the woodsmen who came to purchase the trunks. They often chortled, saying they looked up to Velvl even though he was shorter than all of them.

When Goldah was seven years old, her father took her with him to the forest. "So, *mein liebe*, want to come?" Velvl asked, with a twinkle in his eyes, knowing the response.

Throwing herself into his arms and giggling with pleasure, Goldah said, "Oh, Papa, Mama said I'd have to wait until I was grown up! I've been waiting for-e-ver for you to ask me to go with you."

The early morning dew wove necklaces of diamonds on the leaves of the forest as they started off on their three-hour walk to the area of the forest Velvl was working on. The scent of misted underbrush enveloped them, and the sounds of the forest orchestrated Goldah's nonstop commentary noting the scurrying of a rabbit, the warble and chatter of the birds, and the designs the shadows made by the sun filtering through the trees. Throughout her life, Goldah was to remember those weeks as the best of times. "We slept on cots in a hut made from the earth and ate berries or whatever we found growing wild. It was like camping, but comfortable."

At the end of the week, Velvl and Goldah would once again trudge back the 15 kilometers home, unless Velvl knew the last tradesman well enough to trust him to give his daughter a ride part of the way. The minute after the wood was loaded on the cart, Goldah scrambled up from log to log and sat on the topmost trunk, striding it like a horse, her long golden brown hair flying in the wind. Her eyes shone whenever she told her sisters about those trips, and she rejoiced, "That was the most exciting thing I ever did!"

On her wooden steed, perched too high for the driver to hear or respond, Goldah nevertheless kept up a nonstop stream of chatter.

"We leave early on Fridays to get to Temple," she explained to the tradesman as he drove the cart. "In Tergovitche we have a *shul*, you know," Goldah continued, her chin lifted, taking a deep breath and throwing back her shoulders. "Other villages come to us for *Shabbos*, of course. In other *shtetls*, people pray in someone's home."

Goldah continued chatting away as if responding to a question from the lumberjack. "*Shabbos*…you call it Saturday…it's the Day of Rest! We dress up for Temple on Friday nights. Papa wears a suit and I put on a flouncy dress that makes me look all grown up and…"

The driver said something she couldn't hear, so when the cart stopped at a crossroads, Goldah scrambled down to sit closer to him. She didn't want to miss a thing.

"So, how old are you?" he asked. "I'd say you're already grown up!"

Goldah smiled, "I'm…" holding seven fingers up, "so I get to fill the *chainik* with water and light it just before we leave for Temple."

"What's a *chainik*?"

"Uhmmm…a…what do you call it? You know, a samovar, is what you say. We call it a *chainik*."

"Samovars keep the water hot, for tea. Why do you light it before you go to pray?"

"Jews aren't supposed to make a fire on *Shabbos*, you know. So the little oil flame that I light helps keeps the water hot, you know…so we can have tea even without the cooking fire."

When Goldah didn't get a ride, father and daughter would walk back together to the *shtetl*, Goldah skipping now and then as she struggled to keep up with her father's strong and steady pace. They had to get home early enough to clean up to go to the synagogue. The two were a familiar sight to the inhabitants of the few farms along the way, where they stopped to buy milk and eggs: a short, rather plump, bearded man carrying a rifle in one hand and holding the little girl's hand in the other, intently listening to her observations, often laughing at her comments or earnestly leaning down to explain something to her. The farmer treated Velvl with the utmost respect—Velvl had the Tzar's authority in the forests, and the little girl always made him smile with the questions she asked and the things she came up with.

5.

But when Goldah was 11, Velvl lost his job supervising the felling of trees as the Tzar ruled that the woods were too dangerous to farm. The first skirmishes of the Russian Revolution had begun there, and the forest was constantly overrun with advancing and receding groups of Bolsheviks, White Russians, and Communist combatants.

Once tree farming stopped, the local lumber yard closed down, and Goldah's older brother, Nochum, lost his apprenticeship. The owner promised to find him another job if he would agree to marry his daughter. Nochum refused. Although concerned with the loss of income, his parents were relieved at his negative reply, as Lina, the boss' daughter, was not Jewish.

Velvl and Nochum attempted to find odd jobs here and there, while Tema and the older girls tried to supplement the family income by cleaning and cooking at the estates of wealthy Ukrainian merchants in Umań. Being Jewish, they weren't allowed to live within the town's boundaries, so they were forced to travel by cart 35 kilometers each way to get to work.

Goldah's world turned bleak. Tema, her mother, seemed upset much of the time, lashing out not only at the girls but often even at Nochum, the apple of her eye. Heavy-set Sheine constantly bickered with Feige and only stopped to join the others in picking on Goldah. Velvl, Goldah's beloved father, the only one who took notice of her, became more silent and distant every day, though he was home much of the time now.

"Doesn't Papa love me anymore?" Goldah asked her mother. "Why doesn't he take me to the forest now? Is it because I talk too much?"

"Sha, sha—it's because you ask too many questions and cry too much. You're not the center of the universe, you know!" barked Tema.

"I used to be. Papa always said I was his *goldeneh mazal*. I won't ask another question and maybe he'll love me again."

One cold and dreary Friday afternoon at the beginning of winter, Tema learned they owed the local baker an enormous amount for *challahs* Goldah had taken on account and Tema knew nothing about.

"She's been coming each week," the baker explained, "taking one or two loaves and telling me Mama said it was on account. It's been many weeks!"

Tema stomped home and pounced on Goldah. No matter how long Tema browbeat her or how many blows landed, Goldah refused to say she was sorry. She stood unbowed, only her eyes looking down, biting her lip to avoid crying out, letting the slaps and insults flail over her.

"My sisters and I were hungry. I got the bread to feed us," Goldah repeated over and over.

With a final jab, Tema ensured Goldah would never lie again: "God punishes liars and takes away what they most love."

Goldah sulked in a corner of the kitchen. Glad that the storm of invective had ended, she surreptitiously wiped away tears she would not let her mother see. Goldah had grimly made up her mind, she wouldn't—no matter what—ever, ever cry again. *Papa doesn't love me because I cry, so I won't, I just won't. Nothing is more important than being his favorite, like Papa is my favorite.* She watched her now-calm mother place the finishing curlicues on the *pecorlich* she had baked as dessert for the *Shabbat* dinner at Tzipah's. "You never go empty-handed to eat at someone's table," Tema repeated the instruction, as she often did. As the last rays of the sun began to fade, announcing the beginning of *Shabbat*, the family bundled up and readied to go, and Tema urged Velvl to hurry or they would be late for evening prayers.

"You all go to *mincha* without me. I'm not dressed yet, I simply can't find the strength to get up," Velvl whispered from his bed. "I'd like to see the baby…maybe I can recover and go straight to Tzipah's for dinner. God will understand."

"You should stay in bed and go to sleep then. Maybe an empty stomach is what you need. We'll see you when we come back from Tzipah's. She'll understand too."

"I won't go. I'll stay and keep you company, Papa," Goldah piped up.

"Everyone goes," Tema peremptorily ordered. "Only Papa misses *shul* because he's sick."

<h1 style="text-align:center">6.</h1>

Goldah walked with them to Temple, but at the door, she turned back. She knew there wouldn't be seats for all of them to sit together as the prayers were about to start. They wouldn't notice she wasn't there until the prayers were over. Stubborn as an ink spot, she walked back home and hid in the empty barn, hoping to look in on Papa without his noticing, once he was asleep. The room where her parents slept shared a wall with the barn;

through a slat at the bottom of the planks, she could hear her father's movements.

Afraid that Velvl might hear her or be able to notice the light from a candle, she squatted in the dark and wrapped her arms around her knees. She cocked her head to better hear any sound coming from her father's room. Her attention seemed to amplify the slightest noise so that the rustling of the wind and even her breathing resounded in the stillness, startling her incessantly until she figured out what caused the sounds.

In the darkness, the noise of the rats scurrying across the rafters was suddenly broken by the reverberation of a shot. Goldah ran into the house as fast as her cramped little legs permitted. Her father lay on the bed in a pool of blood, the Tzar's rifle next to him. She shrank back. "Papa, papa, what did you do?" Goldah was assailed by the stench in the room. Blood and gunpowder made a potent mix, her father's distorted face made her stomach rise to her gorge, and her blood hammer her temple, impelling Goldah to retch outside.

When the family returned from their *Shabbat* meal, they found a speechless Goldah sitting by the entrance door. Her sisters went inside while Tema stopped to upbraid Goldah for having disappeared. Tema heard the howls from inside the house and ran in to see what was amiss. She joined in the cries of the other girls as her legs gave way and she fell to the ground, tearing at her clothes. Goldah simply continued staring into space, oblivious of her surroundings, unable to respond, shocked into silence, all the more noticeable surrounded by the wails of woe.

Nochum returned later from visiting with Rachel, the girl he was in love with, and her family. Upon witnessing the distress of his family and the horrific reason for it, Nochum pulled himself together to notify the authorities of his father's death and discuss burial arrangements with the Rabbi. It wouldn't be easy to justify Velvl's burial within the gates of the Jewish cemetery.

There would be a negotiation to have the Rabbi declare the cause of death an accident, so the family wouldn't have to carry the stigma of their father having committed suicide.

7.

With Velvl's death, the family's situation became even more critical. To ease the pressure on their finances, Nochum decided to pledge his troth to Rachel Kostnoff, though they wouldn't have the means to marry until he could earn a living, and he didn't even have a job.

During the *shivah* for Velvl, Nochum got up the nerve to speak to Rachel's father without the customary diffidence required for such subjects. Gospodin Kostoff enjoyed cleverness in language, so Nochum thought it would lighten the shattering of tradition if he approached Rachel's father by using the same word with different meanings.

"This is a *shver* (hard) thing to talk about during *shivah*, I apologize for the directness, *Shver* (father-in-law,)" Nochum said. When Gospadin Kostnoff smiled at the play on words, Nochum knew he had approached the issue correctly. "But the family is facing even harder times when the days of mourning are over and plans have to be made." Nochum knew Rachel's father had been hoarding *kopeks* for his only child's dowry; he'd told Nochum long ago, making a joke of it, "You know, for a long time, I thought I was saving every day for a dowry to get rid of my daughter, now I know I've been saving to buy me a son."

"I understand, my boy," Rachel's father replied. "Times are changing, and I don't like it, but what's to be done? You can't stop the world from turning. The important part is that you and my Rachel are good with each other, and you'll take care of her. With my blessing, there should be enough for passages to

America, and a little more, in case Rachel's cousins, the Belkins, aren't able to put a roof over your head once you get there."

Nochum and Rachel made plans to leave as soon as the traditional month of mourning was over. The period of *shloishim* after a burial gave them the time to make the arrangements for the voyage. As they decided to postpone their marriage until their families were reunited in America, they needed another person as a chaperone.

"I guess we can manage to take one of my sisters. We'll find good jobs there to send back money to help the others survive until we can save up to bring them all over. Once the family is reunited in the *Goldeneh Medinah*, we'll celebrate with a large wedding," Nochum said.

"That way, there'll be three of us working to get the rest of the family over," Rachel answered. Then, with a giggle, said, "And one less to bring, so we can be married sooner."

"Well, I guess Sheine, as the oldest, should be the first to emigrate," Nochum decided.

"I'm making a little money sewing," Sheine refused. "Mama needs me here to help put food on the table."

"I don't want to go without Mama," said Bruche, "so I ought to stay here and wait until we can all go to America together."

True to her disposition, Feigue was ready for an adventure and was more than pleased to go with Nochum and Rachel and join the one million Jews trying to emigrate from Russia and Rumania in the hopes of finding a better life in the U.S.

8.

After a harrowing journey by foot, cart, and train in inclement weather through several countries embroiled in the salvoes of the Great War, Nochum, Rachel, and Feige arrived in Hamburg,

Germany. In March of 1916, they boarded the Pennsylvania. They were registered on the ship's log as siblings.

Most of the 1,254 passengers in steerage were Jews. During the long crossing to New York, the shipmates were neighbors, and the steerage resembled a *shtetl*, not 35 kilometers from the big town, but thousands of nautical miles away. There was no problem collecting the 10 men required to make up the *minyan*. On board, the chanting and buzzing of prayers three times a day provided an anchor to normalcy in alien and disturbing circumstances.

Within the crowded quarters, children zigzagged among adults who read, slept, or played cards. They recreated games they had played in their villages and engaged in the same petty squabbles, their whoops and cries adding to the cacophony of sounds that helped drown out the roar of the sea. As they had at home, the women huddled to gossip about their neighbors.

"I wonder how those three from Tergoviche are related. Handsome young Nochum certainly seems much fonder of the older one, no?" asked one woman.

"Not to be nosey," said a younger one, "but I stole a peek at the captain's log. Nochum is 20 years old, the older girl is 19, and the younger one is 16. He's listed as the women's brother."

"Hmm…sure looks to me as if he's sweet on the older one, and they don't look much alike…" countered another.

"Such an evil mind, you have…" tsked-tsked another. "The younger one looks like him; they might be real family."

9.

In Tergovitche, Tema continued to struggle to make ends meet for herself and the three girls still at home. Bruche brought in a few kopeks by cleaning houses, as did Sheine's sewing, but there was no other source of income. Tema realized that if they were to survive, the family had to be further split up. Soon after Nochum and Feige left for America, Sheine was apprenticed to a dressmaker who gave her room and board. Tema now had to place Goldah, her husband's favorite, who was too young to work and yet another mouth to feed. She was torn with guilt and regret but had to find a way.

"You're going to like it here," Tema said as she led Goldah towards the foreboding grey building on the outskirts of the large town nearest their village. Goldah held back, dragging her feet, wondering, as they walked toward the imposing castle-like structure, what it was.

"It'll be warm inside, with plenty of food. It's only until Nochum sends some money from America," Tema continued.

The thought of food made Goldah salivate. "What about you? Are you staying with me?"

"This place is only for children. Remember, if anyone asks, your parents were killed in Bolshevik skirmishes outside Umañ," Tema said. "This is what I told them you said when I found you roaming the *shtetl*'s roads, famished and in a daze."

Goldah bit her lip, dropped her mother's hand, quickened her pace, turned, and faced Tema to ask, "So, how do you think God will punish you for lying?"

10.

Umañ

At the orphanage, Goldah was registered as Ginya, a name befitting a Russian orphan. It seemed to Goldah, as her mother had threatened, that all good things had eked out of her life since she lied about the bread to the baker. *I wonder when God will stop punishing me. He's not only taken my papa but my mother, brother, and sisters, leaving nothing like it used to be. And now, He's even taken away my name.*

Life at the institution was harsh. The decaying grey walls housed 20 matrons and 450 girls, from infants to 15-year-olds. Chores were meted out according to the orphaned girls' ages. Some of the oldest were put in charge of the toddlers, while others foraged for wood and melted, carved-out slabs of ice from the frozen river to provide water for drinking, cooking, and servicing the outhouses.

The younger ones were sent in groups to scour the streets and houses of Umań, begging for scraps or *kopeks* to supplement what the older ones had foraged. The orphans cooked the scanty meals, washed the chipped dishes, and scrubbed the bare concrete floors. Their work days began in the dark before sunrise and ended an hour before it became dark again. In the last hour before sunset—and only if they completed chores to the matrons' satisfaction—the girls crowded into a large classroom for an hour of lessons.

At least here, there was shelter from the inclement weather within the crumbling building's walls, and something to quell the grumbles of hunger, even if it was slop. The girls who lived there knew residence at the orphanage was their only chance of survival in the harsh winter. Warned they would be expelled at the first transgression, the orphans never disobeyed their keepers: they had nowhere else to go and were well aware other more obedient children waited anxiously to take their place in the dark, drafty, unearthly quiet of the old palace that housed the orphanage.

Because she feared the dire consequences of lying, Goldah almost welcomed the rule that the orphans were to speak only in response to the teachers or matrons. She was assigned to scrub floors, a hard chore for an 11-year-old. But she was delighted not to have to deal with mewling infants or to talk to people and beg for money or food. And while on her knees, she could go over in her head what she had learned the evening before.

Goldah loved to learn new things and each lesson made her look at the world in a different way. History taught her that the Tzar was not a god who dispensed good and bad, but a human who seemed to be having a difficult time keeping power, and who followed rules dictated by a different God than hers. Grammar lessons underlined the difference between the words used at home and the language at the orphanage. Mathematics was the best! It was so precise and orderly, and there was no uncertainty in it: only one answer was correct.

Goldah felt grateful for the hour she was allowed to spend in the classroom. But on days when the matrons found fault with the work the orphans did, class was canceled so they could complete their tasks to the matrons' satisfaction.

To make sure they got to have a class each day, Ginya organized a few girls into a crew. "Come on, you can see that together we can work faster and cleaner. We need to be done or no classes. You probably don't care because you're *dumbkofs*, but at least in class, you'll sit instead of working. I sure want to sit, so let's do it together to hurry up and finish."

"Who are you to order us around?" Tatiana protested.

"I'm the one who will tell on you if we don't get to have a class," Goldah said.

Tatiana stood her ground. "I'll kill you for telling on me."

Goldah stormed up to Tatiana, the others silenced in alarm. Hooking a finger on Tatiana's uniform apron, she stared straight into her eyes and hissed, "I will haunt you for the rest of your life. You will never be able to sleep again as my ghost comes to visit you every night."

They all became afraid of Goldah and trembled at the sight of her piercing blue eyes staring at them; no one said another word and got back to scrubbing.

Required to keep silent in the presence of the caretakers, the orphaned girls spoke to each other only when they were in bed, after lights out. Sleeping in an enormous room with 50 other girls occupying triple-level bunk beds was particularly difficult for Goldah. The others had whispered confidences to exchange, while she didn't dare utter a word, once she had bullied them into working together.

Goldah shuddered, remembering what the matrons said when Irina, the girl they'd turned out, was found dead on the streets of Kiev. "Better a Jewess than a Russian child. She had been taking food and warmth from real orphans, orphans of Mother Russia!"

The thought of Irina's screams "I am NOT Jewish, I'm a good Russian, my father died for the Tzar in the Balkan War" as the security police dragged her off kicking and twisting, was enough to bring tears to Goldah's eyes. She could almost feel the knots in her stomach as she imagined what the girl must have felt while slowly freezing to death or starving on the street. She shook her head as hard as she could, trying to block out the thoughts. She reminded herself she was now *Ginya* in the matron's log. For safety, she had better think of herself as Ginya.

Much as she would have wanted to join in to the whispering in the dark, she lived in constant fear that her awful secrets would be found out: that her real name wasn't Ginya, that her father shot himself, that her mother was alive so she wasn't an orphan, that she wasn't Russian, and that she was Jewish. At best, those reasons would have been enough to keep the doors of the orphanage tightly and forever closed to Goldah Kaminski, and at worst…

11.

Months passed, and on a day when the snow had completely melted, leaving the promise of summer sprouting grass to cover some of the muddy ground, Ginya and her crew scrubbed the cement floor leading up to the office. She watched a dowdily dressed woman walk in and recognized Tema, her mother. Goldah was distressed. *Would the matrons see a resemblance?* She turned her back to the office door, loosened her long hair so it hid her face, and continued scrubbing while remaining close to the other girls.

Addressing the matron at the desk, Tema said, "Months ago, I brought in a girl called Ginya, whose parents had been killed in the forests outside our village. People who say Ginya is part of their family saw the graves of her parents and have contacted inhabitants of the *shtetls* in the vicinity around the graves for information to help find the child."

"It would be good to have one less—we are clearly overcrowded. Tell them to come get her," the Matron said.

"I'd like to ask Ginya if she knows them, whether they are really family, and she wants me to let them know where she is," Tema said. "Maybe I can speak with her?"

"Just for a few minutes. She's doing chores right now. Look for her outside," the Matron said. Then, without getting up, she called out loud, "Ginya, come talk to this woman!"

"Yes, Matron, I heard you," Goldah called out in response. Seeing that Tema came out on her own, she stood up, signaled her mother to follow her, and moved to the back of the building, hoping no one would be able to see them together.

"I'm sorry I haven't come before, but it's difficult to come after I've finished my cleaning job. Bruche is finishing up for me so I could come. I know it must be awful to be here."

"It's just dangerous, Mama. If they find out I'm not an orphan, I get thrown out on the streets. That's what I saw them do to one of the girls in the middle of winter. We think she froze to death. It's better you don't come anymore."

"I came because the money Nochum had promised has started arriving, and soon, we can all be together again," Tema smiled as she pushed back some of Goldah's loose hair.

"Let's see what happens when the time comes," Goldah answered, pushing Tema's hand away. "Promise me you won't come back. And even if I could go back home, how would you explain it to the Matrons?"

"I told Matron your family came looking for you, and when things are settled at home, you can tell them you aren't sure about these people, you need to meet them. We've found one of the wood merchants who knew your father, and we can trust him to come get you, pretending he's your family. Don't you want to leave the orphanage?"

"It's not bad. I get on with it. They let the older girls go out to visit people in town. I can come see you at your job in Umań when I'm old enough."

Tema said, "But it'll be years before they'll let you come. Don't you miss being with us?"

"I gave up on missing anyone since God took everything away from me."

Tema lowered her eyes and kept silent.

"Will you promise to stay away, please, Mama," Goldah asked.

"Yes, if you're so afraid. But money from America will soon begin to come regularly, and then you can come live with the family again. I'll certainly send to get you when that happens."

"No, Mama, I might as well stay here until you've saved up enough for the whole family to join Nochum and Feigue in America. You'll save faster if I stay. So, don't send for me until you are all ready to leave for America."

12.

In the following two years, Goldah developed a close rapport with Raisa Alexovna—one of the caretakers who led her on walks—once she won the right to have them by doing extra work shifts. While they ambled through the local park, Raisa talked about the Communist Manifesto and the ideas of equality contained in it. Goldah was interested in learning more about these revolutionary concepts. At home, she wouldn't have access to even the minimal schooling provided at the orphanage.

Goldah became fascinated by the world seen through Marx's and Engels' perspective and soon began attending communist cell meetings with Raisa. So many of the ideas resonated with her own beliefs about equality among all men and women, dispensing with the mumbo-jumbo that all religions tried to impose and doing away with hierarchical family values. She had more in common with the members of the cell than with her family.

Still, as soon as she was old enough to be allowed out on her own, Goldah went to Umañ to look for Tema, her mother.

"Now that I'm older, they let me come to find out what happened to the family members that were looking for me years ago. They think they should at least pay for the years the orphanage has fed and housed me. I used it as an excuse to come find you," Goldah said.

"I'm so glad to see you. You look grown up now," Tema said as Goldah squirmed out of her embrace.

"I've thought about this carefully and have decided to stay at the orphanage. Raisa Alexovna has offered to find me a position," Goldah answered. "I'm thinking about staying in Russia instead of going to America with all of you.

"What are you talking about?" Tema said, pulling at her cheeks with both hands. "Are you crazy, Goldah? Stay in Communist Russia?" Tema had heard about those unholy notions that promoted no marriage, no religion, and no respect for one's elders. *Who would have thought this would touch me? How could such ungodly ideas have anything to do with my family? After all, we're Jews…and now Goldah is actually spouting these absurd, un-Jewish ideas.*

And worse, topping them with the rude retort, "My name is now Ginya. Comrade Ginya. Never call me Goldah again."

"Your father is turning in his grave to hear you talk back to me like that…" Tema responded.

To Tema, these notions were a perilous cancer from which she needed to shield her children; it was imperative to ship them off to America, even before there was money enough for the entire family to emigrate together. She discussed what she ought to do with her married stepdaughter Tzipah.

"Fancy that *iungatsh* opening her big mouth to me," Tema complained. "I'll show Miss 'my-name's-not-Goldah'!"

"Send my three sisters abroad right away," Tzipah declared in hushed tones to keep from waking her napping child. "Now that it would only be you, I'm sure Sol, my husband, will agree to have you come live with us to help ends meet; close down your house, and later we can all make the trip to America together."

Tzipah knew such an arrangement would both save on their expenses and become an impetus to speed up their plans for the exodus to America. The sounds of war were becoming too loud to ignore, and she feared it would soon be too late to get away.

Tema agreed there was no time to lose. She decided to dispatch the three younger girls out of the country immediately; they could wait somewhere else for the visas Nochum was working night and day to get. Tema applied for help from the Jewish Joint Distribution Committee to smuggle Sheine, Bruche, and Goldah into Rumania. There, they would wait for the papers and money from America and be safe from these un-Jewish, family-destroying ideas. Tema feared the perils of travel less than the dangers of having her daughter become a communist, disrespectful of God and Family.

Kyiv
Lviv
Ternopil
Vinnytsia
UKRAINE
Ivano-Frankivsk
Kosice
Uman
Carpathian Mountains
Chernivtsi
Prut
Debrecen
MOLDOVA
Oradea
Chisinau
Cluj-Napoca
Odesa
ROMANIA
Brasov
DANUBE R.
Galati
Black Sea
Craiova
Bucharest
Constanta

13.

One day, shortly after Tema's conversation with Tzipah, a cart rattled up to next to the river where Goldah was supervising some of the younger orphans while they worked. Seeing Bruche and Sheine, Goldah approached the cart to find out what the matter was. As had been arranged with the JDC, the driver scooped her up and placed her between her sisters, who held on to Goldah tightly between them. The driver urged the horse on.

"What's going on?" Goldah cried out. "I can't just leave the children…why are you here? Where are we going?"

"Shush," the driver admonished, whipping the horses to speed on.

"Why is he doing this?" Goldah demanded of her sisters. "Why aren't you saying anything?"

"Mama told us not to explain until we were far from the orphanage," Bruche said. "She made me put on several layers of Mama's clothes and my winter coat. I brought Mama's coat for you."

"I'm wearing Bruche's clothes which aren't as tight as mine and longer," Sheine said. "I guess Mama thought I'd get even fatter. She said we're going to Rumania to wait for the visas to America. Who knows why she suddenly decided to send us away."

Goldah could guess the reasons for her mother's actions. Only a forced removal would have gotten her to agree to leave the children she was caring for, and without even bidding goodbye to Raisa Alexovna. But faced with circumstances that couldn't be changed, she gave up protesting and "got on with it," settling down into the cart without another word.

The three Kaminski girls traveled for days, changing from cart to cart as smugglers were only contracted for distances within their province, where they would be less likely to attract attention. In some carts, they were wrapped in a scratchy blanket which was then tied under the cart. The blanket gave Sheine and Bruche hives, and their scratching increased the rocking from the horses' gait. Goldah wasn't bothered by the roughness of the blankets, as her uniform had long sleeves, and she could wrap the long skirt around her legs to protect them. She kept her long braid away from the dirty blanket, so her hair stayed cleaner than Bruche and Sheine's short bob. But the swinging of the cart and the stench from the horses' piss and excrement turned her stomach, and she struggled to avoid retching. For once, she was glad they only had bread and tea every night, so she had little to throw up.

Other times, they climbed inside hollowed-out bales of hay, which were then covered with more hay. The bales were transferred from horse cart to horse cart, alongside roads that led from Ukraine, over the Carpathian Mountains, through Moldavia to the border with Rumania. At several points, they were told by the drivers to descend from the cart and stealthily slide in the darkness across a river turned to ice, stumbling every few steps, to board a different cart waiting at the opposite bank.

When they came to the largest river they had ever seen, their guide pointed in the dark towards the other side and said: "This is it. The Danube. Out. Get out quick. This is as far as I come. That side is Rumania. Keep moving as you cross. There are government border guards along the banks. Without a moon, they won't be able to fire at you directly. Ignore any order to stop, or this whole trip will be for nothing. Just keep going. The JDC will take you from the other side."

Bruche and Sheine whimpered with cold and fear. Goldah turned to the driver and, in a shaking voice, asked, "What happens if we're caught?"

"Nothing good—not for you, not for me. On this side, they will find and torture me to tell them who paid me to bring you," he said as he turned the cart around. "With no official permit for travel from another region, you'll end up in jail according to the residence decrees. And if they accuse you of leaving the country, you maybe get a death sentence. Now run so I can get away!"

The darkness was total. The only thing visible was the shimmering ice on the river. As they slipped and slid across it, Goldah heard the pounding of horse hooves on the bank behind them and shouts ringing in her ears. Halfway across, Sheine tripped and fell on the ice. Goldah stooped to help Sheine get up and felt a sting in the back of her leg as a barrage of bullets whizzed over and skimmed the ice, throwing up a cascade of shards.

"Get up, quickly," Goldah whispered. "And try to be quiet, so they can't hear where to aim, and hold on to me so you don't slip again."

Panting, the three girls managed to run and slide to reach the Rumanian river bank. They scrambled up the side, sobbing with relief as they heard whispers in Yiddish from the men who offered them a helping hand. The men signaled silence as they carried the girls a mile inland.

As with the three Kaminski girls, thousands of Jews fled the Russian territory named the Pale of Settlement. In 1882, Jews from "All the Russias" were forcibly resettled there. As long as there weren't government-condoned pogroms, the Jews stayed put in their *shtetls* in the Pale, carefully trying to avoid official notice. By 1916, however, when Russia descended into the chaos that was to culminate in the Revolution, the persecution of Jews was exacerbated, so the Jews made plans to leave before it was too late. Families often began their exodus through relatively democratic Rumania: a reputedly safe point to await their passage to America, the gateway to a better life. Most of them contacted the JDC, who helped arrange ways to get to the border, and volunteers to assist escapees once they were on Rumanian soil.

The volunteers waiting for the Kaminsky sisters had been the welcoming committee for the last few months. By now, it had become a nightly ritual for them. After pulling the exhausted and terrified migrants out, they carried them so they could catch their breath. They placed them on the ground among a copse of trees where a woman helped the girls take off their sopping clothes; their body heat had melted the shards of ice splattered on them. Then, she thoroughly examined their bodies for injuries. Miraculously, none of the bullets had landed on these three. Bruche's cheek had a large welt from a bullet buzzing by it, and Sheine's body was covered in cuts, marks, and scrapes from her fall. Goldah's clothes had been torn by the bullets, but her legs showed only shallow gashes. The volunteers treated the wounds, then helped the girls change into clothes they provided. The sneezing and shivering Kaminski girls were then wrapped in blankets and placed next to the dirt road. The JDC cart arrived an hour later to transport them to the nearby city into safety.

For years after, Goldah shuddered at the first strains of the *Blue Danube* waltz and exclaimed, "I crossed that river once. It's not really blue, you know, and not at all romantic!"

GETTING ON WITH IT

1.

Constanta, Rumania

The representative from the Jewish Distribution Committee knocked on the door of widow Podgorsky's house. The Kaminski girls hovered behind him. Bruche and Sheine stood with their heads bowed, silent, eyes staring at their feet, and nervously kicking the frosty soil like horses shying from unsteady ground. Goldah looked up, inspecting every inch of the outside of the house where the JDC arranged for them to be lodged.

The dilapidated facade of the house attested to the widow's having fallen on hard times after her husband's death. What had once been a mansion, located fashionably close to the busy port, now served as the final stop in the *old country* for the *masses yearning to breathe free* that Emma Lazarus celebrated in the poem engraved on the Statue of Liberty. The smells and sounds of the sea that wafted around the house impregnated its walls, bathed the peeling paint, and seeped through spaces where the plaster had fallen off its inner ribs.

Once the JDC representative took care of the formalities, the three girls were turned over to Mrs. Podgorsky. She yelled out for Manya, the servant girl, to lead the new lodgers to the second-floor bedroom that was to be their home until Nochum sent their visas and passages.

"When we've made our beds, we go look for work," Goldah announced as they walked into the tiny, windowless room that held three cots in a row.

"We could move them around so that we don't have to jump over each other to get to our bed," Bruche said. "Let's take turns to pick where we want to put the cot."

"I'll pick first—I want it behind the door, next to the far wall," Sheine said.

"We're only going to be here with our eyes closed, what difference does it make? Just tell me which one is mine and let's get on with it, let's go find jobs!" Goldah said.

"Why are you so demanding?" Bruche asked. "We just barely got here."

"After all that we've suffered, we deserve to rest a little," Sheine whined.

"At the very least we have to earn our keep so Nochum's money can all be put towards the visas. To get to where we're going, everybody in the family works. Enough with the weak, sickly act, Sheine. We all know how strong you really are and how you find ways to get what you want when you can't find someone—mostly us—to sort things out for you. You're lazy but not weak. Both of you go find jobs. Now!" Goldah harangued her older sisters before she stormed out of the room.

"Why should that pipsqueak be telling us what to do?" Bruche and Sheine asked each other. The two were a year apart; Goldah was six years younger.

After moving the cot behind the door, Sheine plopped down on the unmade bed, her heavy frame making it sag.

"Here," said Bruche, giving her a hand to help her up. "I'll make your bed for you. I don't remember, but…was she always so bossy?" Bruche asked.

Sheine spat out, "How could you not remember? She was *the baby*, as Papa and Mama never let us forget. What she asked, everyone had to do. I hated her and that long hair of hers."

"She was a beautiful baby," Bruche said. "I envied her hair too, but we were told to keep ours short so it wouldn't take a lot of time to get to work. Goldah wouldn't let them cut it, so Papa had me comb her out every day. It wasn't easy."

"Oy…Papa's *goldeneh Goldah*?" Sheine grimaced as she imitated how their father spoke of their sister. "And then he's gone—may he rest in peace—and she gets to go off to school and three hot meals, can you believe? While we work our fingers off and our stomachs grumble…"

"Well," said Bruche, "we're here now, thank God, and Goldah's right, you know. We need to contribute. And you're perfectly healthy and not the weakling you think you are."

"You're always ready to give in to her. What a power she has. Everyone always ends up doing what she orders. You go look for work. I'll wait until I'm recovered. I still have much pain."

2.

With so many refugees streaming into Constanta, work was not easy to find, yet Goldah managed to become a teacher's helper at the JDC's school. However, no matter how much she needled her sisters, they were both still unemployed weeks after having arrived in Constanta.

"You beat me to the only decent job," Sheine accused.

"There is nothing I can do that people pay for," Bruche agreed.

"Rumanians hire other Rumanians to clean their houses. They don't want a Jew."

"You're both *laideggaiers*," Goldah spat out one of her damning epithets at them.

"Who do you think you are, calling us lazy good-for-nothings?" blubbered Sheine as she turned her face to the wall.

"You've got to find a way to earn your keep!" Goldah admonished. "Bruche, tell her she's to stop pretending to be a weakling. She knows she's as strong as a horse."

"So I'm a horse *and* a liar. If we're starting up with the insults, you're a bitch," sputtered Sheine.

"Please, girls, be nice to each other. Sheine, why don't you offer to sew for tenants—you'd have to ask Mrs. Podgosky. I'll put up another sign on the board."

After Goldah's hurtful sermon, Sheine took Bruche's suggestion and asked Mrs. Podgorsky for permission to offer her services to other tenants. The landlady recommended her to a local seamstress in exchange for having Sheine do her mending.

At the JDC, Goldah kept her ears open for opportunities to place Bruche. She pressed her supervisors continuously and wouldn't take "no" for an answer. "Maybe my sister could take new arrivals to their lodgings," Goldah suggested.

"We have JDC representatives who accompany the new emigrants," the director said.

"Yes, but that takes the representatives away from other, surely more important work," Goldah said. "More and more refugees arrive every day, she could help and you wouldn't have to pay my sister much."

Even the few *lei* the three earned would shorten the wait to arrive at their intended destination. At least they wouldn't be tapping into Nochum's remittances, and their savings would add up to meet the $25 entry requirement to America.

Living in the same room at Mrs. Podgorsky's, the sisters were forced into daily contact, and the proximity often produced clashes that sent tempers flaring. Their raised voices added to the cacophony that bled through most of the closed doors of the boarding house; not loud enough to drown out the sounds of the waves crashing against the ships on the busy harbor, but so constant that *the screaming house* became a signpost to direct strangers to the docks.

3.

Their landlady was a miserly old woman. The widow made her living by taking in Jewish boarders emigrating from the Jewish Pale, all who would "soon, very, very soon," they insisted, "as soon as our visas arrive, leave for America." Most of these immigrants, however, stayed on for years. Some never left, dying before the relative in America could scrape together their passage and the $25 required guarantee that the newcomer would not become a burden on the United States taxpayer.

If a boarder's visa arrived after their death, Mrs. Podgorsky auctioned it off to the highest bidder and pocketed the proceeds, contending it barely covered past due rent. There was high demand for the coveted slip of paper: the bidders, anxious to gain admittance to America, were more than willing to pay dearly by taking on another person's name for the rest of their lives. Anything to begin their trip to the Promised Land!

Mrs. Podgorsky spent most of the time sequestered in her bedroom, only turning up after the sun went down on Saturdays. With *Shabbat* officially over, she appeared—a tall, shadowy figure in a long skirt that brushed the floor and a blonde wig slightly askew—to collect the rent. But her presence was constant; even over the boarders' din, she could be heard shouting at or pounding on, Manya, her 17-year-old niece, who seemed to accept the landlady's constant abuse without question. Manya cleaned the dank hallways and common spaces, washed the residents' sheets and clothes, and did the shopping and cooking.

"You *laideggaier!*" Slap… "Didn't sweep the hallway, did you?" Slap… "The bottom of my skirt is now dirty. What a lazy, useless girl you are. You'd be dead if it weren't for me taking you in!" Mrs. Podgorsky yelled. "You should be ashamed of yourself. Do you think someone else should be doing your work?" Slaps punctuated the invective.

Manya's simply covered her face and sobbed.

Goldah pitied Manya, but she simply couldn't understand her putting up with Mrs. Podgorsky's bullying. When they became close friends, she chided Manya to stand up for herself, to stop taking her aunt's ill-treatment, and to grow a backbone.

"She treats you worse than a servant, and you let her get away with it," Goldah insisted. "She has no right to make you do all that housework without paying you."

"I have nowhere else to go. She took me in when my mother couldn't support us. We were all starving," replied Manya shame-facedly. Although she welcomed Goldah reaching out—no one else seemed to take notice of her—she often wished Goldah would just be her friend, not keep pushing her to do what fear of being booted out prevented her from doing.

"But she still has to pay you. Have you ever asked her to?" Goldah pressed.

"I wish I were more like you," Manya sighed in response, scurrying off to complete her chores before her aunt came looking for her and hit her for "lolling about."

At night, exhausted from their long days, Goldah and Manya would sneak into the sitting room to exchange confidences. The front room was seldom used, so their secrets felt safe among the sheet-covered sofa and armchairs that surrounded them like silent ghosts as they huddled close together on the floor to hear each other's whispers.

After years of loneliness and silence, they discovered in each other a like-minded person, a companion who made each feel that someone else cared and was interested in them.

"I was my *Tatte*'s favorite, too," Manya said. "I felt invisible when he died. No one even noticed I was there. No one cared whether I studied my lessons. Soon, there was no food, so Mama turned me over to her sister, Mrs. Podgorsky, who needed a worker. And here it is, five years later."

"My mother not only turned me over to the orphanage but had me pretend to be a different person," Goldah said. "I was always scared they'd find out and I'd be taken away by the

Cossacks. But it ended up being a good thing because I learned about the Communist Manifesto and the idea of being equal and no invented God whose name you can't say..."

Manya interrupted her, "Aren't the ideas in the Communist Manifesto wonderful? My brother, whom I adored, was the first one to tell me about Communism. He ran away with a girl, a Comrade, to Israel and I think they live in a *kibbutz,* I never heard from him again. When I first came to Constanta, I went to communist meetings and we would study the Manifesto there. It reminded me of my brother, whom I miss so much."

4.

Occasionally, Goldah went shopping with Manya, and they took the time to stroll on the boardwalk. Being teenagers, they began to notice boys noticing them. Goldah was fastidious in her dress, taking advantage of her tiny size to wear donated children's clothes that no one else could fit into. Her long, dark hair and sparkling blue eyes were often the objects of the boys' whistles, as was Manya's height and slender, erect demeanor when she was out of her servant's clothes.

After two years of being inseparable, Goldah and Manya found it extremely hard to part when the Kaminski girls' visas finally arrived.

"Promise you'll help me make it happen," Manya implored, wiping a tear with the corner of the rag she used as an apron. "Swear you'll help me get away from here and come to America and see you again."

"Don't be so melodramatic, Manya," Goldah said. "Of course we'll meet again, probably sooner than you think, if you get on with it and stop the *kvetching* and stand up to Mrs. Podorsky and get her to pay you for the work you do."

Manya didn't see them to the dock. Her aunt wouldn't give her the time off. They waved their goodbyes through a window, Manya sobbing uncontrollably, not even noticing the blows her aunt rained down on her. Without looking back, Goldah motioned with her raised arm as she led the procession away, bundled up in her winter coat, even though it was warm, to make room for more books in her suitcase. Bruche, Sheine, and the horse-drawn cart laden with their bundles followed behind.

An hour later, Goldah was back, leading the horse that pulled the cart with a pale-faced Bruche lying in it, moaning loudly. Manya gasped as she watched Goldah tie the horse's reins to a post, shush her sister, wipe the sweat off her brow, and resolutely stride in. Without so much as a glance at Manya, Goldah went straight to the room of one of the paying guests on the bottom floor and knocked sharply on the door. Waving the visa in her hand, she confronted the boarder who lived there.

"Do you want to buy this passage and visa? Decide now," Goldah demanded.

Before the startled woman could reply, Goldah continued, "The Black Arrow is a freight boat, so there is no doctor, and the captain won't allow my sister on board with a broken leg, so she stays. You can take her place if you pack quickly and give me enough money to pay Mrs. Podgorsky to house and feed my sister until her leg heals and my brother can send another visa."

The deal was completed quickly, and the coveted entrance to the land of plenty changed hands. Goldah then turned to Manya, who was standing behind her in the corridor, with one hand covering her mouth and eyes the size of saucers, aghast at the turn of events.

After carefully counting out the money from the sale of the visa and ship's passage, Goldah handed it to her friend. "And you, Manya, will make certain Bruche's well taken care of, in exchange for a visa for yourself as soon as I can manage it," Goldah said.

"Wh…a…a t happ'ned?" asked Manya, stuttering in astonishment.

"Bruche slipped on the gangplank as we were boarding and broke her leg. I took her to a doctor who set it. Now, you make sure you take good care of her," answered Goldah over her shoulder as she hurried out the door. "Have to get back. The captain granted me only time to get Bruche's leg set and settle her in. Have to go, or the boat will leave without me."

Though she was only 15 years old, Goldah figured out how to "get on with it." She had no possibility to consult what to do with her mother or brother. She faced the only options available: all three sisters could remain in Rumania and forfeit their visas, or she and Sheine could board the ship to America and leave Bruche behind. Her sisters, though older, whined, whimpered, wrung their hands, and agreed to do whatever plan Goldah devised, for once glad she was the one taking charge and making the decisions.

5.

Ellis Island

Goldah thought she would not survive the 21-day ocean crossing. Looking back, even her time at the orphanage had been less of a trial. There, at least, it had been relatively clean. The stench in the overcrowded cabin repulsed her: the smell of cooking and the reek of spoiled food, weeks of vomit upon vomit upon feces accumulating on the deck. Most of the travelers had never been on a ship before, many passengers were seasick, and there were no tools to clean up in steerage. The minimal facilities were up a rickety rope ladder. To maneuver walking across a constantly lurching floor forced Goldah into repeated physical contact with arms that grabbed different parts of her anatomy for support, or bodies she, too, was forced to hold on to, to avoid falling. "For sure, if there _is_ a God, he put hell on a boat!" Goldah said to Sheine.

The days seemed never-ending, and at night, Goldah tossed and turned, trying to conjure up sleep amid the sounds of retching and snoring and mumbling coming from other steerage passengers. She kept pushing Sheine away in an attempt to have some breathing space and respite from her sister's incessant moaning. To distract herself from the queasiness in her stomach, Goldah concentrated on repeating English verb conjugations and vocabulary lists from the grammar and composition books she had been given at the JDC. Day after endless day, in rhythm with the swells of the waves, she intoned phrases to remind herself that no pain lasts 100 years…no problem lasts a century… no agony will last forever. As with a mantra, she used it to hold on to the hope that this, too, would soon pass.

And it did. Here, they were finally on a solid surface with the shadow of the Statue of Liberty looming over them—so close to their final destination they could actually see a resplendence of lights in the distance, announcing a town larger than anything they had ever seen. Goldah looked up at the gigantic figure and felt the queasiness in her stomach change for a moment from anguish to excitement as she realized the long trip was almost over. This was the symbol everyone spoke about, the beacon to the wonders of America. All they needed now was to pass immigration and she could start her new life.

Goldah tapped her foot impatiently as they waited to go through the formalities required. The final stamp on their papers would, at last, put an end to their seemingly endless journey to their New World. They would soon be reunited with Nochum, and her brother would take over and help them settle in.

During the processing at Ellis Island, Goldah sat on the long bench and held herself stiffly upright, careful to maintain a distance and a well-positioned shoulder to create a wall between herself and the man sitting next to her. Sheine slumped on her other shoulder, despondent, as she had been during most of the sea voyage. Wriggling to force Sheine to sit up, Goldah felt cheered, anticipating the end of the ordeal. It was almost over. Soon she would be away from the crowds and the filth, and Sheine's constant whining, free of responsibility for anyone but herself. Her brother would take over and she could put the entire ordeal in the past.

But first, they had to get the official papers that would allow them entry into America. Goldah brought herself back to the present and intently watched the goings on in the cavernous hall. Thousands of prospective immigrants sat on the long benches, shuffling along as they moved up towards the row of lecterns at one end of the Great Hall, as spaces opened up when others were called forward for their interviews. Wrapped in long overcoats over layers and layers of clothing and sweating profusely, they pushed along battered suitcases and tied-up bundles, their faces drawn with worry and weariness. Men, women, and children silently awaited their turn at the chance to enter the *Goldeneh medina.*

Eventually, Sheine's number was called. Sheine wouldn't let go of Goldah's arm, so they sidled up together to the tall stand, behind which stood a large burly man in a serge blue uniform which reminded Goldah of every other uniform she had come across: the costume of authority.

"Camen, Jenny? That _is_ your name? Have you ever been to America before? Do you have any relatives here? How old are you? " droned the inspector.

Clearly, the official had posed those and several other rote questions over and over again for days, even though he already had that information in front of him. The number pinned to the girl's coats made reference to the number on the ship's manifesto displayed in the large book on the stand before him.

Neither girl understood much English, but after several repetitions, they were finally able to comprehend what the official was saying: Sheine's first name was being Americanized to Jenny, her last name shortened to "Camen" and only Jenny Camen could be granted the right to enter the United States. Goldah was not old enough; immigrants were required to be 16, and Goldah had just celebrated her 15th birthday. She was to be sent back at the shipping company's expense.

As what the immigration official was saying sunk in, Goldah stopped the sob of desperation before it bubbled up in her throat, shook herself internally, and steadfastly declared that there must be another way.

"That's just the way it is. It's the law," the official informed them. "And since you're sisters traveling together, both of you have to leave together. You'll be deported back to where you came from."

Goldah pulled herself together with a mental admonishment that she could not give in to despair. She had not undergone 21 days of suffering to be turned back within sight of the Statue of Liberty, at the door to America. There was no way she would get back on a ship, much less to return to Rumania! There had to be another option, there always was, if one looked for it and refused to surrender to circumstances.

"Please, Mister, wait," Goldah begged the immigration official, hanging on to his sleeve to prevent him from turning away. She clung on, making the official look down at her. "My sister can go, yes?" The official nodded. "She find brother and tell," she explained.

"It's no use. No one can do anything. It's the law," the official replied.

"Maybe brother can," Goldah haltingly told the inspector. "Only a day," she begged.

Impressed by Goldah's cool-headed approach and her persistence, in spite of her youth, the inspector consulted with his supervisor. They demurred, but since Sheine had met the requirements to enter the U.S. legally, they agreed to hold off writing the deportation orders for a few days, until the next ship was due to sail back to Europe.

Goldah shook her sister hard to shush her sobs and, grabbing her by the shoulders, forced Sheine to look up as she gave her instructions. Goldah believed her sister put on an act of helplessness whenever she didn't want to take responsibility. "You have to get yourself together. You know how to do that! Do you want to be sent back? Get to the passenger landing in Manhattan on that ferry and look for Nochum. Tell him we only have a day before they send us back," Goldah directed.

Sheine stopped crying. In a calmer tone, her voice still wavering, she asked, "What if Nochum's not there? What if I don't recognize him?"

"What if…what if…just go! Nochum will surely be waiting there," Goldah said. "Tell him to go to the JDC for help…"

"Can the JDC do anything? Can they get us in?" Sheine gave up the whine in her voice and a smile spread over her face.

"Have them come up with a solution—any solution other than being deported back to where we came from," Goldah ordered as she shoved Sheine onto the ferry boat to Manhattan.

6.

Saskatchewan, Canada

Goldah lay in her cot in the alcove of the Broiland children's room, wondering whether her pilgrimage would ever end. Nochum had contacted the JDC, which came through once again, arranging for the sisters to become *au pairs* at a Jewish farmer's household in Canada. They would stay at the Broilands' in the province of Saskatchewan until Goldah's 16th birthday when she could be allowed into the United States.

After weeks of the disgusting sea voyage from Constanta in the Black Sea, through the Dardanelles into the Mediterranean, transferring to a larger ship in Genoa, crossing the Atlantic Ocean to New York, a week's hold in the quarantine cells at Ellis Island, and another 10 day's travel by ferry, bus, and train, Goldah had finally arrived to what was to be her home for the next year.

Sheine complained bitterly throughout the train ride; because they had another long trip ahead of them, because she was cold, because it was Goldah's fault that she couldn't stay in America. An early winter storm made the landscape they drove through look dark, dreary, and inhospitable.

Sheine wailed, "We'll be stuck out here on a farm for a year as servants. I'll be even older when I finally get to New York, so it'll be more difficult to get someone to marry me." She traveled with her sister only as far as Toronto. At that stop, she got off the train and announced she was not going further.

"I will not live in this weather, in the middle of nowhere, and slave for food and a place to stay," Sheine said, shaking with cold. "I asked the conductor and he said we just passed the border! I have a new name on the papers that allow me in."

"What will you do?" Goldah asked. "How will you live?"

"It's close to the border, so I'll just cross back," Sheine answered. "With the pocket money the JDC gave us, I can get to the big city. I'll find Nochum, he'll help me. I can sew to earn a living while I find myself an American husband to support me and not ever have to work again."

Goldah was amazed at Sheine's decision but didn't try to stop her; Goldah disapproved of scofflaws as much as of *laideggaiers*.

She never spoke to Sheine again. In Saskatchewan, she told the farmer that only one *au pair* had come and that she would try to be as helpful as possible.

Goldah felt grateful to have been taken in by the Broilands, despite her weariness, the bleakness of the surroundings, and the overarching concern that she might not be up to the job. She swiped out a clearing in the steamed windowpane to look out. Nothing but the searing white of the snow against a pitch-black sky smattered with pinpricks of flickering stars. She shuddered at the thought of the alternative: she would never have survived the return voyage to Constanta. If the sea crossing didn't kill her, the embarrassment of returning in defeat would have.

Although the Broiland farm was 10 miles from the nearest town, Saskatoon, the farmer promised to allow her to attend school once her tasks were completed. Goldah seized on this temporary detour as an opportunity to improve her English, to be better prepared when she was finally allowed into the U.S. *At least I won't be wasting this year…*

Yosie Broiland was a kind, hard-working, 40-year-old man whose wife fell ill and had become too weak to manage the household and care for their children. Having an *au pair* to help with the chores and see to the youngsters would allow them to remain on the farm that had been in his family for three generations. Perhaps in that year, Mrs. Broiland might regain her strength. Besides, as an observant Jew, he believed taking in Jewish refugees from the Pale was a *mitzvah*, God's blessing, as it satisfied the commandment that Jews care for one another.

Being the youngest in her family, Goldah's only experience of taking care of children was at the orphanage. She wasn't particularly warm, and her domineering personality did not favor closeness between her and her charges. But being a stickler about integrity, the determination to keep her end of the bargain was enough incentive to perform her duties efficiently, if without affection. The children were fed, clothed, and supervised adequately, but she never formed much of an attachment to them, nor considered the time she spent with them anything but a chore. Being allowed to attend school was the reward for performing onerous tasks diligently.

Ah! School! Goldah loved learning. Just walking into the school building gave her a thrill. When she first learned that she would be required to sit in a classroom with six and seven-year-olds who were still using picture books to learn new vocabulary, she was appalled. The school authorities expected her to be able to take each grade's final exam before she could go on to the following grade. But after a week, she could review the textbook for that grade and pass the tests, easily demonstrating her understanding of the concepts. By the time classes began after Spring break, Goldah had completed the requirements through 11th grade and would be graduating from high school at the end of the school year. With no more than a smattering of English when she arrived, by graduation time less than a year later, she had completed the 12-year school cycle and would earn her high school diploma with honors.

Notwithstanding her enormous enjoyment of school, the year was particularly trying for Goldah. She was faced with work she detested, forced to care for children she didn't much like, and beholden to the kindness of strangers, which jarred her independent streak. She had also begun to mature into a sensuous young woman, without the benefit of a female family member or close friend to help her deal with the issues brought about by such a life change.

7.

Mrs. Broiland showed displeasure every time her husband talked about Goldah. He admired and felt sorry for the plucky girl who had gone through so much to get here and was thorough in performing the tasks she was assigned. Mrs. Broiland's illness kept her bedridden, so she wasn't able to be present when Mr. Broiland supervised the *au pair*. But she made sure her bed was moved to a position where she could keep an eagle eye and a perked-up ear when they were in the vicinity of her bedroom. Her unhappiness soon became compounded with jealousy and after months of seething upset, Mrs. Broiland accused Goldah in a vociferous confrontation.

"I will not put up with it. I know you are making eyes at my husband, you hussy!" Mrs. Broiland screeched at a red-faced Goldah, showing an unexpected surge of strength.

Hearing his wife's distressed voice, the farmer ran into the bedroom. He sat on the bed and took her hand. "Ellie, dear, don't fret. Your illness makes you imagine what simply isn't true," Mr. Broiland said. "How can you think so little of me—or of you! Please don't say things like that. Goldah has been most helpful to us and attentive to the children!"

"I'll not have her in the house! She must be sent away," Mrs. Broiland demanded. "She wants to steal you away from me. You are to contact the JDC and tell them we want someone else, someone older."

Throughout the confrontation, Goldah retained a stony silence. Upon hearing this, she turned to go and at the door, addressing Mr. Broiland and ignoring his wife, she announced, "I will leave immediately after graduation next week. You'll provide me with a letter of recommendation that includes an honorable discharge. Say you would be happy to keep me here if I were willing to stay. And make sure your wife never utters another word of her ugly assumptions," Goldah commanded. She had planned to leave Canada anyway, when she'd be old enough to be allowed into the U.S. There was only a month to go.

Goldah spent the last weeks of her Canadian residence, from the end of the school term until her birthday in July, in Toronto at a women's boarding house. "I wanted to cross the U.S. border the minute I turned 16," she explained to Nochum when he questioned why she left the Broiland's earlier than planned. "I simply couldn't wait any longer to finally end my wandering."

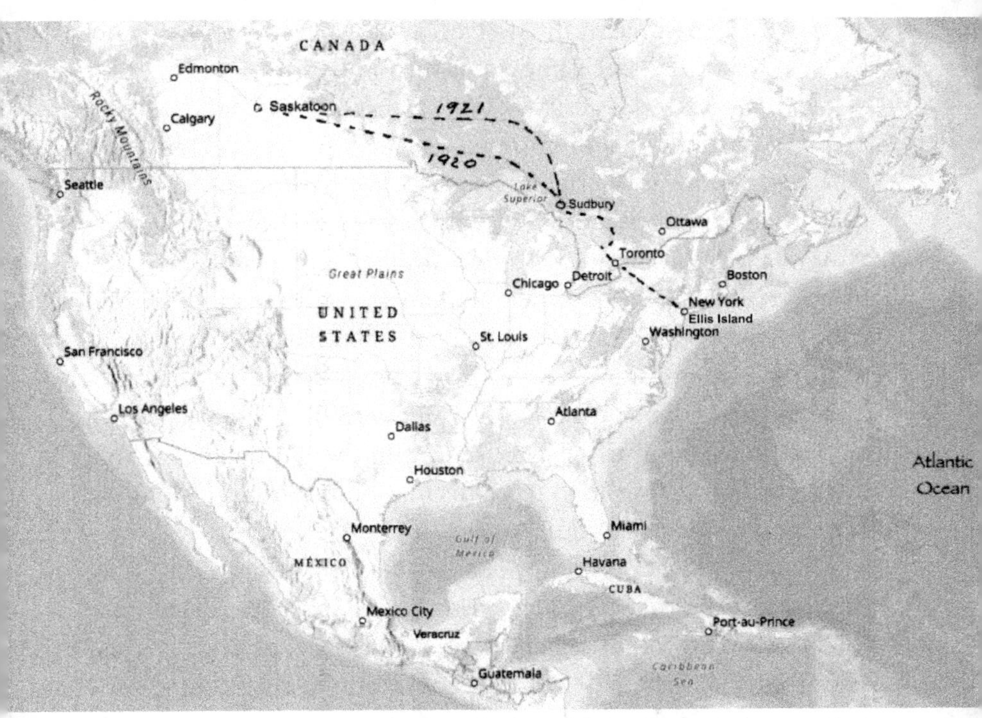

CANADA
Edmonton
Saskatoon
Calgary
1921
1920
Rocky Mountains
Seattle
Lake Superior
Sudbury
Ottawa
Great Plains
Toronto
UNITED STATES
Chicago
Detroit
Boston
New York
Ellis Island
Washington
St. Louis
San Francisco
Los Angeles
Atlanta
Dallas
Houston
Monterrey
Miami
Gulf of Mexico
MÉXICO
Havana
CUBA
Mexico City
Veracruz
Port-au-Prince
Guatemala
Caribbean Sea
Atlantic Ocean

8.

When she entered the United States, Goldah suffered yet another name change: she became Gertrude Camen. The entire family had embraced the Anglicized first and last names bestowed upon them by perhaps well-meaning immigration officials, in the hopes of disappearing their past and avoiding legal conflicts. They hoped to reinvent themselves, as they overwrote the names by which they had been known in the old country.

Her brother Nochum Kaminski, now Nathan Camen, owned a "Chinese" laundry on Nostrund Avenue, and he and his wife lived above it. Gertrude came to live with them, and they called her Gertie. Because it was Brooklyn, she became Goittie.

Goittie's childhood adoration for her father was reenacted in her feelings for her brother. Nathan was still the kind-hearted *gutte neshumah* as always. He was instrumental in helping his sisters make the transition to their new lives. Nathan put them up, loaned them money, called in old favors to find them jobs, and helped them enroll in school. Reuniting the family and getting them on their feet seemed to be his main interest in life, and the laundry provided the funds for it.

At first, Rachel was supportive—Nathan promised to have their wedding as soon as his sisters had emigrated. But once she became his wife, Rachel resented his "squandering" of their resources and wished he wouldn't constantly be supporting some new member of the family's voyage and integration to America.

"We're not the Jewish Defense Committee, you know," Rachel muttered incessantly under her breath. "We should be saving and planning for our children!"

"It's okay, sweetheart, it won't be for very long now," Nathan tried to soothe her. "And don't forget, we were helped too…if your cousins hadn't opened their home to us and loaned us the money to get into business, we couldn't be helping others."

Goittie overheard her sister-in-law's complaints and noticed how much they hurt Nathan. She couldn't fathom how anybody would want to cause Nathan upset; he dispensed such joy and support to everyone that he came into contact with. She disliked Nathan's wife almost as intensely as her sister-in-law disliked her, so relations in the Camen household became increasingly strained. As soon as Goittie was able to talk Nathan into allowing her to move out, she went to live with her sister Fanny, who had emigrated years earlier together with Nathan and Rachel.

9.

Fanny lived in a one-room apartment with her friend Tillie, and they welcomed another roommate to reduce their share of the rent. Fanny taught Goittie how to seamlessly sew on buttons, turn shirt collars, and mend minor tears so she could support herself by helping Nathan in the laundry. But Goittie was determined to continue her education and not to let her high school diploma go to waste. *I'm not about to spend the rest of my life repairing shirts.* She enrolled in bookkeeping courses at Brooklyn College's night school.

Goittie worked an eight-hour day at the laundry, six days a week; and in the evenings, she either attended school or studied for her classes. On weekends, she volunteered at the JDC to establish connections that would help secure a visa for Manya, the girl she had befriended in Rumania.

Goittie kept up a sporadic correspondence with Manya; in Canada, she wrote to make sure Manya was caring for Bruche, the sister she had been forced to leave behind. Once in the U.S., Goittie learned from Manya that Bruche returned to Umañ when she heard of the obstacles her sisters had had to overcome to enter the Promised Land.

"I can't face all that on my own!" Manya reported Bruche said. "Now that my leg is healed, I'll go home and wait there with my mother and Tzipah's family for the visas for all of us."

"What about the visa your brother is sending for you here?" Manya asked.

"Give it to the boarder who bids most and then send the money back to my brother in New York," Bruche replied. "I'll wait to go to America together with the rest of the family, when he can get all the visas together."

Manya hadn't heard from Bruche since she went back to Tergoviche, so she couldn't provide up-to-date information on her or Goldah's mother's whereabouts. Goittie wrote to Manya and assured her that she still intended to help her emigrate to America, even though Bruche was no longer Manya's responsibility. "You can count on it no matter how long it takes. I promised, and I always keep my word."

THE DESTINED ONE

1.

Brooklyn

One night, a year after Goittie arrived in the United States from Canada, she returned home late from school to find a dirty waif on the stoop of the brownstone building where she lived. Sheltered in the corner created by the heavy wooden door and the side wall on the landing entrance, her head resting on a tattered makeshift bundle, her arms embracing a battered suitcase. The crumpled figure looked up, eyes bleary with sleep. As Goittie climbed the steps, the waif scrambled up and flung herself at a startled Goittie, smothering her in hugs and sobs.

Goittie pushed the intruder away to see her face and gasped, "Manya???" The being was unrecognizable.

"Take it, it's yours…American money—I changed the *lei* to dollars at Ellis Island," Manya said, pressing bundles of bills into Goittie's hands. "You know I wouldn't steal from you…I just had to get away."

"Stop. Enough! Let's go inside," Goittie said. "You should know better than to make a drama in the middle of the street."

"Please, please don't turn your back on our friendship. Don't send me away," Manya begged as Goittie shoved her aside to unlock the front door.

"Stop the sniveling. Put that money away. Let's get upstairs. I'll help carry your bundles," Goittie cut her off. "You'll clean up and then we'll talk."

Mindful of Goittie's strict views on what was kosher and fearing a rebuff, Manya blew her nose, bit her lip, and trailed after Goittie, whimpering up three flights of stairs into the one-room flat Goittie shared with Fanny and Tillie. While Manya had a bath, Goittie was relentlessly bombarded with questions from her astounded roommates.

"Who is this person?" demanded Fanny.

"The sisters and I boarded at her aunt's in Rumania while we were waiting for the visas to America," replied Goittie.

"And why is she here now?" asked Tillie.

Goittie's face clouded over; she turned away to hand Manya a towel through the curtain and glowered, "To wash up!"

Fanny knew better than to press further when Goittie was annoyed. But Tillie wasn't used to being cut short. "And after she's clean, what happens? Where is she to stay? There's no room for her here!" Tillie insisted.

Goittie's brow scrunched up for several minutes. The room filled with a tense silence. The only sounds in the room came from behind the curtain where Manya scrubbed herself clean.

When Goittie finally broke the heavy silence, she enunciated slowly, struggling to control her impatience for having been interrogated, "Manya cared for Bruche when we had to leave her behind," she explained. "It's our turn to return the favor."

Goittie then turned to Fanny and continued, "She'll stay in your bed and you two will go over to Nathan's, while I figure out how to deal with this unexpected arrival."

Stunned at being turned out of her own home, Tillie waited for Fanny to protest. But, familiar with her sister's style, Fanny signaled her friend to gather a few necessities and leave without asking any more questions. Fanny was well aware that no further explanation would be forthcoming. The prickly silence in which the two women collected some clothes was only pierced by the sounds of water sloshing against the tin in the washtub. As they walked out, Goittie shut the door sharply behind them.

Once they were alone, Manya confessed her ethical transgression in a flurry of justifications alternating with bawling entreaties for forgiveness. "When Bruche's visa arrived, I don't know how…but I armed myself with courage and broke into Auntie's cash box and took the money to pay you for the visa and the passage on a ship. I kept reminding myself what you said, that Auntie should have paid me for all those years I worked for her… so I wasn't stealing…I was taking what she owed me as back wages."

Goittie listened, inserting an occasional "Stop!" or "Enough with the *kvetching*!" She repeatedly pushed her friend away as Manya tried to hug her or reached out to take her hand. "Finish with the story, already."

Trembling, Manya said, "Then I boarded the ship to New York and came to find you here. Please, please…"

Waving both hands in the air, Goittie stood up and said in a commanding tone, "Get <u>ahold</u> of yourself! Let me think!" The blubbering was reduced to whimpers, then snivels, and at long last, sniffled to a stop. As Goittie paced, Manya awaited the verdict in downcast silence.

"I'm guessing that what your aunt owed you for all those years of work," Goittie said in a softer voice, "would make you the highest bidder for Bruche's visa and passage." And with a smile that quelled Manya's terror, "You delivered the payment in person. It's fine. And now we're finished with that subject." Thus, she and Manya were reunited, as Goittie had predicted years earlier, much sooner than either expected.

2.

In the days following Manya's arrival in New York, Goittie hatched plans to rearrange her living situation in a way that suited her better. As a roommate, Manya would be more compliant, argue less about the division of labor, and never question Goittie's authority. The following afternoon, Goittie left work earlier than usual so she could stop in at Nathan's to speak to Fanny before night class began.

"Fanny," Goittie asked her sister, "is Jenny working? Did she find a husband?"

"So you're finally going to talk to her? How many years has it been since you two spoke?" Fanny asked. "It's about time you should make up—after all, we're family!"

"No. Never. She has no integrity; fancy a sister of mine sneaking out in Canada and leaving me to explain to the Broilands why only one *au pair* arrived in Saskatoon. I will never speak to her again," Goittie retorted. "I thought if she's not working or running a household, she could take my place at the laundry."

"Why? How will you make a living?" said Fanny.

"I found jobs for Manya, who is now Mary, and me in a millinery shop in Manhattan. And a little flat close to the shop, so Mary and I'll be moving out at the end of the month," Goittie informed her sister. "You ask Jenny if she wants to move in with you and Tillie and help in the laundry in my place."

Jenny and Fanny didn't know how to oppose Goittie any better now than when they were younger. "You know," Fanny said, when Jenny at first refused, "it's not a bad plan...we should go along with it."

"No, the plan is not bad, but she could have asked me herself," Jenny said. "She's still thinking she's the boss in the family."

"She rules everywhere...I told her once that if she keeps on ordering people about, she'll never get a husband...she answered there are no Jewish nunneries," Fanny frowned, remembering how Goittie had put her down.

"What does that mean?" Jenny retorted.

"It means Jewish girls don't remain single!" Fanny said.

Both girls knew that marriage was vitally important to Jews. Remaining single was not an option, as one of the primary aims in a Jew's life is to marry and "form a family."

"No use opposing Goldah," Jenny said, spitefully using the *greenhorn* name to belittle her sister, which would have enraged

Goittie, who worked so hard to assimilate into America. "You tell her I said Goldah is a Cossack who always gets her way."

"Good. So you'll move in with us," Fanny said

Now, Goittie felt she was making headway. A millinery shop in Manhattan seemed at least a step or two up from a Chinese laundry in Brooklyn. Certainly, having a boss and co-workers made it more of a professional occupation than sewing for her brother. Also, earning a wage she had negotiated meant she had to budget instead of having her brother cover her expenses. Budgeting gave her the impression that she was, at long last, gaining control over her own life.

The most salient improvement of Goittie's new circumstances was having Mary as a roommate. Sharing with only one person, and a friend at that, was infinitely better than living with her sister and her sister's friend.

With the move from Brooklyn to Manhattan, Goittie's days became even longer. She continued to work six days and attend night school twice a week, but now she had to travel to classes back and forth between the City and Brooklyn. Still, she liked the courses and used the traveling time on the subway to study for them. She enjoyed the pulse of Manhattan, abuzz with excitement, the *today* that promised a better *tomorrow*. Manhattan had the vibrancy of youth, while Brooklyn seemed the place where one ended up: in the staid, tranquil life of those who have settled down.

3.

Yet, she found her work tedious. Sewing headbands into men's hats eight hours a day, surrounded by chattering females, was certainly not a fulfilling routine. Most of the girls were immigrants and spoke Pidgin English with a thick accent, while Goittie prided herself on the breadth of her vocabulary and the correctness of her pronunciation. The buzz of mispronounced words grated on her ears. She looked down upon her coworkers because they "sounded like greenhorns." *Greenhorn* was a new addition to her insult epithets: New arrivals who hadn't lost their thick accents probably because they did not work at speaking correctly— Goittie despised them.

The surroundings were bleak, as well. The back room of the shop, where the women sewed, had no windows and four blank walls with metal tubing forming intricate webs of silver strands against the concrete; the labyrinth of joints and fittings connecting over their heads seemed to compress the seamstresses' breath, so the air was stifling and reeked of their sweat. The hum and crackle of the pipes added to Goittie's irritation.

Goittie tried to devise ways to distract herself from the monotony of the repetitive labor as well as the frustration of having to listen to her coworkers' grating attempts at speaking English. She wondered if the owner would permit her to work in the front room. Watching the customers might alleviate the boredom and would get her out of the other women's company. Also, the front room's large window suffused the space with natural light and provided a view of the street.

"Why don't you let us take turns sewing behind the front counter," she suggested to Mr. Kepl, the owner. "It'll save you paying for a counter girl and be good for business if customers watch the hats being hand-stitched."

"Ya' maybe. But don't you go thinking I'm paying anyone more for sitting out here," Mr. Kepl said. "Maybe we can give it a trial run."

The activity in the front room offered Goittie endless entertainment. After a few turns at the counter, she began helping the men who came in to shop, which pleased Mr. Kepl no end, as it allowed him to concentrate on his newspaper. In addition to diverting Goittie from the monotonous stitching and removing her from her peers, helping the customers decide which hat best suited them and their pocketbooks provided fodder for her elaborate daydreams.

Even when she was cooped up in the back, Goittie amused herself imagining the sort of gentleman who would buy the hat she was finishing. Out front, she could watch the man who actually purchased it and try to imagine what kind of person he was…how would he angle that hat? Where would he wear it? Where would he put it when he took it off?

From there, it didn't take long to come up with an even more entertaining—and much more daring—game. With her rarely-heard, deep-in-the-throat giggle, she confided her plan to Mary.

"I'll write little notes and tuck them into the headbands. A fellow who buys the hat will either discover the note or not. If they find it, it'll pique their curiosity, and if it does, they might come back to the hat shop looking for whoever wrote the note," Goittie detailed her idea one evening.

Mary listened with her mouth agape.

"If the fellow turns up, I'll already know that he notices things, so he's got some wits and is a doer who takes his future into his own hands," Goittie continued, weaving inferences from the imagined responses to her note.

"Also, I'll have aroused his interest. If he comes looking for me, it's because he wants the kind of girl who did that. Then I won't have to deal with the jerks who want an obedient and brainless servant to breed and raise children," Goittie declared, piling on reasons to justify what she feared Mary might misconstrue as brazen behavior.

Certainly, this method was an efficient way to increase Goittie's chances of finding the sort of companion she wanted:

a man who displayed intelligence, curiosity, and ambition; one who was not shy, and one who was willing to look for adventure. That type of man would surely appreciate those characteristics in his sweetheart, not consider them unseemly in a woman.

Mary was aghast at the plan. "Where do you get such hare-brained notions? Aren't you scared? What if Mr. Kepl finds out? What if the fellow who found the note is an axe murderer?" Mary asked.

"What if…what if…what if!" Goittie shot back at her. "It's just for fun, and if you must be a killjoy with your 'what ifs,' why not 'what if' my *bashert*—my destined one—sees the note, and that's how we find each other?"

Despite early clashes with the Jewish mores she had grown up with—which had been the impetus for her mother shipping her out to America—Goittie's experiences had developed into conservative views which included Jewish values. At 19, she had tired of opposing the tenets her mother believed in. And for a woman, that required finding "a nice Jewish boy who can provide."

Thus, a young Jewish woman's dream of coupling became reality with the *bashert,* the "destined one." Goittie believed any action that increased the odds of this taking place—albeit stratagem or ruse, daring or reckless—was kosher.

Faced with Goittie's angry dismissal, Manya gave up trying to deter her from putting the scheme into practice. Still, she refused to join in and convinced Goittie to keep this note business a secret. She feared Goittie would lose her job if the boss found out, and she worried what the other girls in the shop would think of Goittie's derring-do.

"Fine," Goittie said, agreeing to keep her plan to herself. *By not telling them about it, I can also put notes in the bands they sew, and increase my chances of finding the right fellow, someone who is a "gutte neshama," a good soul, like my brother.*

4.

This thought reminded Goittie that she hadn't visited Nathan in several weeks. He seldom saw Goittie once she moved to Manhattan. Given the mutual dislike between her and her sister-in-law, Goittie found excuses to decline *Shabbat* dinner at their house. She missed Nathan a little and felt guilty a lot, so now and then, Goittie stopped in at the laundry after night school to visit with her brother. Tonight, Nathan wanted to talk at length. He was upset, reporting the latest failed attempt to locate their mother and sisters in the old country. Years had passed since they'd had any word from them. Goittie had come to the conclusion that they were dead and had given up expecting them to turn up.

"I'm so disappointed," Nathan said, "I paid the JDC to send someone to search in Umañ, thinking they might have moved there. I just heard from the JDC, who said they haven't been able to trace any of the Jews that lived in Tergovitche; the *shtetl* was destroyed in the Revolution."

"What terrible news, Nochum," Goittie used his old name like an endearment. She hugged him and stroked his hair. "You should stop spending money to look for them—it just upsets you. Give up looking. Maybe they will contact us."

"That's also what Rachel says. I can't even talk to her about my unhappiness anymore. She starts up with, 'You're wasting our savings to find and bring the whole world to the U.S. And then you have to borrow to help them get settled in'," Nathan confided reluctantly. "*The whole world*…it's my mother and my sisters and my nephew and niece and her father! It's our family, and I must do everything I can to be together again. Family is family," Nathan sobbed.

Goittie did what she could to cheer her brother up, although by now, she was convinced that the family members who remained in the old country were not alive. In the years after she left, several *pogroms* had taken place in the county of Kiev where their hometown was located.

It took a long time for Nathan to unburden his woes. When he looked at the clock blinking on and off on the neon marquee of the building across the street, Nathan realized how late he had kept his sister. He tried to convince Goittie to stay the night and not ride the subway home as late as it was.

"I can't stay. I'd be late for work in the morning." Goittie repeated. "I'll be fine, don't worry about me," she insisted until Nathan let her leave.

On the almost empty subway ride home, Goittie wished she hadn't stayed so late in Brooklyn. After a full day's work and a two-hour lecture on tax law, plus the depressing conversation with her brother, she felt drained and just wanted to get home. By the time she pulled herself up the stairs of the station at Second Avenue, it was close to 11:00 p.m. She was bone tired and still faced the eight-block walk to her apartment.

"No use thinking about it," Goittie told herself, "just get on with it."

With her throat tightened, lips pressed together, head and shoulders straight and high, chin charging forward, frown lines on her brow and around the eyes; her stance displayed the unwavering certainty that it—whatever it was—could be accomplished by taking herself in hand.

Goittie stepped out of the exit onto the sidewalk and stumbled, almost tripping on a large black dog with curly hair. Both let out a yelp. The man holding the rope tied around the dog's neck let out a roar of laughter mingled with an apology. As she looked up from collecting the spilled contents of her bag, Goittie couldn't help but laugh too. *He looks so much like the dog, they must be related*, she thought. Their hair was a mass of shiny black curls and both had twinkling brown eyes. The stranger tried to help her pick up her belongings, but the dog kept getting in the way.

"You could train your animal better," she huffed, trying to pull a straight face over her mirth.

"It's not my dog," he answered contritely in an English tinged with a slight Yiddish accent.

"Then why are you walking it?" Goittie asked, moving away with as quick a stride as her short legs would allow.

He trailed behind her as closely as he could, trying to keep the conversation up while maneuvering the dog.

"When I came out of the subway after work, there he was. I like animals, so I talked to him."

"Talked to it?" Goittie asked, starting to walk faster to discourage him from following. "Such *meshugaz*."

"Well, you know, he looked so sad and lonely. Everyone needs a word of kindness at the end of the day," he said as he caught up with her. "He followed me all the way home. I fed him some scraps which he wolfed down. I felt sorry for him because my mother insisted I should put it out—she didn't want it in the house. So I found a rope and tied it around the dog's neck. I've been walking up and down Second Avenue, hoping his owner would be looking for him."

5.

Though she disliked animals, Goittie was struck by the earnest young man's kindness, so she allowed him to walk her home.

In introducing themselves, Benjamin Gesheft and Gertrude Camen commiserated: they had both endured the indignity of losing the names by which they had been known, forced to take on different identities because immigration officials were unable to pronounce their birth names.

"Do you mind going by an invented name?" asked Goittie.

"Nothing good ever came from that other name," Ben replied without a moment's hesitation, "maybe the new one will be more lucky!"

"So you think having a different name brings luck?" Goittie asked. "Then my life should have much improved, having answered to so many different names…"

"I've always wondered what names mean. I love books and only wish I'd had more education, so for fun, I go to the library here. The library is another thing that makes America wonderful! I've looked up what names mean in the library. Are you interested in names?"

"I'm very interested in words, names, the names of people, the names of things…" Goittie said.

"I thought I was the only one who liked that sort of thing," Ben said with surprise. "Had a talk about this with Jake once, back when he was called Yankl…which was how he wanted to be called instead of the name he was given—Jacob— which means *he who has an in with God*. But he preferred the nick-name Yankl, meaning both *deceiver* and *yokel*…which seems to fit his character better than the original name. He became a card shark. He had another chance at getting his name back when he was registered at Ellis Island; his Americanized name was Jacob. But again, he wants to be called *Jake*, which means pretty much the same thing as Yankl. Who knows if the name turned him into a deceiver?"

"Well whatever a name means, it's what we've got now," said Goittie with determination and a little sadness.

"By now, I think of myself as Ben, and I'll go look up Gertrude and let you know what it means."

"It's funny, but no one calls me Gertrude. I'm called Gertie but pronounced Goittie because that's how they say it in Brooklyn. I guess luck or not, it's easier to fit into this new world with a name that sounds American."

"So, you live in Brooklyn, Goittie?" Ben laughed, imitating a Brooklyn accent.

"No, I go to night school and some of my family lives there. I moved to Manhattan about a year ago and live at 2nd Avenue and 7th," Goittie said.

"Why we're neighbors, almost. I live at 2nd and 9th." Ben waved his free hand with excitement. "You see, my good luck."

"It's just a coincidence. Most Jews come to live in this neighborhood. I bet you also came from Ukraine, where I was born…" Goittie laughed.

"I did…so another coinci…whatever you call it…I came from a *shtetl* near a big town called Umań. Do you know that region?" Ben asked.

"I know Umań well. That's the town from where we left to go to Rumania…"

"So did my family." Ben said, jumping up and down with excitement. "See, it was meant to be, it's *bashert* we should meet."

"It may have been Destiny that we meet, so now we'll have to wait to find out what we met for…I'll say goodnight. Thanks for walking me home."

Ben almost danced his way home. He felt the same bubbly feeling inside and a similar surge of awe as he had on the boat when the Statue of Liberty came into view. This girl might be *it*—the one who would understand and support his need to be the boss, be looked up to, and be called *Mister,* what would have been *gospodin* in the old country.

6.

Goittie bought a massive, second-hand black trunk with ornate locks that were more decoration than protectors of its contents. It was the kind of thing that gave the room the character Goittie wanted. She loved it because it had obviously been used by someone like her who had traveled by ship from the old country. It was versatile: so she first stood it up and turned it into a cabinet to put her clothes away; as soon as she could afford an armoire, she emptied the trunk of clothing and used it to guard photographs and mementos of the moment and placed cushions on top to use it as a window seat.

The black trunk, which was put to various uses through the many moves in Goittie's life, held multiple photographs dated throughout the summers of 1925 and 1926. Goittie's distinctive, spidery handwriting labeled the location on the back of the photos: Unity Camp, Martindale, Ferndale, Fallsburgh, Monticello, Rockaway, Napinach Prison, and Coney Island. Goittie was pictured embraced by various young men, always beguiling: a tiny, attractive young woman with long hair, worn loose trailing to the ground or braided and pinned like a coiled snake around her ears.

The trunk also held multiple postcard photographs, portraits of her beaux of that period, inscribed with admiring notes, annotated with the dates and places to which they escorted her. "To Miss Camen, for remembrance from her friend Morris Merker;" (took me to see *Dearest Enemy*.) "To Gertrude Camen from her best friend, and wishful–Abram Silverberg." This one, she told Mary with a wistful sigh, "I would have accepted his offer of marriage if only he hadn't wanted a lot of children."

The memorabilia in the trunk painted pictures in sepia of the lifestyle Goittie and her friends enjoyed during three years after she met Ben. They usually went out in large groups. Goittie included her roommate Mary, who introduced Harry Wine to the group. Ben's sisters, Esther and Ruth, and his brother Jake, tagged along. Fanny brought Tillie who invited Rich Silver. And there were a few others—Ethel and her sister Rose, the Cussis girls, and their brothers. All were in their 20s, all Jewish, most of them recent emigrants from the Pale, the area to which their Jewish grandparents and parents had been forcibly resettled during the Tzarist *pogroms* of the 1800s. The 20-somethings worked hard during the week to earn their livings, but on weekends they splurged, enjoying the riches and variety of entertainment New York offered. It was the Roaring Twenties, and they played at being *Guys and Dolls*.

There are no individual photographs of Ben during this period. He was part of the crowd of friends. Goittie kept refusing Ben's offers to become "my sweetheart," although she made sure to ask him to join in her weekend plans.

Although Ben and Goittie spent most weekends together, it was always as part of the group. She would chat with him, but she chatted with everyone. She danced with him but with the other fellows as well. She flirted with Ben but wouldn't go out with him alone. She encouraged his chasing her but wouldn't allow herself to be caught.

Ben had found his mate. Goittie seemed to be everything he liked: strong, decisive, and assured. She had a brilliant mind and enjoyed discussing many subjects. Ben made his interest in Goittie crystal clear to the group—he hoped peer pressure would help persuade her to accept him as a husband. "She's so tiny; she only comes up to my chest. And I could circle her waist with my hands," Ben described Goittie's figure. "If only she would let me," he sighed. But Goittie still demurred.

"Why do you keep asking him to join us, when you don't want him as a beau," Mary asked.

"I'm not about to settle down yet—especially with someone who dreams of being a millionaire. Life is complicated enough without adding the stresses of owning your own business, which is all Ben wants to save up for. It's like an obsession to him, wanting to be called *Gospodin* Gesheft."

7.

For Goittie's 21st birthday, Ben planned what he thought would be an ideal present: a surprise birthday party. But, there was one problem; he knew Goittie's ideas about propriety were not the mores of the Roaring Twenties. She had previously declined his invitations, saying, "It wouldn't be proper to go to a fellow's house. If a girl does, everyone will expect them to get hitched." Ben wouldn't have minded that: he had found the girl, and soon could support a household; but every time he brought up the subject of marriage, Goittie refused to even talk about it.

Ben asked his sister Ruth to help him trick Goittie into coming to their house.

"You know Goittie's rules," Ruth said. "And her temper. Don't do it; she'll throw a fit."

"Oh, come on, Ruthie, you can invite Rich Silver to the party," Ben wheedled. "He's friends with Goittie, so you can invite him and he won't think you're too forward."

Ruth was in love with Rich Silver and was determined to have him propose marriage. They had been considered an "item" since the previous summer, and now she yearned for their relationship to be closer to official. If Rich came to her house, it would symbolize his agreement to a more permanent, publicly avowed pairing.

"OK, I'll help you fool Goittie," Ruth agreed. "But I hope you don't regret it."

On the day of the party, Ruth called Goittie to let her know Ben couldn't come to meet her after work as they'd planned because he'd had a minor accident. He was sorry he couldn't take her anywhere to celebrate her birthday but asked Ruth to persuade a reluctant Goittie that, as he was hurt and would really appreciate seeing her, there was nothing wrong with coming to visit him at home. The whole family would be present, and certainly, no one could interpret it as something unseemly.

Goittie reluctantly agreed, and as she walked into the Gesheft's apartment, she heard the shouts of "Surprise!" Her face clouded over and her mouth puckered in distaste. She visibly pulled herself together and hissed over her shoulder as she turned to walk out, "I wish you *had* had a crippling accident. I have told you many times how I hate to be surprised."

Ben tried for several months to obtain an audience with Goittie to attempt to get her to accept his apology. It took hundreds of messages, daily rounds to her apartment, and multiple intercessions by Nathan and Mary to get Goittie to consent even to see him again. She agreed to grant Ben a 10-minute appointment after work; he was to meet her on the steps in front of the public library.

Dressed in his Sunday best, Ben paced along 42nd Street at the bottom of the library stairs, awaiting Goittie's arrival. As he watched her carefully descend each step, he felt rivulets of sweat run down his back.

"Hello, Goittie, you look er…wonderful," Ben said when she reached him.

"Well, I see you're still healthy," Goittie replied, looking away from him at the lions guarding the entrance.

Visibly taken aback, Ben stammered, "L..l..look, sweet'art, I just…I only…I wanted to please you. I'll do…anything, <u>anything</u> to make you happy…the party…I didn't know…"

Goittie turned her gaze fully on Ben, her eyes flashing, "What 'didn't you know'? That I dislike lies even more than surprises? Don't lie to me!"

"I mean, I didn't think…I thought…I believed…you'd like a party…in your honor…with your friends," he continued piteously.

"I don't much like parties, and I hate surprises! <u>Any</u> surprise! No one really likes surprises. In every situation, I like to know exactly what to expect, so as to be prepared to deal with it. You should know I mean every word I say!" Goittie cut him off and began to stride away.

"Please, don't run off! I was wrong. Tell me what I need to do to make up for it…just tell me what you want…I'll do whatever…I promise," Ben pleaded.

"Promise? Do you even know what a promise means?" Goittie spluttered. "Nothing is more important than 'keeping your word.' Doing what you say you will do is all that counts!"

"Yes, yes—I promise! I will keep my word!" Ben said.

8.

Although Goittie appeared reluctant to be "Ben's girl," she liked him better than her other swains. He was certainly the most tenacious. She liked that because, in her mind, it showed he could be counted on. He also seemed the most willing to accept her requirements. "They all have to be bent to comply—it's a woman's job to do so. I'll have to work less to train Ben, and he's nice enough," So she accepted his promise, and after 1926, the pictures collected in the black trunk showed Ben and Goittie in various poses of intimacy. In one, he carried her, her long hair flowing over his shoulders; in another, they looked up at each other—attraction, love, and belonging rolled into a glint of longing. Ben shooed the other Romeos away and gave up trying to change Goittie's mind or daring to go against her express wishes.

There were no photographs of their continual spats. Goittie and Ben were in agreement about very few subjects: Even though they had become an *item,* friends and family were never sure whether they would turn up together the next time the group made plans to go out. Their values were clearly different, and Goittie was not one to compromise.

Outside of pursuing his unwavering aim to become an entrepreneur, Ben was a happy-go-lucky follower, relinquishing control over any decision to whoever wanted it. With his jovial, expansive, bellowing laughter, Ben loved nothing better than silly pranks. "Impractical jokes," Goittie called them. For her, life was a very serious matter.

Perfection was what Goittie demanded—from herself and others. And to achieve that pinnacle, one followed clear-cut, unbending rules, stated as universal principles. Ben thought life was imperfect and derived pleasure from it anyway. Goittie delivered her tenets in a well-modulated voice, looking out at a faraway point in space as if lip-synching a deity's commandments. These weren't *her* rules or beliefs, but universal, absolute truths.

So Ben and Goittie argued. They argued about right and wrong. They bickered about the object of marriage. They discussed family, disagreeing about the number of offspring to raise. They belittled each other's likes and dislikes. He loved opera; she liked silence. He was gregarious; she was a loner. She wanted his full attention when she demanded it and his "on-call only" proximity when she had other things to do.

"Why do you keep seeing Ben?" Mary often asked. "You don't see eye-to-eye on much of anything. He's also pretty short on education. I've noticed how you often correct his language— whether it's English, Yiddish, or Russian."

"He's sweet on me, you know. He just doesn't stop calling," Goittie replied. "And, he's not a bad fellow. Like all men, he just needs to be shown who's boss. Which is what you should start doing with your Harry; particularly when he informs the world how you roped him in!"

Ironically, the hatband ploy that Mary had been so adamantly against attracted Mary's own *bashert*, She met Harry when he came looking for the daring woman who had placed a note inside his hat. That was after Goittie was Ben's sweet'art. But Mary liked Harry and told him she'd written the note. And Harry rubbed in her ploy often, calling her a brazen hussy, but Mary never defended herself. She never let on that the game had been Goittie's doing.

9.

Ben continued to try to convince Goittie that they'd stop quarreling if they got married. When in early 1927, she finally accepted, they decided on a triple wedding the following June, the traditional month for weddings. Ruth and her Rich, and Mary and Harry Wine would also get hitched on a Monday, which was the lightest workday of the week. All six marched off to City Hall on June 5th during their lunchtime, served as each other's witnesses, said their "I do's," and split the expenses. They had no celebration or a honeymoon—they just got back to work.

This minimalist approach held true in Ben and Goittie's lifestyle as well. Married life was not much different than when they had been single. After the wedding, they continued to live on the Lower East Side, still worked at their same jobs, and spent weekends with the same crowd. To Goittie, it felt almost as if she had simply moved to a different apartment and changed roommates. But Ben loved being married to Goittie. He admired how she had given up opposing his need to save as much as possible to open his own business. "My earnings will also go into the savings account," Goittie said. "What business are you thinking of?"

"Anything where I don't sell my time and the only thing that counts is what I decide what to do," Ben said. And with a catch in his throat, "Before becoming a foreman, I spent every day making holes on the right side of the shoe tops. I want what I think to count! I want to do deals."

"You have plenty of time until we save up enough for your grandiose plans, but you should start thinking of what the business should be," Goittie said. "I think plans need to be made before you can get on with it, but you believe in Destiny. I do have to admit, you haven't done so badly until now…"

BEST LAID PLANS

1.

Brooklyn

A few weeks after the wedding, Goittie completed night school. Although proud to have an official document that would open doors to finding a respectable position away from the millinery shop, she adamantly refused to "make a fuss" about the degree.

"Graduation, ballyhoo! Why would anyone want to go to a boring ceremony?" Goittie answered when Ben asked how many tickets she could get. "It's rude to ask the family and our friends to spend time and money…and the tickets are expensive!" Goittie went on when Ben wondered whether there was anyone they *should* invite. "No one. If I didn't have to, I wouldn't go either."

Her brother, however, insisted that the first person in the family to graduate from college was to be properly celebrated. As she had derailed Nathan's plan for a wedding reception by eloping—as he called the hasty ceremony at the City Registrar's— and wanted no one at the graduation ceremony, Nathan insisted he wanted to organize a luncheon to celebrate. After demurring, Goittie finally agreed, and Nathan rented the small back room of Junior's Deli on Flatbush Avenue.

On the first Sunday after classes were over, Goittie followed Ben as the restaurant hostess led them down between the gaudy, orange leatherette-covered booths toward the private room in the back. The odors from the kitchen were overpowering; the strong smell of hot grease permeated the front room, which was packed with Sunday diners shouting to be heard above the clatter of plates and cutlery and the tinkle of glass.

It was a sizzling July day, and the ancient blades of the fan whirred and whooshed incessantly, failing to provide relief from the heat but adding to the noise. Ben wished he hadn't decided that the remarkable occasion merited wearing his suit and tie, but he didn't want anyone to think he was anything but proud of Goittie. He wanted to show he wasn't embarrassed because his wife had more education than he did, so he suited up for it.

By the time they reached the back room, Ben was sweating profusely and thankful for the slight respite provided by the more modern whirring fans on this ceiling. The assembled guests rushed up to congratulate the new graduate, and Ben moved away to allow Goittie center stage on her own.

Waving away the congratulations, her blue eyes twinkled and she called out, "Thank you all for coming. It's nice to see you." And looking to make light of it, Goittie announced, "Now, hopefully, all that book learning will help us manage our finances."

Turning to thank Nathan for the party, Goittie added, "And I can now be the official bookkeeper at the laundry. What you now pay the certified bookkeeper, we'll deposit in a separate account, so we can draw from it to continue trying to reunite the family."

Nathan's wife muttered under her breath, "Finally! Someone in the family gives *us* something! Although it's more good money thrown out." Goittie pretended she hadn't heard Rachel. No point in dressing her sister-in-law down; it would only ruin Nathan's pleasure in celebrating his little sister.

Those attending were not surprised that Goittie minimized the achievement they came to celebrate. Within the space of a few weeks, she had not only changed her marital status but had become the first college graduate among them. For Goittie, completing her schooling was simply another step to "get on with," yet she had loosened her long tresses from their usual tight braids. The hair flowed down her back to her knees and betrayed her sense that this was *an occasion.*

From that day on, Ben handed Goittie the envelope with his weekly paycheck from the shoe factory and she doled out $2 from it for his transportation and incidentals for the week. She added her wages into the envelope, minus $25.00 for food and the rent. The envelope's contents went into their savings account so that one day Ben could start his own business. Ben loved Goittie for keeping them organized. He admired her knowledge and appreciated her total support—even though he knew she was not keen on his focus on becoming a magnate, a *gospodin*.

Though their friends constantly teased him about being hen-pecked, Ben never seemed particularly bothered by Goittie ruling the roost. Turning down a gin rummy night with the boys, he said, "Sorry, fellas, Goittie expects me home in the evenings." To the men's peals of laughter and cracks about being tied to the wife's apron strings, Ben replied, "Goittie doesn't wear aprons; you all know she wears the pants." His eyes twinkled. And with almost a bit of pride and a deprecating finality, he put an end to the conversation: "Every now and then, she'll let me try them on, but they fit her better."

Goittie took every opportunity to provide Mary with an illustration of how to gain the upper hand with one's mate. It was the usual subject between them as they waited for the bus home after work. Standing at the corner of 8th Avenue and Jane Street, they watched the buses pass by, looking for theirs. One of them advertised on the side panel the final days of *The Cherry Orchard* at the Imperial Theater.

"You know how much I've been talking about wanting to see that," Goittie reminded her. "It's been on for years…even before you got here; I think it was just a few months after I arrived from Canada that the show opened."

"Yes, Harry and I have really wanted to see it, too. I read reviews that even the Russians think they've done a great job with Chekhov's play," Mary said. "But the tickets cost a fortune!"

"Well," Goittie's eyes shone thinking of Ben's show of affection, "my old man tried to take me to celebrate moving into our new apartment."

"What do you mean, *tried*?" Mary asked. "You lucky girl! When did you go? Did you love it? What did it cost?"

"Ben told me it took him from the beginning of the year, saving on train fare by walking to or from work, and skipping lunch a couple of times a week," Goittie responded to the last question first. "Lost some pounds I guess…"

"Wasn't that nifty! So tell me how the play was…" Mary insisted excitedly.

"Here's how it was…" Goittie answered, reaching into her pocketbook and grabbing the torn ticket remains and handing them to Mary.

Mary scrunched up her face, wondering if she had understood, looked intently at the tiny scraps, and confirmed they came from theater tickets. "You… tore them up? Oh, my, my, how could you? Why, on earth…" she sputtered.

"I told him many times how I dislike surprises…once I forgave him after that awful time when he threw the surprise birthday party because he promised never to surprise me again. I said it over and over. He promised, then broke his promise and bought the tickets without asking when—or even whether—I wanted to go. I bet that's the last time he'll ever try that," Goittie said.

"OH! What did Ben do?" Mary asked.

"He just lowered his head and said nothing. What could he say? He knew I was right. One way or another, to keep control, husbands must be taught, or they won't listen to you."

2.

Now that Goittie didn't have classes to attend, her evenings were free and she hankered to put her degree to good use and bring in extra cash. Finding a bookkeeping position had turned out to be more difficult than she had expected. The *red scare* was just dying down, and who knew if there were any records of her Communist connections. The Ku Klux Klan was growing in numbers and hated the Jews as much as the Blacks. Many laws against immigrants were being instituted and the rumblings of a new war were echoing from Europe. It was not a good time for employers to risk hiring a naturalized Russian woman who was Jewish to boot. Nevertheless, Goittie made sure every potential boss was aware of her background. After months of her applications being turned down, she decided to set up on her own. As before, she turned to Nathan for help.

"Do you think the *heshboiness* are in order?" asked Goittie when she delivered the August accounts.

"I know the accounts are right to a penny, without even checking, Goldah," he responded, using her childhood name.

Goittie winced upon hearing him call her Goldah. She had come to talk business and was loath to be reminded of the days before she became a professional. She squirmed against the ladder-back chair Nathan pulled out for her and waited for the trundle of the passing streetcar to stop so that he could hear her request. The dank room smelled of sweat and chemicals, forcing her to take off her jacket and hold her handkerchief to her nose. The rattling from the street died down and Goittie rose to stand in the path of the fan that steadfastly refused to give up its ineffectual job of cooling the steaming locale.

"So, would you recommend my services to your customers and to other shopkeepers?" Goittie asked in a diffident voice, afraid to be rebuffed.

"You really mean to work at this bookkeeping, eh?" Nathan replied, his eyes shining with pride.

"I could have business cards made and you could give them out to your customers. We'll put half of any business that comes from the cards into little Gertrude's college fund," continued Goittie, warming to the subject.

Goittie frequently babysat Gertrude. If nothing else, babysitting helped Goittie reciprocate Nathan's kindnesses throughout the years. Before she married Ben, it also provided an acceptable place for courting in times where there were few venues or opportunities for a couple's privacy.

Goittie had a particular fondness for Nathan's daughter, which stemmed from the fact that the little girl bore her name. "Gertrude" had been selected when she was born because Nathan's wife had turned down every other name Nathan suggested, reminding him that a living relative on her side of the family had that name.

"You know Ashkenazi Jews name their children only in honor of the dead," exclaimed Rachel. "You can't call her Libe, Aunt Dorfman's name. Auntie'd think we wish her dead!"

Goittie pooh-poohed the custom, calling it a silly superstition. "I'm young and healthy," she said, "and would be honored if you name the baby after me."

"That is a very generous offer, Goldah, and it could mean a lot of money if all my customers hire you," Nathan joked.

"You wouldn't mind, would you?" Goittie was so anxious that she didn't hear his "yes."

"You make the cards, Goldah, and I'll keep them on the counter so the clients can see them," Nathan said.

Although Nathan felt uncomfortable pressing his customers, he was delighted to call upon his many friends and acquaintances. He encouraged them to take advantage of an expert bookkeeper with a degree, who could keep accounts straight, was honest, and wouldn't set them back much.

As little Gertrude's college fund grew, even Rachel, Nathan's wife, was less combative with Goittie. Soon, Goittie had enough clients so that she would have been able to say goodbye to Mr. Kepl's establishment. But she hesitated to give up on the steady income it provided. However, the departure was brought on by another event.

3.

Goittie and Ben had agreed to put off having children until their career plans had advanced further. But, as Goittie ruefully said with a shrug of the shoulders when her pregnancy began showing, "Some women just have to *look* at a pair of pants, and they become pregnant…"

Leah was born in September of 1928, a little more than a year after their marriage. Goittie stopped working at the millinery shop; what she earned keeping the books for people Nathan had recommended helped to pay for household expenses, while Ben's salary from the shoe factory went straight into savings.

Ruth, Ben's youngest sister, had given birth to her first child in June, so the young mothers spent a lot of their time together, trying to keep themselves busy while supervising the toddlers. They generally sat in Thompkins Square Park after pushing the girls in their baby carriages in a brisk trudge through the grimy streets of lower Manhattan. They picked two benches and placed both carriages between them. Ruth sat on one bench with her wool and needles or a finished sweater and strings of spangles and sequins to embroider it.

Goittie extricated the large, lined, album-size red books where she kept her clients' records and a footstool from the back of Leah's pram. She spread the book on the other bench and sat in front of it on the footstool. They worked in silence. Ruth created mini works of art with her knitting and embroidery, while Goittie kept track of the finances of businesses that employed her.

In the summer of 1929, the two families rented bungalows on Rockaway Beach, joining in the yearly ritual to avoid the stultifying heat and humidity of the City. The migration to the rustic, rural seaside community—the summer destination for working-class New Yorkers—began on Memorial Day weekend.

Less than an hour's subway ride on the "A" train and a short walk brought them to their "court," as the cluster of 10 tiny wooden A-frame bungalows built around a courtyard was called.

Goittie breathed deeply, savoring the idea of two wonderful months to watch a silvery sea stretching out to the horizon and feel the coolness of the ocean breeze rising up over Jamaica Bay. Across the Bay, she could see Manhattan's skyline and was reminded how lucky she was not to suffer its sweltering heat and that her clients agreed to wait for their accounts until September.

Entering her summer abode through the door of the narrow, screened-in porch, Goittie sighed. The bungalows on either side were so close that even whispered conversations next door could be heard. Only the clotheslines that ran between the bungalows offered some semblance of privacy. *I'll make sure to keep towels and sheets hanging there all the time,* Goittie promised herself. Inside was a daybed covered by a madras bedspread, a kitchen table with a brown tablecloth, and, in the back, two bedrooms, separated from each other by paper-thin, head-high wood partitions. Bare light bulbs hung from a cord fastened to the pine rafters. The bathroom was the size of a closet.

The husbands and some friends arrived on Friday evenings, turning the weekends at the beach into enjoyable communal gabfests. Dinners became large parties on the sand, with people streaming back and forth fetching dishes from the bungalows to bring them to the beach, even though women in bathing suits were not allowed to leave the beachfront without covering up.

The mouth-watering scent of cherry blintzes from the cafés suffused the warm evening, and the sounds of screaming riders on the Thriller roller coaster at Playland added background noise. The adults sat on the beach past midnight, the moon lighting up the scene like a spotlight; some dashed into the sea for a swim to cool off during sultry August nights, even though swimming after dark was also prohibited. The lifeguards—undisputed lords of the beach—who would have prevented it had long since gone home.

Many of their conversations centered on worries about the relatives who remained behind in what was now Ukraine. "We haven't heard from Mama since Stalin's *pogroms* began last year," Ethel Grinberg said. "The family took too long to try to come to America," her husband pointed out. "Yes, visas are now impossible to get," Rich Silver commented. "The immigration laws have locked the borders down," added his wife Ruth.

Goittie had come to the conclusion that her mother and sisters were dead, but Ben's tyrannical brother Menashe and his family still hoped for visas. When they heard that Menashe's father-in-law, an intellectual and principal of a *gymnasium* was detained and exiled to Siberia, the Geshefts realized that it was too risky for any Jew to remain in Russia.

Unable to get visas into the United States for Menashe's family, the Geshefts pooled resources to book them passages on the first ship bound for Veracruz out of Eastern Europe. Mexico would be a safer place to wait for the U.S. visas to come through. Ben couldn't help but derive some satisfaction from Menashe being forced to publicly own up that he had made the wrong decision by staying behind.

"Now," said Ben, "that bully owes me again."

4.

That year, after Menashe, Shoshannah, and their child arrived in Mexico, Jake, Ben, Esther, and Ruth once again split the cost to pay for their eldest brother to visit them in New York. Menashe hadn't seen his father in 17 years and his mother and siblings in eight. He arrived on October 22, in the middle of the stock market crash.

The siblings gathered at Yosef and Malkah's home to welcome Menashe after many years of separation. To ease the added tension brought by the changes that took place since they were last together, Goittie suggested they keep the reunion to the original members of the family. She was eager to avoid an evening where everyone would vie to display his achievements during the years they hadn't seen each other.

"In Mexico, the streets are paved in gold," Menashe said. As ever, he won at one-upmanship; with his brothers and sisters listening agape, he told stories of the wonderful business opportunities available in Mexico.

"All you need is a couple thousand dollars and you open a business and become rich. Look at me," he crowed, "only been there less than a year, and already I can afford a full-time maid to help Shoshannah look after the child."

Ben's eyes glittered with desire, jealousy, hatred, and envy as the family sat around the dining room table listening to Menashe's fascinating stories of a country of outlaws and innocents.

"Anyone with a little money and a brain can easily be wealthy in a minute," Menashe said.

Ben felt his entrails twist with frustration. He had both a little money and brains, yet once again, luck had favored his tyrannical brother landing him in the right place. Although Ben had, with great foresight, left for the land of plenty just in time, now everything seemed to have flip-flopped. With the stock market crash, Menashe had ended up with the better deal even though he had been a *dumbkof* to have decided to remain in Russia.

Walking home from his parent's house that night, Ben was as distraught as on the ride from Vinnytsia to Krasnoe when he had been caught carrying gold. This was just such a crossroads—and now that Menashe had opened up other possibilities with his talk of opportunities for wealth, Ben could no longer stay in the United States. His days were spent in constant worry—about whether the shoe factory would close, whether he would lose his job, and whether the money they had scrimped to save would now be worthless.

As he had on that long-ago train ride, Ben concentrated on all possible options and methodically discarded those he felt wouldn't work. After much consideration, he decided they'd go to Mexico to make their fortune and return to the U.S. once the country's economic situation had sorted itself out. Ben knew the formula to follow: ensure his and his family's livelihood, so he could grow the next enterprise.

By the time he arrived home—he had walked up and down Second Avenue for hours—Ben had figured out how to overcome the central obstacle to moving to Mexico: getting his wife to agree to be uprooted once again.

Ben knew Goittie's determination and admired her intelligence. If she backed the move wholeheartedly, she would help him map out a plan of action that was even more well-thought-out than any he could have possibly come up with. He felt energized and thrilled that this brilliant woman was his partner. If she approved of the move, everything else would surely fall into place.

For her part, Goittie hated being a *hausfrau*. She disliked not having a regular job, just contributing to the financial support of the household with the bookkeeping income. When they married, Ben and Goittie intended to delay raising a family and planned to both continue at their jobs to save towards economic independence instead of just salaries. Besides, she found caring for the child and keeping house boringly tiresome.

Although she enjoyed watching the baby grow and delighted in the notion that she was responsible for the proper upbringing of a new little person, Goittie yearned for intellectual stimulation. She often complained that she and Ben weren't able to go out together anymore. Ben knew that the idea of having a maid to take care of Leah would certainly appeal to his wife. They would have live-in childcare, Goittie could go back to work, and they'd be able to go out in the evening now and then, without having to pay for babysitting or enlisting one of his sisters to keep an eye on the toddler.

Ben arrived home so late that Goittie had gone to sleep. He waited impatiently for Goittie to wake so he could command her undivided attention. Goittie was impossibly testy about the little things—she would have barked at him if she realized how late he had returned, for example— but she was incredibly calm and resourceful about the big things. After all they'd been through to get here, becoming immigrants in yet another—and more exotic— country was definitely a big thing.

5.

Goittie woke and saw that Ben wasn't in bed. Seeing the light on in the other room, she shook herself awake. Ben wouldn't be up with the light on if it wasn't something serious. These were the times she felt closest to Ben, when she might be needed and appreciated for her insights and capacity to envision the big picture. She wrapped a robe over her nightclothes and went into the other room.

As Ben expected, when Goittie came in and saw him pacing, still in his street clothes, she sat down and listened in silence while he spilled out the issue and outlined his idea.

"After just a short time in Mexico, Menashe claims to have a profitable business selling things made of leather. He says he sells easy and makes enough profit to pay rent and food and even a maid to help Susannah with the house and the kid," Ben reported. He gulped and the thickness in his voice betrayed his envy of Menashe's fortunate turn of events.

Goittie didn't say a word, but her intent look signaled she was meticulously taking the mental notes that enabled her to repeat what was said, *verbatim*. She waved Ben on.

"The whole business world here is falling apart. And that *mamzer* claims anyone with a little *gelt* and some brains can do what he's done because the country is just bursting with demand, and they import most goods. We have more than a few dollars and brains! You have 20 times the *zeijl* he has," Ben sputtered.

"And…?" prompted Goittie, as Ben stopped, wondering how much more to say.

"We can start a business down there. I'll have to figure out what, but that shouldn't be too difficult! We'll need a steady income until the business starts producing. So I thought we could invite my brother Jake to be a partner—he doesn't have anyone to support, so his paycheck would be his contribution," continued Ben.

He could see Goittie got the gist of his notion. He had natural business instincts and knew when to stop selling an idea and wrap it up with a succinct summary to close the deal. "As things are bound to get more and more difficult in New York with the financial difficulties, we should make plans to move to Mexico and start our business there." Then he closed with the sales *ask*— "So, what do you think?"

"Let's sleep on it," Goittie said when she saw Ben was done. Without another word, she went back to bed and expected him to follow. That was typically her first step when she wanted to think things over—unless she disapproved outright. If so, she declared her opposition in no uncertain terms.

Ben was satisfied for the moment. At least she hadn't said "no" right away. He had learned that there was absolutely no point in bringing up anything that went *against her principles* because nothing would get Goittie to budge when that was the case.

Ben waited for several days while she mulled over the idea of moving to Mexico. One never rushed Goittie's decisions; she needed to sleep on it for as many nights as she considered necessary. By the time she finished working a problem over, Goittie had researched options, explored multiple avenues, created scenarios about various possibilities, and ranked each one for the probability of success. Then she selected the option that had the highest ranking and eliminated all others. Only then would she be ready to reach a decision and respond.

As Ben told Goittie, he decided to ensure their livelihood until their enterprise in Mexico could support them. To have a certain source of income he would invite his brother Jake to become their partner in whatever business they decided to set up. Jake would remain in New York and provide their stipend from his salary. A monthly check and his savings would be Jake's capital investment. Ben and Goittie would invest their savings and be the working partners. However, until Goittie handed down her decision, Ben couldn't talk to Jake because if she nixed it, there was no point in inviting the family's ridicule. So he waited nervously for Goittie's answer to come.

In the meantime, he calmed his anxiety by spending every free minute at the library, quizzing the librarian, reading up on Mexico, and trying to figure out what he could produce that Mexicans needed to buy.

6.

A few days later, Goittie said without preamble: "You'll go to Mexico first. You've told me about Menashe's tendency to exaggerate, so you need to check it out. Once you know first-hand what it's like, and whether it'll work for us, Leah and I will follow. Depending on how long it takes to check it out, my brother

Nathan said we could stay with him. Your idea to involve Jake as a partner is sound: he's single and his salary can support us during the first year or two while we are growing the business and have no income."

Not a word about the backwardness of the country, or the enormity of readjusting to another migration, this time with a little child, or, once again, having to learn a new language and adapt to a new culture. In those few curt and definitive sentences, Goittie let him know she was fully behind the move. Ben's optimism was fired.

Now Ben could let the combination of intention and imagination lead his questioning to choose the enterprise and how he would set it up. Menashe had started a belt factory and Ben wanted to get as far away from his brother's business as possible. Leather reminded Ben of shoes, and he felt it was symbolic of the old country and their enslavement to selling their time rather than becoming owners benefiting from the profits. He wanted something better and more lasting than leather as the raw material. In the end, he decided to manufacture stainless steel cutlery which he learned Mexico was importing from Japan.

"Everyone needs utensils to eat," Ben said. "The more civilized they become, the more they use forks and spoons. Probably a bigger market for cutlery than belts. And the Mexican government will close the border to Japanese imports as soon as I can request it once production is flowing."

Once he decided on the product, talked it over with Goittie, and she concurred, he started his quest. He needed to learn about stainless steel as a raw material and take a crash course in the cutlery manufacturing process. After easily winning Jake over to the partnership idea, Ben approached the foreman at the shoe factory. The foreman steeled himself for a confrontation; every worker was on a short fuse—they were all worried about being laid off. The economy was rapidly failing, shops and factories were closing daily, and the hunger lines were growing.

"Things are getting harder, right? Soon, you'll have to get rid of some of us, won't you?" asked Ben diffidently.

"Yeah, but you won't be among the first," the foreman assured him.

"If you can offer that to my brother Jake, maybe I'll go try my luck somewhere else. That way, he can help out with the family in case it takes a bit for me to get it together," Ben replied.

Because the foreman had, on occasion, witnessed Ben's rarely displayed temper when he was deeply upset, he was relieved to have avoided the face-off he had expected. He agreed to try to keep Jake on as long as he possibly could.

Ben and Goittie spent the next several months doing research. She read books and articles and consulted with one of her long-ago teachers at Brooklyn College to help make the business plan, and then briefed Ben about what she learned.

He visited factories to learn about the workings of the machinery and to make connections with machinists. At the National Silver Company, he offered his services without pay to the foreman and worked for a couple of months. In his gregarious and inquisitive way, Ben quickly learned certain machines were about to be scrapped because the factory had ordered newer ones to modernize before the economic situation became gloomy.

With his innate business instinct, Ben was able to purchase the machinery as scrap metal; the equipment was slightly outdated but in excellent working condition. However, he still needed to have cutting dies—which, of course, National Silver refused to sell to him.

The cost was huge: $10,000! They pooled savings from their single days and Ben's full salary since they'd married. Goittie's bookkeeping provided the basic household needs. The savings came from the hundreds of hours Ben had walked the shop floor as foreman of the production lines and Goittie's many hours of stitching and accounting they hadn't spent on basics. Now their capital seemed much less substantial and Ben worried that they might not have enough to make it before the cutlery production had money flowing in.

Ben approached the top machinist at the factory and asked if he could make dies from a sample at a reasonable price; the machinist agreed to moonlight to make them. Ben went to the Five and Dime and bought a five-piece set of cutlery, imported from Europe, with a design that he liked and featured a knife, salad and dinner forks, soup, and dessert spoons.

Once Ben had the dies and tested them, he felt as prepared as he could be. He would leave for Mexico as his father had gone to America—to begin a new life and bring the family once he dug in a foothold. The day before his boat was due to sail, Goittie and Leah moved into Nathan's home in Brooklyn.

"Would you and Rachel mind babysitting Leah until tomorrow, so the wife and I can be on our own and I can take her for a quiet farewell dinner?" Ben whispered to Nathan while the women were out of the room.

"What a question! You know we yearn to have that little doll spend time with us," Nathan answered. "But has Goittie okayed this scheme?" Everyone was aware of Goittie's aversion to surprises.

"I didn't ask until now that it's all arranged so she <u>will</u> approve," replied Ben. "And if she doesn't, nothing is lost."

Nathan nodded, glad Ben wasn't springing it on her; his little sister was in good hands. But still, he worried, "You'll have to stay in town. Won't she be upset?"

Ben was glad he made all the plans before speaking with Nathan. "The couples who wanted our apartment were all willing to pay the "latch money" I asked for signing the sublet. So, I used some of it to reserve a room in a nice hotel not far from the docks," said Ben, answering both questions at once. "I guess I'd better go ask your sister if she's okay with the plan."

Asking for money in exchange for turning over a lease to secure hard-to-get living quarters underlined Ben's instinct to obtain profit from perceived value and be successful. *After all, my last name does mean "business."* Ben felt more confident about living up to his surname; setting off to start his own *gesheft* was the first step towards achieving the status he yearned for as a youngster. He felt well on his way to earning the honorary title of respect he craved. *Gospodin Gesheft…sounds perfect. I wonder, how do they say gospodin in Mexico?* he mused.

WANDERING JEWS

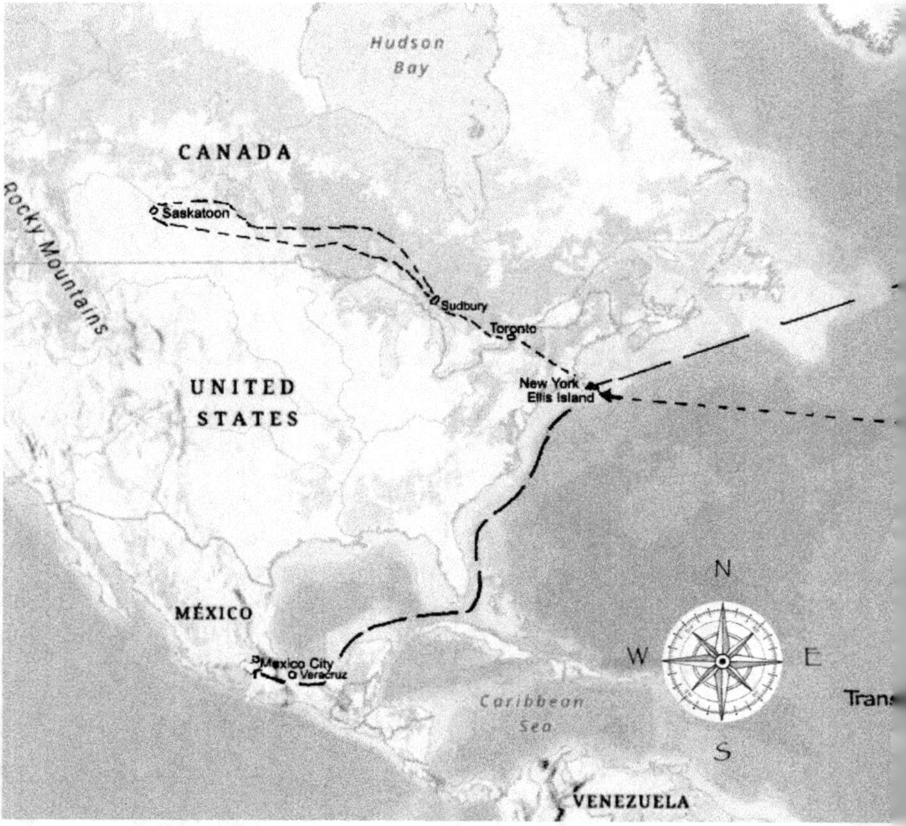

Goittie's Routes: 11,800 miles

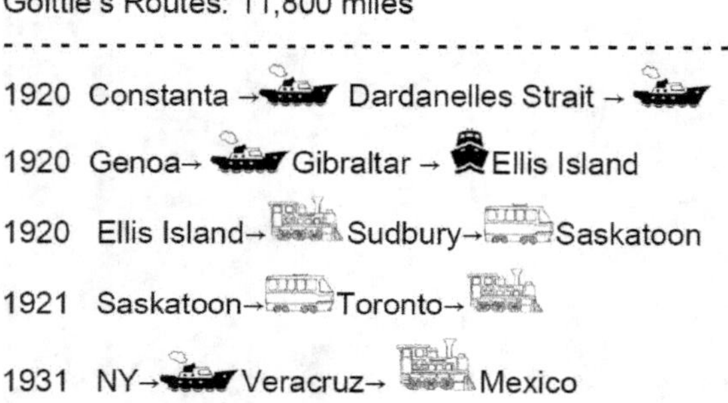

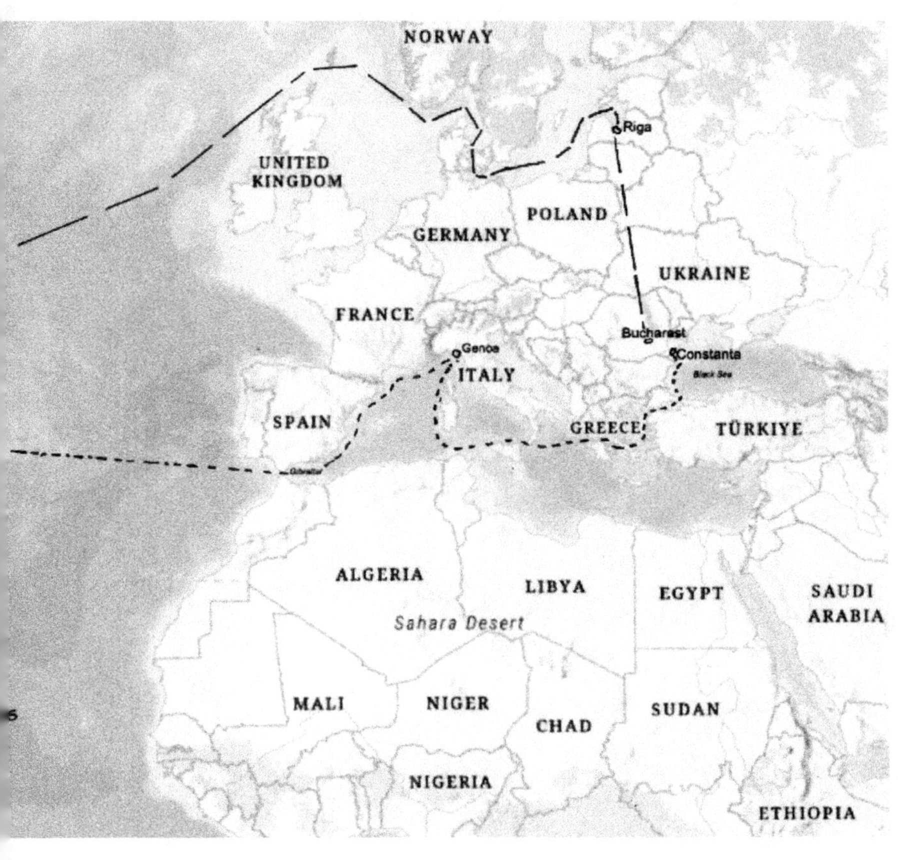

Ben's Routes: 9900 migration miles

1919 Vinnytsia→ Bucharest → Riga

1924 Riga→ 'the Estonia'→Ellis Island

1931 NY→ Veracruz→ Mexico City

1.

*I*n May of 1930, Ben was one of the 1,200 passengers ready to board third class on the <u>White Star</u>, sailing from New York to the Mexican port of Veracruz. Ben and Goittie had their farewell night, and Goittie came to the dock to see him off.

"I'll send telegrams as things fall into place and let you know when you and Leah can come," Ben said. "I won't write letters so I don't annoy you with my bad spelling." Goittie burst out in one of her rare chuckles and simply wished him a safe voyage and a quick settling in.

Once aboard, Ben stood on the deck and looked out at the receding Manhattan skyline. He felt wrenched, nearly as desolate as six years earlier when he'd traveled in steerage from Rumania to New York. *I didn't stick around too long, did I?* Once again, he saw himself as a caricature of the Wandering Jew. *Will I ever be able to put roots down? To call some place "home"? Are we Jews forever cursed to keep wandering?*

Dejected, he turned away from the view as the city faded into the horizon and went below to crawl into his cot in an attempt to calm the swells of nausea and make the hold stop spinning. The stench of unbathed bodies and the stale air brought back the nightmare of the crowded, windowless space in which he had come to America. Ben fought back the waves of despair those memories brought back and stifled his gagging by making mental lists of the things that made the current situation different. *At least, this voyage is just a few days, not weeks, long,* he sighed.

He also felt free of the fear that had haunted him then: that he wouldn't be allowed in and sent back to the horrors of anti-Semitic Eastern Europe. Now he had a U.S. passport and was an American investor. He had a connection in the new country already—even if it was his detested tyrant of a brother. Menashe could, at the very least, provide a place to stay for a few days. Above all, Ben had a clear plan blessed with Goittie's support, and promised steady income while they got on their feet. He had the machinery and a little money to begin operations.

"No need for charity or some Jewish organization to help with the first steps; things are more than better," he cheered himself up. *Once we're fully running, I'll try to get a tax on any imported cutlery—then we can be the only manufacturers of cutlery in the country.*

Ben figured it would take dealing with government officials, but he had learned that Mexicans were as notorious as Russians for bending the rules. In one of the books about Mexico, he had read that Alvaro Obregón, a Mexican war hero who became President of Mexico—was quoted as saying. "Not even a general will resist a $50,000 cannonball." *I hope I'm carrying enough cash to bribe my way in and enough sense to offer as little as possible.*

When he wasn't retching or attempting to lift his spirits, Ben lay ruminating on his bunk bed or dozing off and half-listening to the incessant chatter around him. Steerage was crowded with immigrants from the old countries, also in search of a better life, with a hope that Latin America would provide the means to it. As it had been six years earlier, Yiddish was the dominant language in steerage and the sound of *mameloshen*—his mother tongue—lulled him into a hypnotic state.

Something awakened him and as Ben shook off his lethargy, he realized it was the accent of a young man across the hold who was proudly announcing, "I'm on my way to marry a 'Mexican Jewish princess.'"

Ben was flabbergasted to hear someone have speech patterns he remembered from his childhood. Unable to stand up and walk with the rocking of the boat, he gingerly sat up on the cot and waved to the young man who spoke about his upcoming marriage, beckoning him to come closer.

"Where are you from?" Ben asked between wave swells. "You sound like a *lantzman*."

"From Russia," the young man replied. "Born in a *shtetl* in the Pale, not far from Kiev, and you?"

"We must have been neighbors, then. Our *shtetl* was close to Vinnytsia," Ben said as he held onto the side of the cot in an attempt to sit up and continue the conversation.

"Vinnytsia! That's only as far as we were allowed to go from the *shtetl* where I was born!" gasped the young man. "My name's Shuster," he continued, holding out his hand.

It was Ben's turn to sputter with surprise, "Shuster! Shuster from Krasnoe? The Shuster I worked with was a shoemaker."

"Small world, indeed," exclaimed Saul Shuster. "I can't believe you used to work for my father!"

"No," corrected Ben, "your father worked for me!"

"Either way, it doesn't matter...he was killed *alevay levasholem*, may he rest in peace, in the first *pogrom*. We tried to come to America. But we couldn't get a visa...at *shul* someone told me about how Mexican families who emigrated to Latin America made their fortunes and wanted to marry their daughters to nice Jewish boys. There weren't enough of those in Mexico, so it became popular to import suitable candidates among the bachelors who wanted to leave the old country. It was simply a question of offering a dowry large enough to pay for passages for the future groom's family."

"Nu, are you a nice Jewish boy?" Ben asked. "You're going to marry a girl you've never even seen?"

"I saw her picture, and we've written. She's never seen me either. Her family is respected and they'll keep their word and help me bring my family over."

"Ah… so that's why you're going to Mexico?" Ben said. "You *are* a nice Jewish *boychik*."

"Mexican law allows citizens to obtain residence visas for family members three generations back. So, when my Mexican princess and I produce an heir, our child can ensure legal permanent residence in Mexico to my mother and sisters. My wedding is a passport out of the horrors of Stalin for my family." Shuster replied. "And you, why are you going to Mexico?"

"Things aren't so good in the U.S. and my brother who, like you, couldn't get a visa to America and feared for his life in the Pale, went to Mexico," Ben explained. "He says 'the streets are paved in gold,' so I'm going to try to start a business, and my family will come later."

"Good luck to both of us in our new life," Shuster said. He hugged Ben and said, "Remember we are friends for life—not only from the same town, *lantzmen*, but brothers at sea, *shifsbruder*. Those are the deepest of ties."

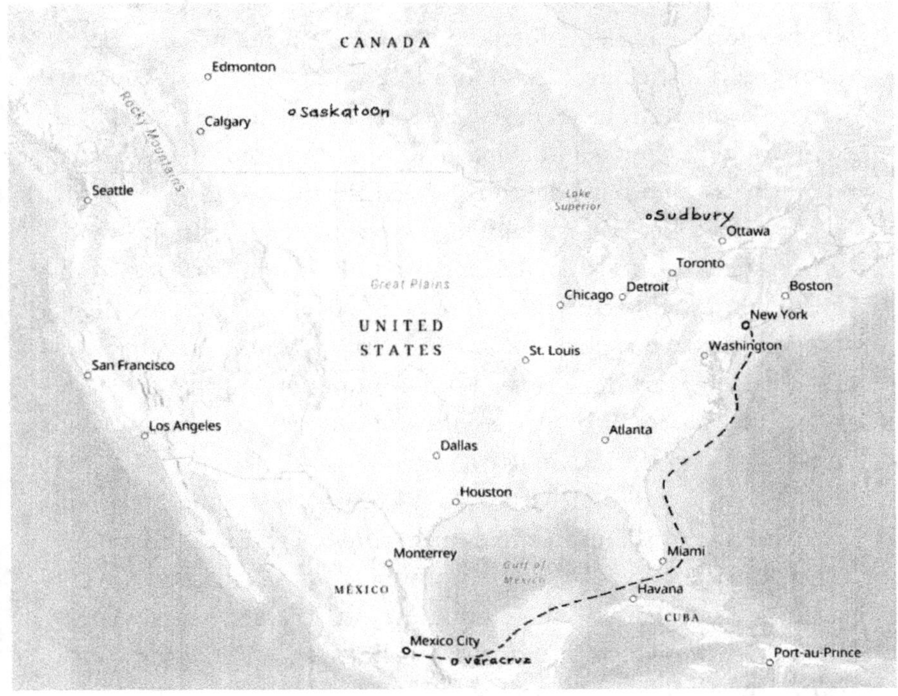
CANADA
Edmonton
Saskatoon
Calgary
Rocky Mountains
Seattle
Lake Superior
Sudbury
Ottawa
Toronto
Great Plains
Detroit
Boston
Chicago
New York
UNITED STATES
St. Louis
Washington
San Francisco
Atlanta
Los Angeles
Dallas
Houston
Monterrey
Gulf of Mexico
Miami
MÉXICO
Havana
CUBA
Mexico City
Veracruz
Port-au-Prince

2.

Landing in Veracruz was nothing like arriving in New York. There was no grand old Lady Liberty to greet Ben, nor was there the excitement of the concept of America, the *Goldeneh Medina*. He remembered his eagerness then to reach the front of the line of immigrants waiting to pass the final hurdle before entering the land of plenty. For a moment, he relived the feelings of devastation he felt back then, when the New York immigration officers subjected him to their harsh and insensitive—if not downright cruel—treatment. He believed the gatekeepers to the land of the free would be kindly and helpful. Why, they weren't much better than the hated official despots back in Russia!

By now, Ben's illusions had disappeared; he thought of all government officials as the enemy and simply watched with great interest the cruelty and venality displayed by the Mexican officials. Here, he was in no hurry to be the first in line. By observing how they treated other immigrants, he could learn how little was enough to grease the officials' palms to circumvent their obstacles to, or denials of, entry.

What he knew of Mexico was confirmed by the apparent indifference of the uniformed authorities to the thievery going on before their eyes. Scoundrels posing as porters relieved unsuspecting passengers of their bundles and suitcases, leaving the newcomers to watch in despair as their meager belongings were carted away, never to be seen again.

Finally, Ben took his turn in line. He didn't want to be last, either, because if the officials' "take" was disappointing, they would surely try to extort a larger sum from those at the end of the line. The immigration officers were unable to trump up anything wrong with Ben's entry papers to justify a bribe. But when Ben communicated with gestures and words looked up in his little dictionary, that he brought crates containing equipment with him, they began shaking their heads.

Although their words were unintelligible to Ben, the tone and manner was quite clear. He would be unable to unload the crates without a large "deposit." Ben was aghast at the amount they were demanding; it would be years before he could put together such a sum. Unable to speak the language to talk these *Cossacks* into letting him get on with it, he began jumping up and down in intense frustration, waving his arms, cursing in Russian, shouting in English with a few *mamzers* thrown in. Everyone in the vicinity flinched and held their breath at Ben's tirade. An eerie silence enveloped the scene, and only his shouts resounded throughout the boardwalk.

3.

Saul Shuster was met off the ship by his future wife's family. Upon learning that the man creating the commotion was their new son-in-law's *lantzman*, they all rushed over to where Ben was vociferating. Stepping between Ben and the officer, Shuster's father-in-law motioned to Saul, who said to Ben, "Meet my *shver*, Señor Zimmerman, my future wife's father."

Ben sputtered one last invective and pulled himself together as he turned towards the older man and stuck his hand out. "Name's Gesheft, Benjamin Gesheft. Do you have an 'in' to a supervisor? Or do you know someone here who's in charge?"

Ben knew he could sell tulips to the Dutch and had never learned to take "no" for an answer. He had long ago developed his strategy: continue to demand to speak to the "one in charge" until he got to the person with the authority to countermand what underlings had refused.

"Or can you help translate from English or Yiddish or Russian or even Rumanian into Mexican?" Ben insisted.

Mr. Zimmerman, Saul Shuster's prospective father-in-law, roared with laughter. "The language they speak here is Spanish —there is no 'Mexican' language."

Ben's face blazed red at his mistake, and as he searched for cover for his embarrassment, he realized blustering would not produce the desired results. With a deep breath, he recovered his jovial countenance and listened carefully to the man who seemed to have experience in dealing with the local authorities.

"What you need is a professional to handle the import details for you," Mr. Zimmerman said.

"They're called customs agents," Itzhoc, Shuster's future brother-in-law added, as he approached and introduced himself.

"We'll locate a reputable one who can help you finagle the lowest import duties at a reasonable cost, including his fee."

With the Zimmermans' help, Federico Gonzales, customs agent, was engaged. Once the deal was closed, the Zimmermans rushed Ben out toward the dock to pick up their baggage and the rest of their group to catch the next train to Mexico City.

"You'll come with us, of course," Saul Shuster said, patting Ben on the back. "We've just got time to get to the train station. My father-in-law tells me it's been all arranged. Bravo! And you'll get the machinery in Mexico City. It's all arranged."

"What do you mean, get to the train station?" Ben asked. "I'll go on the train my equipment is on. Thank you and your in-laws for all the help, but I'm staying here until Gonzalez gets the machinery through customs."

There was no way Ben would part from his crates, especially when he learned it might take several months for the formalities to be met and the proper palms to be greased. He knew personal follow-up was the best tool to cut through red tape and no agent could possibly be as interested as he in getting the matter resolved.

So Ben remained in Veracruz, following the customs agent's every move, knowing that it would stand him in good stead to learn how one dealt with the Mexican bureaucracy. As he hung around, he listened intently, trying to pick up words in Spanish, reading Mexican newspapers, asking Señor Gonzalez, his assistants, and anyone who would respond, "What is that called?" And as he learned the intricacies of language (such as that the *h* was silent) he discovered nuances that provided clues to the status of the person addressed.

Ben learned that the correct way to address someone was Señor, Señora or Señorita (corresponding to mister, madam, or miss) before their last name, depending on their gender and marriage status. Only those you spoke to using the informal *tu* should be called by their first name. The informal *tu* was used only for intimates, children, or those below you on the social scale. The formal *usted* was reserved for those whom the speaker considered an equal or of a higher social status, *Don* and *Doña* were generally used as honorifics, indicating that the person thus addressed was accorded a higher status than the ordinary "Mr." or "Mrs." It also indicated that the speaker was lower on the social or economic scale than the person addressed.

By the time all constraints had been met, a few palms greased, the bureaucratic machine mobilized to provide the final approval required, two months had passed. In the meantime, Ben acquired sufficient rudiments in the language to understand directions and get himself and the crates containing the machinery on board the train to Mexico City.

Señor Gonzalez claimed it was Ben who taught him how to deal with bureaucrats. "Señor Gesheft just never stopped pestering the officials; he changed his tactics every day. He alternately begged, demanded, entreated, and appealed to their patriotism by pointing out that by establishing his manufacturing plant, he would be creating jobs for Mexicans. It behooved them to let him unload the machinery so he could do so."

"In the end," Señor Gonzalez roared and slapped his thigh each time he told the story, "the government officials gave in just to get him off their backs."

4.

Back in Brooklyn, Goittie waited impatiently for news from Ben. She had received the telegram letting her know he had docked in Veracruz, but no word since. Mexican communications were notoriously slow and quite unreliable. Although she steeled herself not to expect to hear from him in weeks, almost four months had passed since he had sailed and she began to worry. She was sorry she hadn't encouraged him to write letters, but his lack of schooling annoyed and embarrassed her, although she wouldn't admit it. She felt like a harpy each time she corrected him, and just couldn't help doing so.

Around her, everything seemed to be falling apart. As the domino effect of the stock market crash brought one crisis after another, relatives and friends lost their jobs and were forced out of their apartments, placing many in dire straits. Fortunately, Jake was still working and providing the weekly stipend. But, as the economic situation became more unstable with every passing day, there was no certainty that he could continue to do so. Most of her clients closed their doors, so she had very little income from her bookkeeping. Goittie braced herself. *No use worrying, let's just get on with it.*

Goittie had accepted her brother Nathan's offer to live with them while Ben got established in Mexico, even though it meant having to put up with her sister-in-law. Once Goittie had moved into her own apartment in 1923, the two women hardly ever spoke to each other. Goittie remained close to her beloved brother in spite of her distance from his wife.

"Necessity eats all pride," Goittie said when she agreed to move into the house on Flatbush Avenue, while Nathan's wife took their children to a rented bungalow on Rockaway Beach for the summer.

Nathan's "Chinese" laundry was surviving in spite of the Depression, and in the summer of 1930, there was still enough discretionary income for the family's customary holiday plans. With Rachel and the children away, Goittie didn't feel she imposed as much, and she was able to help earn her keep by working in the laundry in addition to maintaining the accounts. She was also pleased to have moved further away from the Gesheft in-laws, who kept pestering for news from Ben, and making snide remarks that he had probably found himself a young *shiksele*.

Going back to her brother's house was a regression for Goittie and she didn't take to it kindly. Returning to live in Brooklyn brought back memories of when she had been a "greenhorn"— which, in Goittie's vocabulary, had the force of the worst expletive. Now that few of her clients still had businesses, she hated being dependent on her brother's good will again, even though, generous man that he was, he derived great pleasure from hosting "his little sister" and her child.

Goittie promised herself that, no matter what, she would be out of her brother's home before a year was up. Through painstaking research, Goittie discovered that, during Easter, only first-class passengers traveled; since the following year Passover happened to partially coincide with Easter, fewer Jews would be buying spaces at that time. She discovered that to fill up the boat, shipping companies would be open to negotiating discounts on steerage space if she booked early. To seal her promise to herself, she booked passage to Mexico for Easter week the following year.

Nathan tried desperately to talk her out of it. "You can't just take off with a baby for a strange backward land. You don't speak the language and can't foresee what to expect in Mexico! You're welcome to stay here as long as it takes for Ben to get his footing before you join him."

Nathan might as well have been talking to himself, and he knew it—no entreaties, sinister warning or logical argument could sway Goittie. Once she'd set plans in her mind, postponements or alterations were denied consideration. A promise was a promise, and she would simply make sure to find a way to keep her word.

"At least wait until you hear from Ben before you book the passage. You don't even know whether he's alive," was Nathan's final attempt at dissuading her.

Goittie felt he was right, but convinced herself Ben would certainly be in contact before the ship on which she had booked was to sail. After all, March 1931 was months away!

"All right, I won't go unless I've heard from Ben," she reluctantly agreed.

Every night, she debated whether to send Menashe, Ben's brother, a telegram to ask about Ben's whereabouts. Goittie ended the inner debate with her classic "I'll sleep on it."

And every morning she would decide to wait one more day before foregoing her strength of will, swallowing her pride and giving in to her anxiety. Thankfully, between a precocious toddler who required constant care, supervising the employees in the back, and laundry customers demanding intermittent attention, there was little time during the day to allow her to dwell on her predicament.

Goittie didn't particularly like children, frequently expressing a dislike of youngsters in general and badly behaved ones in particular. But Leah was a delightful child who helped lighten up her mother's generally dour mien and occasionally made her laugh out loud. In the evenings, Goittie would sometimes regale her brother with the day's anecdotes.

"You should have seen her, toddling up to the refrigerator door, asking for 'beddybutah wifout bed'," Goittie recounted, with her rarely heard giggle. "She may end up rolling instead of walking with the gobs of butter she eats."

Although Goittie mostly didn't take notice of holidays, pretended she cared nothing about them, and tended to belittle celebrations, birthdays were milestones she always observed. When Leah's birthday came and went in September without a word from Ben, she shifted from concern to anger about his silence and sulked. At the end of October, on a sweltering day at the laundry, the tinkle of the door chimes finally brought some respite. When the mailman handed Goittie a brown card that announced a package at the customs dock, she knew it must be Leah's belated birthday present from Ben.

Her heart grew lighter at seeing the card, confirming Ben had not disappeared. She was glad she hadn't lost face trying to contact him, and that neither he nor anyone else would ever know that she had at any point doubted she would hear from him. Above all, it gave her relief to have a return address where, in March, she would send the telegram informing Ben of her eventual arrival.

5.

During the time she lived in her brother's home, Goittie stayed away from everyone in Ben's family, mostly to avoid the inevitable questions and snarky comments about the harebrained scheme of immigrating to Mexico.

Occasionally, the Geshefts called to complain about how long it had been since they had seen their grandchild. Goittie responded with the definitive tone which allowed no contradiction or further questions: "As you know, the distance from Brooklyn to Manhattan makes it difficult and expensive to visit."

Since Ben left, she had seen only Jake when he came on Saturdays to deliver the agreed-upon weekly stipend. But, once she heard from Ben and firmed up her departure date, Goittie agreed to join the Geshefts for *Shabbat* dinner at Malkah's on the following Friday. At some point, she needed to inform her in-laws of her imminent departure, and it was an efficient way to do so to all of them at the same time.

Goittie dressed Leah in a trouser suit bought expressly for the occasion. *They'll probably spend a lot of time criticizing the outfit. I'll bite my tongue; better they should concentrate on belittling Leah's clothes than calling me a fool for taking her to a backward place—and not even knowing the language!*

The following Friday night Goittie walked in to the Gesheft's, letting go of Leah's hand as they crossed the threshold. She kept her palm on the child's back both to provide support and gently prompt her to bow as they had rehearsed. Only the grandfather clapped. The awkward silence was broken by Goittie's *Gut shabbos*! greeting.

"So, you finally brought Leah to see us. I don't think she was walking the last time, right?" Ruth dripped venom.

"I thought little girls were supposed to wear dresses," Jake said.

"Like Dora. See, Ruth knit her dress herself, doesn't she look adorable?" Esther pointed out.

"Did you sew on the frills to your nephew's castoffs?" Malkah spat out, cattily underlining that Goittie lived on her brother's generosity.

Goittie allowed the torrent of barbs wash over her only by sheer will reinforced by the pleasure of knowing she deliberately provoked it. The ruse worked: by the time the in-laws exhausted their verbal attacks on her choice of Leah's outfit, they were cowed into surprised silence at the news that she'd heard from Ben and their move to Mexico would proceed as planned.

Goittie delivered the announcement that they were to sail in March, turning the evening's attacks into a fluster of embarrassed congratulations and grudging good wishes for the success of the adventure. Leah commanded center stage, looking like the poster for a trendsetting doll, saying "please" and "thank you," dutifully kissing each relative upon arrival and departure, and not cringing when Esther pinched her cheek or when Rich Silver laughed uproariously and showered her with spit.

Once they sat down for dinner, between mouthfuls of *gefilte* fish, Yosef surreptitiously pressed an envelope with well-worn dollar bills into Goittie's hand. At the end of the meal, as the others sipped their glasses of *chai*, he walked over to the mantel, took down the daguerrotype portrait of himself, and with tears in his eyes, handed it to Leah as he hugged her and said, "Remember your *zeide*, because I will never forget my *kukla*, my little doll."

Jake didn't balk when Gottie informed him he was to continue to deliver the promised weekly stipend to Nathan when she was gone. Nathan offered to advance several hundred dollars for her to take in cash until new financial arrangements could be made, and Jake's weekly remittances would begin to pay off the debt. After the Crash, no one had much confidence in banks. And at any rate, Goittie wasn't certain whether Mexico even had a working banking system.

6.

Veracruz

Goittie swayed down the ship's plank. After five miserable days at sea surrounded by the stink of vomit mixed with the rankness of unwashed bodies on the ship, she had hoped for a breath of fresh air. Stepping out, however, she was forced to hold her nose at the stench wafting up from rotting vegetables and rancid fish, the sweaty clothes of the stevedores, and the mounds of debris littering the filthy Veracruz boardwalk. *At least, the ground isn't rocking; I swear, I'll never step on anything that floats again.*

With two-year-old Leah in tow, Goittie peered anxiously at the people milling about on the dock, blinking in the blinding sun, and trying to locate Ben. Unable to spot him, she thought perhaps she forgot what he looked like. It had been more than a year since she last saw him, and who knows how little he had kept up his appearance with no one around to remind him he needed a shave and give him a haircut, and maintain his clothing in spiffy condition. *Maybe he'd gotten "black" from being out in this merciless sun, with no one to make him put on a hat.*

Goittie waited dejectedly for about an hour, percolating her doubts into anxiety and finally erupting in the "how dare he do this to me" fury that often gave her the motivation to solve apparently insurmountable situations. This was Passover week, and as Goittie looked at people in line waiting to be interviewed by the immigration and customs officers, she was unable to detect any other Jewish passenger to approach for assistance to manage the formalities of immigration or how to get to Mexico City. Having expected Ben at the dock, she planned only as far as boarding the ship and surviving the voyage. *But I've sorted things out in the past, and I'll do it again. I've got to figure out how to get to Mexico City to find that good-for-nothing husband of mine.*

Goittie surveyed the people standing around the dock. She based her decision of which stranger to ask for help on her core belief that all *dark-skinned* people were to be distrusted and that men who cared about their appearance were less likely to be ruffians. In spite of her outstanding intelligence, Goittie held her prejudices openly, claiming that "any Jew was more trustworthy than the best goy." But with no Jews around, she decided to count on the legendary gallantry of Latin men and hope that Leah's tugging at her hand would protect her from unwanted advances. Goittie approached the most light-skinned and well-dressed man on the dock.

The man spoke enough English to grasp the predicament she was in. With the expansive kindness of Mexican males towards señoras in distress, Señor Suárez helped Goittie find an immigration official who spoke some English and was willing to get her through the formalities. While the questioning took place, locals who made a living out of filching immigrant's possessions made off with Goittie's two suitcases, leaving only the black trunk that was too heavy to cart away.

Before leaving New York, Goittie had packed the trunk and suitcases with the only possessions she deemed indispensable. So many uprootings conditioned her to travel light. Tergovitche, Umañ, Constanza, Saskatoon, Brooklyn, Manhattan, Brooklyn, and now Mexico. She had carefully triaged and then decanted her selection, selling off or giving away what she felt wouldn't be immediately needed or could eventually be replaced.

Watching half of one's most prized items disappear would reduce most to an uncontrollable stream of tears or invective. But Goittie curtailed her emotions and methodically surveyed her options: she had an exhausted two-year-old and was in desperate need of some trappings of security; she could hardly communicate with the kind stranger who was helping her, and theft was observed with indifference by the officials in charge.

"*Policía*? *Donde*? to report," Goittie asked slowly, looking up the words in her little dictionary and punctuating them with hand signals.

The officials shrugged and said the station was closed for Holy Week. There seemed little she could do to get her possessions back. In her inimitable fashion, Goittie shrugged, muttering, "No use crying over burnt toast. Let's get on with it."

Goittie and Leah's ship docked on Good Friday, one of the most somberly observed holidays in this very Catholic country. Only one train to Mexico City was scheduled and it had already left. They would have to stay the night in Veracruz. Although Goittie traveled halfway across the world, she never stayed at a hotel on her own before and had no idea how to pick one appropriate to her circumstances. Deeming it improper, however, she refused Señor Suárez's kind offer to put her up for the night and insisted he should just point out a decent hotel that was within walking distance to the train station. She would take the first train available the following day.

Propriety dictated Goittie's personal Commandments, fashioned through the prism of her rather naïve and intractable belief system. She had implacable rules for everything, and one of them was that you didn't go to a man's house if he wasn't a relative. She was also incapable of accepting random kindness. "Favors end up costing much more than money," was another of her dicta. She operated on principles of duty, appropriateness, and value for money. When she thanked him and turned to say goodbye, Goittie further insulted Señor Suárez by pressing dollars into his hand, insisting on paying for his services.

Mexico City

As the train chugged into the central station in Mexico City, Goittie felt at the end of her tether. What was she to do? She could hardly speak Spanish and hadn't the slightest idea what happened to Ben. Sailing from Manhattan, she concentrated only on attending to her child and keeping down what little she ate. All she had to do was keep herself together until they docked in Veracruz. Then, Ben would take over, having recently gone through the immigration ordeal, he would have organized what to do next. It had never occurred to her that he wouldn't be there to meet them, and she would have to manage all of it on her own. And "all of it" seemed to require more and more steps!

The city was bustling. It brought the Lower East Side of Manhattan to Goittie's mind. It was dirty, noisy, and crowded. Carts full of merchandise competed with pedestrians carrying huge baskets, like enormous wasp nests, over their heads—baskets so heavy the carrier was bent double. Ignoring them was impossible, as they hawked their wares in strident tones seeking to out-shout one another. Dirty street urchins with snotty noses pulled at her clothes. Not understanding their chatter, Goittie couldn't make out whether they were begging or selling. Whatever it was, she swatted at them as if at annoying insects.

"Do all immigrants create the same mess, wherever they end up?" Goittie mumbled to herself. "It's as if they have no ownership of their new environment and feel they can just trash it without consequences."

Peering up and down the street outside the train station, Goittie saw a beat-up car proudly displaying "Taxi" on a hand-painted placard balanced against the windshield wipers. "I don't know what I would have done if the word for 'taxi' had been something else in Spanish," she said when she told the story of her arrival.

Steeling herself, Goittie motioned the taxi forward. She forced herself to stop the litany of "what ifs" assaulting her mind and directed the driver to load the black trunk. Half of it stuck out of the car, but with emphatic gestures, she insisted he tie it down. Then she showed the driver the envelope with Menashe's address and imperiously waved him forward as she settled Leah and herself into the back seat. Even without language, she managed to direct people to do her bidding.

The trip through the narrow streets of Mexico City was a harrowing, jolting series of screeching brakes and whirring acceleration, as the driver narrowly missed hitting other cars or knocking over cyclists or jaywalking pedestrians. Goittie claimed her decision never to learn to drive stemmed from that grueling first experience with Mexico City traffic.

The cab finally stopped on a narrow, cobblestoned street. The driver got out and began struggling to release the trunk from its ropes. Goittie gulped, realizing she still didn't know what to do, now that she had gotten to Menashe's address. She refused to entertain any explanation for Ben's not having turned up. *There might be a logical reason for his absence. No point in getting worked up. First, I need to find that no-good Benjamin Gesheft. Then I'll listen to his story of what actually happened. I'll hear him <u>very</u> quietly. Then, I'll respond appropriately.*

Goittie held out a sheath of peso notes to the taxi driver, motioning him to take what was owed. Then added one more note as a tip and turned to the massive portals of Soledad #3, the address on the note that had come with Leah's birthday package six months earlier. She pulled the string that rang the bell. From inside the heavy oak doors, she could hear the clang of the bell echo the pounding inside her chest.

STREETS PAVED WITH GOLD

1.

One of the massive door panels creaked open, allowing a slit wide enough for Goittie to see a very young, dark-skinned girl, her pitch-black hair woven into braids hanging down to her knees, peeking through. She stared wide-eyed at the newcomers. A gruff voice trumpeted behind the girl, *Quién ays?* Though the tone was off-putting and the Spanish words baffling, Goittie breathed a heavy sigh of relief. That was not the voice of a stranger. She was at the door of Ben's brother, Menashe.

"I'm looking for Benjamin," Goittie called out in Yiddish, hoping the mother tongue would bring him to the door, so she wouldn't need to continue talking through the half-closed portals. Flocks of birds in the trees added a screeching racket, so Goittie felt she needed to shout for Menashe to hear. Passersby were beginning to congregate on the sidewalk, curiously eyeing the large trunk and the disheveled woman and child, adding embarrassment to her frustration and fatigue.

Goittie pretended nothing was amiss and avoided eye contact with the onlookers. The heat of the midday sun was becoming oppressive; she leaned against the oak doors, feeling faint. After what seemed an eternity, Menashe shoved the maid away, opened the door wider, and stared at the newcomers.

"Benjamin who?" Menashe demanded, his round moon-like face contorted with dislike.

"Ben Gesheft. You know, your brother," Goittie replied, stiffening her spine, raising herself up to her full four feet eleven inches height, the set of her shoulders announcing his bluster and pretended ignorance would not cower her.

"He's not here. I haven't seen him for weeks," Menashe barked, his boot-clad foot planted firmly in the door crack.

"Stop pretending you don't know who I am. Will you let us in? I guess Ben didn't know we were arriving," Goittie sighed wearily. "Did you give him my telegram?"

A beautiful woman tiptoed up behind Menashe, timidly inquiring who was at the door. Taking in the situation at a glance, she squared her shoulders, gulped and looked skyward, and muttered, "Let them in, for the sake of *Adonai*. Can't you see they are worn out with traveling? Don't you know it is a transgression of the Jewish Laws of Hospitality?" edging Menashe aside, she opened the door wide and picked up the bedraggled Leah in her arms. The little girl was so tired she didn't protest when the blonde stranger carried her inside. The woman called out for the maid and signaled her to bring the trunk inside.

Menashe's jaw dropped; for a moment, his wife's unusual daring to countermand him appeared to disconcert him, so he didn't respond. Then, his face twisted in a dark scowl, he turned abruptly and stomped away through the patio towards the back of the house, his boots clacking menacingly.

2.

Goittie wearily followed the woman with a wan smile, gratefully acknowledging that she'd had the heart to take them in—even if it was only out of religious piety. In the overgrown patio, the jacaranda trees were in bloom, permeating the air with a sickly smell of fallen blossoms, trampled as they walked through. The birds celebrated the beautiful day.

The house was a massive, dark hacienda-like structure, set back across the overgrown garden, with high stone walls surrounding the very large property. *Looks like Menashe's tales of gold on the pavement and easy living weren't exaggerations,* Goittie thought.

Inside the dark house, Shoshannah led Goittie onto the sofa in the living room, where Goittie crumpled down without a word, lacking the energy even to thank the beautiful woman—whom she guessed was her sister-in-law—for her kindness. Leah placed her head on Goittie's lap when Shoshannah carefully put her down next to her mother.

As if she could plumb the depths of Goittie's fatigue and desperation, Shoshannah quietly ministered to the weary travelers. She once dreamed of becoming a doctor and had actually been the first female to fulfill the entrance requirements to medical school at the University in Odesa.

In a milieu where most women were housebound, dour, and obese, a bright, vivacious blonde beauty with a youthful figure like Shoshannah's had men swarming around her like locusts on a hot summer day. Away from home for the first time in her life, and tired of swatting suitors away, after a year, Shoshannah consulted with her father about the best way to avoid their pursuit. If only she hadn't allowed her father to convince her to give up what he considered unattainable aims for a medical career and come home to "fulfill her destiny as a woman," she would never have married Menashe. Shoshannah brushed her reveries away and turned to attend to the visitors; she knew exactly what they needed.

She called out to Maria, the maid, and with elaborate gestures, directed her to run a bath, while she went into the kitchen to warm up something for them to eat. Once the chicken soup and hot bath had exerted their miraculous restorative powers, Leah—scrubbed clean and sated—fell asleep next to her on the couch, and Goittie finally spoke.

"Thank you for your hospitality. After Menashe's lack of welcome, I thought I'd have to stay on the street. When Ben didn't meet us when the boat docked in Veracruz, I had no idea where to look for him except here, where he told me he was staying. You did know he had a wife, didn't you?"

"I didn't think you were a *shnorrer,* a beggar," chortled Shoshannah, trying to make light of Goittie's predicament, "and I guessed you were our sister-in-law, Ben's wife!"

"Not for much longer, unless he turns up soon with a good explanation!" Goittie said, gritting her teeth.

Shoshannah nodded with relief; the spunky response indicated Goittie had recovered, was back in charge, and she and the child would soon be able to leave. The sooner they were out of the house, the easier it would be to face Menashe's wrath. He had let it go at the portal because people were watching, and he wasn't about to continue providing a spectacle for the group congregating outside his territory. But the longer Goittie and the child stayed, the more stringent a punishment he would dispense for having done something for Ben. He'd sort Shoshannah out for her effrontery when the unexpected visitors were dispatched.

3.

Menashe was an irascible man under the best of circumstances, and where his brother was concerned, his anger was deranged. When Ben had turned up a few months earlier, Menashe grudgingly allowed him to lodge with them. Shoshannah was very pleased to finally reunite with a member of Menashe's family, whom she had known for so short a time in the old country. More than anything, she was delighted to learn that Ben and his family were planning to try their luck in Mexico.

Since they had emigrated almost two years ago, Shoshannah had been desperately lonely, not knowing anyone, not speaking the language, with only her little girl, Dinah, to talk to. Her husband had never been much of a companion and, as the years passed, seemed to have less and less of an inclination to speak.

Menashe communicated in grunts and gestures and made no effort to chat even with the customers who came to the little leather shop he set up at the end of the walled garden. Shoshannah no longer expected her spouse to provide anything other than sustenance. With Ben's arrival and the promise of his wife and child to follow soon, she could look forward to the beginnings of a community and a playmate for her daughter.

Ben proved to be a considerate guest; in the mornings, he left the house as soon as the sun was up and was gone until the evening. Upon his return, he sat at the wooden kitchen table while Shoshannah directed the maid in the dinner preparations. He gave her details of his efforts to find an appropriate locale to set up the factory, to interview potential workers, and to get the lay of the land.

"I met with Juan, whom I might hire as a foreman. Knows plenty about machinery and is not too expensive. He reminds me of Rich, my sister Ruth's husband," Ben said, with a smile.

Shoshannah hadn't met the New York relatives, so she asked Ben to tell her about her husband's family. She enjoyed their conversations because he interspersed his remarks with jokey asides that made her laugh.

"When Rich Silver speaks, he spits," Ben continued. "And today, I couldn't help but tell Juan the same thing I've said to Rich Silver: 'I'll get rich from saving the cost of a shower being around you."

Shoshannah laughed. "It's a good thing the future foreman doesn't understand what you said!" Still, she kept looking out the window and perking her ears for the sound of Menashe's heavy tread through the patio announcing his return. As soon as she heard his footsteps or the yelp of the dog being kicked out of the way, Shoshannah hastily excused herself, asked Ben to ready himself for dinner, and ran to ostensibly look in on Dinah, who had been put to bed earlier.

Menashe had made it clear to Shoshannah that it was under duress that he had allowed Ben to stay with them. He issued strict instructions to provide the unwanted guest with no more than a room to sleep in and an evening meal. Whether he wanted to extend his hospitality or not, Menashe simply couldn't face the opprobrium certain to come from others in the family if he refused his brother shelter until he and his family had settled in. But he wasn't about to make Ben feel at home and certainly didn't want his wife "making friends" with that *mamzer*.

"It's not about making friends," Shoshannah said, lowering her gaze, yet shaking her head, "but we must observe the Laws. One of them is to make our guests welcome, and family is family."

Although Menashe had managed to cower Shoshannah into obedience in most areas, he was never able to break her from the observance of religious and social dicta: God seemed to provide her strength to stand up to her husband's demands when they contradicted Jewish law. She appeared willing to take the most extreme penalties to honor her beliefs.

It infuriated Menashe to return home after a 10-hour work stint at the shop, to see Ben and Shoshannah chattering away, to watch his wife's face light up in response to one of Ben's comments, or hear the silvery tinkle of her melodious laughter at one of his jokes. Shoshannah's cheeriness was what originally attracted him to her, but once they were married, her gaiety had seemed to peter out slowly and had completely disappeared by the time they emigrated to Mexico.

Shoshannah tried her best not to cross her husband, terrified of his vile temper and its consequences, and knew that to see her chatting with Ben would provoke him. So she regularly made sure that she was not in the same room with Ben when Menashe came in. But Menashe found fault with any exchange between them, and after a few weeks, he began casting about for a legitimate excuse to require Ben to leave; *he'd had enough of that brother of his taking advantage of his generosity!*

Having worked himself up thinking about how to be rid of Ben, Menashe came in one evening in a worse mood than usual. He slammed the door behind him, announcing his arrival. At the sound, Shoshannah scurried out of Dinah's room. "Dinner's ready; how soon will you be wanting it?" she asked, hurrying into the kitchen.

Menashe's grunt acknowledged he had heard her. He nodded in Ben's direction and lumbered over to the table, indicating his response. He was ready to be served his meal and expected the others to follow if they intended to eat as well. Menashe was as tight with words as with money. Chattering irritated him and he seemed to use words only when issuing an order, hurling an insult or demanding an answer.

Ben waited for Shoshannah to come in with the soup tureen and, after pulling her chair out, walked around Menashe, who was at the head of the table, to sit down.

"Harrumph! Quite the gentleman my brother has become!" Menashe muttered without addressing either of them directly,

Ignoring the jibe, but uncomfortable with the silence that followed it, Ben asked Menashe, "So, how was your day?"

"It was—and now it's over," Menashe replied between noisy slurps.

The click of the quarter-grandfather clock's minute needle pierced the silence, and Shoshannah felt it was her turn to say something. "I was telling Ben about Dinah's little Russian song…" She stopped herself mid-sentence as the impatient clack-clack of Menashe's spoon against the bottom of the bowl indicated he was ready for the next course; she signaled to the maid to bring the meat in from the kitchen.

"I see we're now rich enough to throw money out on flowers," Menashe spat out, still addressing neither one, as he gestured towards the daisies on the dining room table. "I guess I'm too generous with the wife's allowance."

"I brought them," countered Ben, "to thank Shoshannah for the hospitality; women seem to like flowers."

Menashe sputtered and his face slowly turned red—at first just a flush, but deepening and extending until it exploded into splotches of fiery carmine—while his eyes became so enlarged they seemed ready to explode from their sockets, and a vein in his temple throbbed as if about to burst. He stood up and staring at Ben, pointed menacingly at the door.

"Get out!" thundered Menashe. "Where do you get off, bringing my woman flowers? Get out right now! You can pick up your belongings later. I don't want you in my house for even another instant!"

Although a grown man, Ben was no more able to stand up to Menashe than he had been when they were children. His elder brother still intimidated him, and Ben responded as he always had, by giving in. Shoshannah made no attempt to interfere; she had lived through Menashe's jealous rampages before. He would scream at her, reminding her that in Mexico, the law considered murder a crime of passion and absolved the husband if his actions were prompted by jealousy. Menashe would use any attempt she made to dissuade him from throwing Ben out as further evidence that he had reason to be jealous of their relationship. Both the law and the family would justify Menashe ousting Ben from his home.

"So, are you going to tell me where Ben has disappeared to?" Goittie said, bringing Shoshannah back from her thoughts.

"Ben left one night weeks ago," Shoshannah said. "I've only seen him once since then, when he stopped by to pick up his things, tell me where he was staying, and asked me to let him know when a telegram from you arrived. He went to stay with the Zimmerman family—but it's been a long time and I don't know whether he's still there." Shoshannah answered, deciding to provide only that much information.

"A long time? How long?"

"Weeks…many weeks…"

"So he never heard when we would arrive in Veracruz?" Goittie muttered. "You didn't give him my telegram?"

"I didn't know there had been a telegram." Shoshannah covered her face with her hands, realizing Goittie would eventually have to be told the reason why Ben had gone to stay somewhere else.

4.

The night Menashe evicted him, Ben went in search of the only other people he knew in Mexico City. Saul Shuster's new family, the Zimmermans, offered him a place to stay when he first met them in Veracruz; but Ben hadn't wanted to impose on them any further. Menashe was his brother and *owed him*, so he went to Menashe's instead.

Given his brother's jealous fit, now he didn't have a choice and decided to take the Zimmermans up on their offer, hoping it was still available. It was a long way to their house but Ben decided to walk. It would give him time to clear his head, calm himself down, pull his countenance together, and come up with an explanation for having changed his mind. He'd ask Saul Shuster to help him present his case.

Ben's thoughts marked the rhythm of his steps: *Should I tell them what happened? No way! Dirty laundry is washed at home! No need for the whole world to know there's such bad blood between that bastard and me, and it sure doesn't look good to be thrown out of your brother's home. Now I'll have to make a decision about where to locate the factory without consulting Goittie. Goittie! It's been so hectic that I haven't even written to her since I let her know I'd finally gotten the machinery to Mexico City. How would she react if she knew I was thrown out? Best not to tell her…time enough for her to find out when she gets here…*

Ben decided that the first order of business would be to install the machinery and make arrangements for their living quarters. He looked at many options, and came to the conclusion that to start out, the best arrangement was one similar to what Menashe set up: a property that provided both living quarters and space enough to install the factory on the premises. Menashe mostly sold his leather goods to individuals—which is why he needed a shop—but Ben had every intention of selling the cutlery to wholesale distributors who would buy in large quantities to resell.

As the darkness closed in around him, Ben felt the bite of the wind blowing down from the twin volcanoes, silent sentinels over the valley where the Aztecs founded Tenochtitlán. Even in the dark, the snowcapped Popocatépetl loomed over Ben although, in reality, the volcanoes were many kilometers away at the end of Calzada Tlálpan, the long avenue down which Ben walked. That very morning, he had been shown an old manor house whose side wall abutted Calzada Tlálpan, the busy four-lane thoroughfare that traversed the length of the city from its central square, the Zócalo, to the foot of the mountains that surrounded the valley. Trolleys in both directions circulated down the middle of the street, underlining the importance of the avenue.

The entrance to the manor house was on Albert Street, a narrow side street lined with trees. The eastern portal to the City stood in that neighborhood during colonial times, so the area was called Portales. From Albert Street, it was only a few kilometers' drive to the Zócalo, where the commercial center of the City had developed, and was conveniently serviced by the trams that ran the length of the avenue.

Ben stopped in front of the property. When he saw it earlier, he thought it had enough possibilities to put it on a list to show

Goittie when she arrived. *Now I don't have the luxury of comparing and consulting, so I might as well negotiate a one-year lease on this one. If Goittie doesn't like it, we can move in a year. Surely she'll understand that, given what's happened, I needed a place to live… there was no time to dither. Yes, I'll call the landlord in the morning, haggle on the terms a bit and sign a year's contract.*

The decision acted like a gale that blew all clouds away. Ben's dejection evaporated and his footsteps lightened and quickened, thoughts racing as he built upon his initial selection of locale to imagining a fully-installed factory. His optimism returned full blast: *I guess being kicked out of Menashe's may yet end up being a good thing. Now I can stop debating whether to hire that foreman whom I wasn't sure about. I'll hire him tomorrow morning, after signing for the space. And as soon as I buy a bed, I can sleep there, so I won't need to ask Shuster to put me up for more than a couple of days.*

By the time he reached the Zimmerman's house, Ben fully recovered his amiable outlook on life and knew exactly what he would do to settle in. It was late in the evening and he hoped it wouldn't upset the Zimmermans when he rang their doorbell.

"Shalom, Gesheft, what a surprise!" Saul Shuster exclaimed when he saw who was at the door.

"Shalom, Shuster, I hope it's a <u>welcome</u> surprise and that it's not too late," Ben replied.

"I've been deciding whether to rent a property at Albert #3 or not, so I thought I'd just walk and see how close it was… and ended up walking around for hours," Ben babbled hurriedly. "Hope I'm not disturbing…I don't even know the time."

"Never mind the time, you're always welcome! Will you eat with us? We were just about to sit down," Saul replied, ushering Ben into the dining room where the family gathered for the evening meal.

"We're real Mexicans, as you can see," Mr. Zimmerman explained, his appearance contrasting his words. *I don't think*

I've ever seen a more typical Jewish family sitting together around a dinner table, Ben thought. As if he'd read Ben's thoughts, the patriarch at the head of the table explained, "During the week, we eat dinner no earlier than 10:00 p.m., like Mexicans do. We sit down to eat when everyone is home from work."

He pumped Ben's hand heartily and turned to Mrs. Zimmerman, a smiling, rotund middle-aged woman wearing the traditional wig used by married Jewish women. "My dear, meet Ben Gesheft, Saul's *lantzman,* and new friend. He's the man I told you turned the port of Veracruz upside down when we were there to meet the new son-in-law."

Ben lowered his eyes in embarrassment, remembering that meeting. *I must have looked like a child throwing a tantrum.* Itzhak, the Zimmerman's eldest, whom Ben also met in Veracruz, clapped Ben on the back and said, "But it got him what he wanted and it makes a great story, so never mind." He walked Ben to the foot of the long table to greet his mother. "I have your husband to thank for many reasons," said Ben, "and I'm very pleased to meet you. I seem to be a specialist in 'turning things upside down'…I sincerely hope I haven't done that to your dinner."

Everyone laughed and stood up to welcome Ben, whom Saul led around the dining table, introducing him first to his wife, Masha, then to Masha's older sister and her husband. Finally, Ben was seated next to Itzhak's wife.

"So, tell us what's happened since we left you in Veracruz. I heard from Gonzalez that you got the machines through— it's been months since then! And we haven't heard a word from you," said Mr. Zimmerman.

"Let the poor man get a bite first, *mein man,*" interjected Mrs. Zimmerman, as she waved to the maid to serve Ben.

"Ben's telephoned a couple of times to let me know what he's been up to," said Saul, "Sorry I forgot to tell you. But with the wedding and everything that's been happening, it just completely slipped my mind."

"You should be sorry—I would think you would have enjoyed someone from your old *shtetl* being at your wedding!" Mr. Zimmerman chastised him.

Ben broke in to distract Mr. Zimmerman, "I've almost decided where to install the plant. I'm thinking of leasing a large, old house not very far from here, where we can put the machinery on the bottom floor and live upstairs. If you have time, I'd really like to hear what you think of the plans, but not now. Now, I want to congratulate Saul for the wonderful family he married into and hear more about all of you."

Saul gave him a look of gratitude for changing the subject. The family soon continued with the normal course of their chatter over the meal, easily including Ben in the conversation as part of the group. When the dinner was over, the men moved into the living room with their glasses of tea to light up cigarettes, while the women remained at the table to engage in "women talk."

"So you're all set up to start business, Gesheft?" asked Itzhak.

"Not quite *all* set up yet; but yes, I've got the foreman, and I'm closing the deal on the house at Albert #3, just off Calzada Tlalpan," replied Ben. "May I ask what you think of the location, Mr. Zimmerman?"

"Call me Srulik, and I'll call you Ben—in this country, we call equals by their first name—and I'm not that much older than you!" said Srulik Zimmerman. "And you'll also have to learn to use the informal *tu*—it's not that different from our *du*. Anyway, it's good we all speak Yiddish! Spanish comes later."

Ben nodded, thinking how lucky Saul was to be part of a family as amiable as this, instead of someone like Menashe. He wondered how he could break it to Mr. Zimmerman—*er* Srulik—that he wanted to accept his original offer to put him up until he had settled in.

"Very well then, Srulik, what do you think of that location for a factory?" asked Ben. "And what do you think of living in the same place as the factory?"

"It's not a bad idea. It allows you to keep an eye on the workers, saves on travel from work to home…it's a good way to begin your business life," Srulik said. "As for living in the same place, well…it depends on whether your wife minds—does she?"

"I don't know. I haven't talked to her about it; she's still in America. I didn't want her and our baby to come until I had the arrangements made for when they get here. My brother has no room for all of us, and I think even I have already used up my welcome there," answered Ben.

"Then you can just come stay here, if that's the case," responded Srulik.

"That's very kind of you but…I may not be able to afford such first-class accommodations," Ben quipped, hoping the Zimmermans would get that he was joking.

"As you can see, we have plenty of room, and I love having every room occupied. I even pay some of my children so they stay with us," Srulik replied in the same bantering tone.

"Under those generous terms," beamed Ben, "I'm delighted to take up one of your rooms, starting tonight, but for no more than a couple of weeks, and you certainly don't have to pay me!"

Consistent with the age-old tradition among Jews to help each other out in times of need, the Zimmermans once again came through. In addition to putting Ben up, in the busy days that followed, the men provided Ben with the services of their lawyer, who counseled Ben and prepared the contracts with his landlord and the workers, while the women of the family helped him by selecting basic furnishings for the living quarters.

Once he installed the machinery and the bedroom was furnished, Ben felt things had advanced far enough along that he could now send for Goittie and Leah. He composed the telegram in his head months ago, working assiduously to keep such enormous news within the confines of the 10 words allowed in the least expensive Western Union telegram: *Everything arranged stop telegraph arrival date to meet in Veracruz.*

5.

Portales

Ben pulled the chord of the bell outside Menashe's oak portals with a flourish. He wasn't sure whether the bubbliness he felt inside was nerves or excitement or a little of both. He rushed over as soon as he got the message that Shoshannah called the Zimmerman's house. *Goittie was already here! With the baby! How could that have happened? Surely, she must have sent word to let him know when she was coming! Why hadn't there been a telegram? Of course! Menashe had received it and kept it from Shoshannah.* Volleys of thoughts bounced around in his head and he found it difficult to swallow through a throat closed down with fear. Would Goittie believe Menashe's notion that Ben was "making eyes" at Shoshanna?

Ben was about to pull the chord again, when Goittie opened the door; she held Leah in her arms. The baby howled when Ben tried to hug them both; he leaped back with a grimace. The little girl turned away from the strange man at the door, hiding her face in her mother's neck. Goittie cooed and patted Leah's back until her sobbing slowly diminished, became hiccups, and at long last subsided.

Once Leah quieted down, Goittie said, "I understand you have a place for us to live." Ben took a step closer while an enormous grin covered his face. "We'll go get some rest there and then figure out what's next," Gottie told Ben curtly as she pushed him away. "From what Shoshannah tells me, we don't want to stay here any longer. So get a taxi and we'll get going. I've invited Shoshannah to come along, so we'll put off telling our stories until later."

Ben realized he needed to follow Goittie's directions. It was obvious she learned of Menashe's actions and the details of what his ire unleashed. Goittie would need to be mollified and he trembled at the thought of how she would respond to what ensued. Until she reached her conclusions, Ben feared he was to be subjected to Goittie's "ice treatment," a refusal to speak to him directly. He hoped it would only be *days* of nothing but clipped exchanges of questions, requests, or demands. Ben sighed. Marriage to Goittie wasn't easy!

The taxi turned right off Calzada Tlapan, into a residential enclave of tree-lined side streets. Away from the hubbub of busses, trains, and autos circulating on the giant avenue, the quiet streets provided a welcoming silence to the newcomers.

"This is a nice neighborhood," Goittie said to Shoshannah as the taxi lurched along the streets of the Portales district.

"Everyone says it is very well located; it's quite close to the *zócalo*, the central town square," Ben noted.

Goittie ignored his comment, "Does *Portales* mean anything?" she directed her question to Shoshannah.

"Portales means the portals," "Shoshannah replied. "It's where the entrance to the City was in colonial times."

"The gates used to be right here, where our street ends," Ben added as the taxi drove into Calle Albert.

"Oh! It's so nice…there are trees on both sides of the street," Shoshannah exclaimed.

Goittie descended from the taxi and, still speaking only to Shoshannah, she mused, "I like the house being in the shadow of the original portals to the city. They seem to mark the entrance to a new life."

Ben led them on a tour of the hacienda-like structure. In typical Mexican colonial style, the house was built around a central square, the patio. "The surrounding walls keep us isolated from the outside world, locked gates keeping intruders out, and" Ben patted Leah's head, "little girls in."

"The patio lets light into the many rooms that open out on it," Shoshannah approved.

"From what I've seen," Goittie added, "the patio is used for storage, as a vegetable garden, and a playground for youngsters, the dog's run and the cat's sunning area. Quite useful, I thought, when I looked at Colonial architecture books to get an idea of where we'd be living might look like."

"You are really clever, Goittie," Shoshannah said.

"Didn't I tell you, Shoshannah? Goittie is the most intelligent person I know," Ben said.

"I just don't like to be surprised, so I try to prepare for what comes next," Goittie said.

Following the Zimmerman's advice, Ben housed the cutlery factory on the ground floor, installing the machinery in the largest area. Ben smiled when he heard Goittie designate the use for each room they looked into. "In this room, we'll store the sheets of raw material," and as they moved to the room next door "the finished product can be stacked here."

When she opened the door to the smallest room, she announced: "That's where I'll have the office."

The living quarters were on the second and third floors. A vaulted corridor with an elaborate design cutout on the wooden barrier ran the length of three sides of the square created by the patio. The rooms were all entered from this corridor; the drawing room or parlor contained a classic three-piece suite with a sofa and two armchairs arranged around a center table that held ashtrays and the obligatory fake palm. The dining room was next to the parlor, but they weren't connected, so to get from one room to the other one had to exit into the corridor. Next to the dining room was the kitchen, which was adjacent to the bathroom in order to share the plumbing. The two rooms next to the bathroom were the bedrooms. The third floor had two more bedrooms and a bathroom over the one below. Once they could afford it, this is where the hired help would sleep.

When the tour was over, Ben let out a deep sigh of relief. Goittie hadn't balked at sharing the living quarters with the factory and had seemed pleased with his choices. He hoped Goittie's expansive response to their new living arrangements signaled a return to normalcy between them.

But shortly after he returned with the taxi he hailed for Shoshannah and they said their goodbyes, Goittie informed him, "I've put Leah to bed and will join her now. First, I must have some rest to regain my energy. I've got to work out whether there was something one of us could have done…something to prevent what happened from happening. I'll be sleeping in her room until I figure out whether Menashe just went crazy or you gave him a good reason to throw you out.

PREGNANT PAUSES

1.

For weeks, Goittie continued to ignore Ben's overtures; they worked side by side in strained silence to get production going: that was job No. 1. There was work for many pairs of hands; too much work, never-ending work. A manufacturing business was much more complicated than Ben imagined, requiring complex and intricate decisions. *Yet here I am, so I'll have to learn to make those decisions!*

Ben recalled the old days when making a living was a simple question of following instructions from the boss, not spending more than you earned, and saving for a better future. *But I want to be the boss—so maybe what we need is some employees!* Ben asked Juan, the foreman, to bring in other workers to help advance factory production. As soon as he trained them, the workers could run the machines so Ben could concentrate on selling the finished product. Juan's wife, Estela, was hired to help with the household chores, and one of their daughters was brought in to watch Leah, which freed Goittie to set up the administration of the business. Slowly, the cacophony of sound increased, attesting to a busy crew manning an assembly line in active production of knives and forks, soup, and dessert spoons.

Having paid help and the factory on the premises allowed Goittie to run both the household and the cutlery production; her instructions were followed without question. In spite of her limited command of Spanish, the diminutive figure in a simple housedress unwaveringly directed the machine operators and the women who cooked and cleaned and kept an eye on Leah. Ben spent his days negotiating for raw materials and contacting wholesalers to distribute the finished product. By the time evening came, both were exhausted, too tired to do more than eat a meal in silence and go to bed, in the hopes that they could recoup their energy to do it again the following day.

Although Goittie continued not speaking to him, Ben kept trying to entice her to respond—to laugh at his funny stories, to agree to or rebut his ideas, to allow him to hold her. She rebuffed him repeatedly, but Ben didn't give up. *After all,* he thought, *she can't keep avoiding me forever.* However, it was beginning to feel like forever. It had been a couple of months since Goittie arrived and almost two years since he left the States. *Surely, she must miss the physical side of their marriage.* So Ben decided to stop trying to cajole her into dropping the ice treatment. There were other ways to connect besides talking!

One night, after they both retired, Ben waited until he heard Goittie snoring—which she did quite loudly—took his slippers off, slunk through the corridor, took a deep breath, and tiptoed into Leah's bedroom, where Goittie was sleeping. He was very quiet as he knelt by her bed and lightly touched her, stopped her yelp of surprise with a kiss, and was thrilled to feel her respond. He slipped his arms under her body, lifted her gently from the bed, then carried her back to his bedroom.

They caressed and made love in silence, and in the heat of the moment, Ben could not extricate himself before ejaculating. Goittie pushed Ben away and jumped out of bed to dash to the bathroom to rinse herself off. Ben followed, but she closed the door in his face and didn't come out until Ben went to his bedroom.

The next morning, Goittie didn't even say a ritual good morning; she pointedly left the room as Ben walked in and spent the entire day ignoring any of his attempts to reestablish communication. Apparently, sexual closeness wasn't going to change Goittie's upset. On the contrary, she seemed even angrier than before and Ben wondered whether he should confront her and ask how long she intended to continue the freeze and whether there was anything he could do to shorten the punishment. But she gave him no opening until six weeks later when she unexpectedly turned to him after she had put Leah to bed.

2.

"Come to the office. Sit. We need to talk," she said. Ben was startled as she'd caught him in the midst of his bedtime preparations. He wondered what had happened to help break the ice treatment and why she summoned him to the office. "Now?" he asked. "It's after 11:00 and we have to be up very early so I can get to my appointments on time."

"Yes, now," Goittie answered, waiting for him to follow her down the hall to the office. She sat at the desk and motioned Ben to sit down across from her.

Ben sat and waited for Goittie to speak. The silence was strained, broken only by the ticking of the clocking-in machine. Goittie looked down at her intertwined hands, then cracked her fingers backward and forward several times. She lifted her gaze, started to say something, hesitated, then pursed her lips. After a few aborted attempts at speaking, she turned bright red, stood up, and peered out the window as she blurted out, "As if things weren't hard enough, there's more to deal with…" She gulped, "I'm pregnant."

Ben remained silent, uncertain what to say. All he could think of was that he would need to increase sales so income could start coming in right away instead of, as he had imagined, having some time to make contacts and grow distribution by selling wholesale. "Well, I'll start going door to door tomorrow, selling the product. Now that I'll be the father of more than one, I'll have to work twice as hard!"

In spite of her embarrassment at having allowed the ice treatment to thaw long enough to let him into her bed, Goittie couldn't help laughing out loud. Worrying about increasing sales was not the response she imagined Ben would have. She was most unhappy when she realized she had missed her period. She pondered what to do and debated various options. Mostly, she berated herself for having allowed Ben into the conjugal bed. She would have to come clean, once the unavoidable evidence that her silence hadn't precluded marital cohabitation began showing, it would be too late to do anything about the pregnancy.

All I have to do is <u>look</u> at his pants and he makes me pregnant… babies…they're nothing but complications…I don't know why any-one wants a baby, I mustn't think about things like that, I wish I was like other women who yearned for children…but even if I did, certainly now is not the time…maybe I should try to lose the baby. But she didn't know anyone she could trust to ask whether they had a connection to a provider or whether abortion was legal in Mexico. So she decided to inform Ben and get his reaction so as to reach a decision.

"Now that I'll be the father of more than one, I guess that makes me a patriarch! How very exciting to be the head of a growing family!"

3.

With the pointed silence abandoned, Ben and Goittie could concentrate on the daunting challenge of making <u>Cubiertos Gesheft, S.R.de L</u>. profitable. As planned, they took no salary and depended on Ben's brother Jake's agreed-upon monthly stipend for food and rent. They projected that during the first year of operations, sales would cover the expected expenses of the start-up business. But the product wasn't selling according to their projections. It took several months of nightly strategy sessions to figure out what the problem was.

They sat in the darkened parlor, where only the floor lamp was turned on, spotlighting the back of the armchair where Goittie was perched, her arms resting atop her ballooning belly. Ben sat across from her, his elbow on the sofa arm, his hand holding his head. He sighed, "I just don't understand it. Mr. Morales really liked the quality and was particularly happy with the price. He told me we beat the Japanese product hands down."

When Ben first arrived in Mexico, he used the dies cut from the cutlery samples he bought in New York and pushed production. However, few of the wholesalers he approached wanted to distribute the cutlery and those who did canceled subsequent orders because their customers were returning them.

"Well, you can't blame buyers for canceling the orders; if their customers don't buy our cutlery, stores won't buy more from us," Goittie replied, rustling in the chair in an attempt to make herself more comfortable. "We need to know why the end customers don't like our product."

"How can we find that out?" Ben asked, taking off his glasses to rub his eyes.

"We'll have to ask them. I'll write out some questions in the morning." Goittie said. "Now that we have a plan, let's sleep on it."

To overcome their limited ability to speak Spanish, Goittie wrote out scripts of the questions to ask housewives and store clerks. Then she read the prepared scripts to the machine workers and Marta, the young woman who took care of Leah, correcting the text as they made suggestions to make the questions easier to understand. Goittie and Ben then took turns making the rounds of shops where cutlery was sold, to ask why their cutlery wasn't selling.

After many false starts, Ben and Goittie were able to determine that customers preferred the design of cutlery they bought in the past. "Soup spoons too heavy, too fat..." customers responded. Ben set out to find a toolmaker to copy the Japanese designs and turn them into manufacturing dies. He hung around for days at different factory sites, striking up Pidgin conversations with the workers as they came out during the lunch hour or at quitting time. He didn't even know what the thing he needed was called in Spanish. "What do you call that?" *¿Cómo se dice?* became his mantra.

"*Hola, mano*," Ben tried at a factory that utilized dies to cut metal into various shapes for hinges. On earlier occasions, he addressed one of the workers as "Señor" and watched the worker flinch. Ben sensed it had created a distance between them, instead of opening the listener up to further conversation, so he had moved on and listened intently. Overhearing workers call one another *mano*, he assumed it was the accepted greeting.

"*Hola, Señor*," the worker replied. Ben sighed. It would take a long time to learn the social graces of this country.

Because the worker couldn't understand what Ben was asking, he was taken to the boss. "So, vat iz it you vant?" Mr. Hasse asked. Recognizing the German accent, Ben made use of his Yiddish to tell his story and explain his needs.

"Mexicans are used to the small, rounded spoons and flatter forks the Japanese make," Ben told him.

"Ha-Ha! Ja-Ja! Crasy, isn't it? Vat do they know about forks? They don't even use them." Mr. Hasse said, choking with laughter as tears rolled down his face.

"Yes, but Mexican consumers think the European style of large soup spoons is much too big and the tines of the forks are too curved. I have to have new dies made. I can tell by the great design of your hinges that you have a talented machinist. Can I talk to him? Maybe he can help me."

"Sure, if you vant, maybe you can take the machinist to work with you—I'm planning to close the factory one day," Mr. Hasse said as he introduced Ben to Ingeniero Baños, the machinist at the plant, who agreed to tool new dies for the spoons and forks copying the shape of Japanese cutlery sold in local stores. Since they were starting from square one, Ben figured it was the moment to experiment with an idea he'd been kicking around in his head when he was speaking with customers about the product. He wanted to make the knife from a single piece of metal instead of having a blade inserted into a hollow handle made separately from the blade. *It'll make the knife sturdier and longer lasting as well as less expensive by requiring less metal and production time.*

Ben asked Baños to redesign the shape of the knives to those specs rather than using the Japanese sample. The single-piece blade-and-handle knife was very well received and became one of the breakthrough notions for the increased sales of <u>Cubiertos Gesheft</u>. Baños was impressed with Ben's capacity to visualize design improvements, and Ben admired Baños' ability to deliver to minute specifications. So they decided to collaborate in creating dies for other manufacturers. Ben found the clients and Baños manufactured the dies from the scrap material of the cutlery, which increased the factory's income.

Once the new shapes went into production, sales started to pick up, although it would be many more months before the factory became profitable. Ben divided his day, contacting distributors and stores that carried cutlery during the mornings and selling door-to-door in the afternoon and into early evening when housewives were more available. He made sure to stop knocking on their doors when the *novela* started: no one answered the doorbell when the soap operas were on. Mistresses and maids alike were glued to the radio.

Goittie continued to manage production, taking phone orders and making sure the room that contained the finished product stack grew daily. Neat stacks of brown cardboard boxes with six elongated small white boxes lined the walls. Each white box held half-dozens of knives, forks, soup, and dessert spoons in the design created with the new dies.

Ben and Goittie's routine to make the business successful continued day after long day without respite. Soon, however,

Goittie would need to cut down on the number of hours she worked. As her belly distended, she felt more and more tired and planned ahead to avoid going up and down the stairs as little as possible. Her anxiety increased as she knew she would need to have someone fill in for her for a few weeks when the baby was born in the New Year.

Early in December, Goittie had a precipitous fall as she was coming down the stairs, causing her to go into labor. Due to the fall, the doctors believed, the baby turned around in the womb and needed a C-section to be delivered on December 10th, almost a month before the due date. Mother and child remained in serious condition: the baby remained in an incubator and struggled to keep his weight up, and Goittie contended with infection from the C-section.

In spite of his lack of religious observance, and his concern over Goittie's health and his baby son's delicate condition, Ben was overjoyed at Mario's birth. "Now I have my *kadish* assured," he smiled, "every man needs to know that when he dies, his son will fulfill the requirement that male children say a prayer in his memory every day for a year and once a year for the rest of the son's life."

At the end of January Goittie was, at long last, allowed to leave the hospital, but Mario had to be left behind until he gained a bit more weight. As the taxi trundled to the gate of the old manor house, a very thin, pale-faced Goittie smiled weakly. She had large, dark circles under her eyes. The surgery and the weeks she spent in the hospital had taken their toll.

"I'm so glad you are back," Ben mused.

"It is good to be back. I'd forgotten how much I like this little street," Goittie said.

"I wish we hadn't had to leave the baby at the hospital," Ben said. "Leah will jump up and down with joy to see you, although she'll be disappointed her baby brother didn't come with us.

She's been begging to go see him. Surely they'll let us bring him home very soon."

It was well into summer before Ben and Goittie were able to bring Mario home, after finally having brought his preemie weight up. Even then, he received adequate care for a premature infant but not much affection from a mother recovering from childbirth and a complicated surgery.

Mario was over one year old when Ben and Goittie were finally able to eke out a living from Cubiertos Gesheft and felt that they could bank the stipend that Jake had agreed to provide as his partner's share into the business.

The economic situation in the U.S. continued to deteriorate, and there seemed to be no end in sight to the Depression. Jake was making noises about giving the money to his parents instead of continuing to provide his share to Goittie and Ben. The rest of the family in New York repeatedly asked Menashe and Ben for help.

Scraping by during the Depression bread lines, Malkah, Joseph, Ruth, Esther, and Jake considered that Menashe and Ben and their families were "living the life of Riley" in a place where, obviously, the streets were really "paved with gold," as Menashe declared years earlier. Every Friday night, they mulled on the subject over their spartan *Shabbat* meal.

"Why, Menashe's the boss of his own leather goods factory! And Ben has stopped selling door-to-door," Jake commented as he slurped the watered-down chicken soup.

"Yea," said Esther, her voice dripping discontent, "he just sits at a desk, waiting for customers to phone their orders in, while I work my fingers to the bone and can't even put enough to eat on the table."

The comparison list of benefits grew every week.

"Why, they eat fresh fruit and vegetables every day!" whined Malkah as she picked at the wilted mush of carrots on her plate.

Jake added, "Ben can now afford a *second* child. And he's ensured his *kadish*."

"And both Shoshannah and Goittie have servants to help with the children!" Ruth chimed in as she ran off to chase Dora. "This girl just doesn't stop!"

Esther groused, "While we slave and clean house for others, if we're lucky to find someone who still has a house and is able to pay!"

With each passing week, the in-laws became more and more restless as their complaints increased. Finally, they decided to pressure the "well-to-do" brothers to provide boat passages to Mexico for all of them. One of the Geshefts needed to go down there to get their brothers' commitment. Jake was sent to inform Menashe and Ben that it was time for them to share the Mexican bounty with the whole family.

4.

Jake's arrival, bearing the urgent message of the family's dire need, forced Ben and Menashe to put aside the fact that they weren't on speaking terms. Both brothers knew it would be more effective and would cost each of them less if they worked together to get their relatives settled in.

Menashe called Ben to say he had a specific solution to propose. "Given that the rest of the family is determined to descend upon us, we should organize it effectively, or we'll go bankrupt."

Ben agreed to listen to Menashe's proposal. "You come to discuss this personally, here, at my office." He wanted his brother to understand this was to be nothing more than a business arrangement. Ben hadn't spoken to Menashe since the night he was thrown out, and he would never forgive the upset Menashe caused when he kept silent about Goittie's telegram.

"Look, we don't need to be friends. We need to decide what we can do to house seven people and find them ways to earn a living. And we do it together because we have to," Menashe said.

They met the next day. Juan, the foreman, let Menashe into Goittie's little office, where an unsmiling Ben sat at the desk and signaled Menashe to sit across the desk from him. Dispensing with any niceties, Ben jumped right into the subject. "This is a business arrangement that will fulfill the family obligations with a smaller personal cost to each of us."

Menashe's mouth twisted into a semblance of a smile: he liked that approach. "We need to take this in steps, agreed?"

There was no pretense at reconciliation. They would figure out how to solve the issues raised by the entire family expecting help. Once their situation was settled, Ben and Menashe could return to not speaking to each other.

"Agreed. Jake has bought into the partnership with us, as you may or may not know…so we only need to find a wife for him so he can get legal residence."

"Shouldn't be a problem. Plenty of Jewish girls in Mexico City needing a husband," Menashe said.

"And a bride would bring a dowry, so it would cost us less to set Jake up," added Ben.

"We could line up some candidates for Jake, and during the holidays, he can look them over at Temple," Menashe said. "Trouble is, Jake's not a *boychik* any more…no one would consider him a 'nice Jewish boy' at his age."

"He'll have to do with an older woman, and he can't count on too much of a dowry," Ben said. "What about Sheine, Srulik Zimmerman's cousin's sister-in-law?"

"I don't know…she's an *alteh moid* and her name is probably what cursed her to be an old maid! Her parents must have been blind, calling her Sheine! *Beautiful,* she definitely isn't," Menashe cruelly reminded Ben.

"Yeah…naming children is always risky. Names are important; even the Book tells us we are our names. But names can change, as we both know." Ben smirked.

Menashe ignored him and continued. "But your friends, the Zimmermans, are very wealthy, and maybe the cousins are too so that they might cough up a passable dowry. After all, it's a *shandah*—a shame—that both her younger sisters are already married and have children. The family will be happy to have Sheine off their hands."

Menashe was right. When Ben spoke to Srulik Zimmerman about making the introductions, Srulik was delighted. To the Greenbergs, the offer was quite welcome. They had almost given up marrying Sheine off, and she was ever so pleased to have the recently arrived foreigner interested in her. She agreed to meet him to discuss the possibility of marriage further. Even though the Greenbergs were of modest means, as Sheine was the last of her siblings to find a mate, her entire family chipped in to make her a more attractive candidate to the "American" suitor. Once the arrangements were discussed, Jake and Sheine were pointed out to each other at Temple on a Friday night. Both agreed to meet officially. Sheine and her parents were summarily invited to dinner at the Zimmermans so they could meet Jake, who was accompanied by Ben and Goittie. The invitation paid homage to a tradition from the old world, where such a visit was customary in Lithuania, and known as *Bashoyen di kallah*—the "checking out the bride."

Although everyone expected some nervousness from the main characters, the onlookers were astonished: Jake greeted Sheine with a hug, to which she obviously responded. He then led her to a seat and held her hand while he proposed.

Ben couldn't wait to ask how Jake had made such a quick decision, so he asked to speak with him alone for a few minutes.

"Before I left New York, I bought the ring. I made the decision to marry whoever would say 'yes' if I dared to ask. You all made it easy for me by making the introductions. But Menashe's warning that she was ugly put me off and I changed my mind and thought I would wait and see if a prettier candidate could be found."

"We could have looked for others but you jumped right in and asked her to marry you!" Ben shook his head. "Now you can't back out."

"I don't want to. Ever since I saw her at Temple, I thought Sheine was quite a prize. She has more to offer than beauty: she provides me the legal right to remain and work in Mexico and a respectable dowry to set up our household. She smiles a lot and is still young enough to have children."

"You've surprised everyone. Deciding to marry someone you don't even know."

"I just want to get married and there wasn't anyone before Sheine who would have me. And maybe getting to know each other over a lifetime is what it's about, anyway."

"Maybe you're right. Sheine seems pleasant enough, but I guess you're OK with how she looks?"

"As we walked into the room, I saw myself in the huge mirror hanging behind her…it reminded me how little of a beauty I am: a hunchback bald man with a glass eye who has no other interests than to win at gin rummy. Her greatest beauty is that she's willing to marry me."

"For all we know, Sheine has the same idea. She is way past marrying age and apparently didn't have many offers, or at least any offers she was willing to accept. Gratitude is not a bad basis for a marriage."

Sheine and Jake were engaged and the wedding date was set for the following February. The task for Ben and Menashe now became how to arrange for the rest of the Geshefts in Mexico.

The brothers were going to have to pay for the rest of the family to come from New York for the wedding.

"We might as well make arrangements for them to come to stay permanently," Ben said.

"But we should complete our original plan first. Let's find someone to marry Esther."

"Then we can figure out where the rest will live. I have some ideas," Menashe said.

A widower with a 9-year-old child was enlisted to marry Esther. The brothers talked Esther into the advantages of a ready-made family and offered to provide a dowry. "You're already 32 years old," Ben argued when Esther demurred. Menashe added, "And you're probably too old to have kids anymore. It's a great opportunity unless you want to remain an old maid."

"I'm only 25," Esther retorted, ignoring the rolling of the siblings' eyes.

"From now on, when anyone asks how old I am, I'll say "You have to ask my older sister," Ben quipped.

Esther made a face and turned to Menashe, "Is the fellow a nice man? What about the kid? What happened to the mother?"

"I didn't ask." Menashe retorted. "He's a school principal. That's all I know!"

"Esther insisted. "Is he well-to-do? Does he ask for a dowry?"

"Questions, questions!" Menashe thundered. "You want to stay in Mexico with the family, this is the only way to get papers. You'd think you had other options. You don't and should be glad that Moishe, the principal, is even entertaining the possibility. So, decide." In the end, Esther agreed to meet Moishe and his daughter.

The match was furthered when the child asked Esther where she had gotten the beautiful sweater she was wearing and Esther told her she had knitted it.

"Would you show me how to knit one…" Juliet went over to Esther and whispered in her ear, "For my dad?"

"I'd be happy to. You'll have to come visit me soon. We can go pick the wool and the needles together."

That was the source of meetings between the three of them. After a few weeks, Moishe asked her, and Esther happily consented, to become Mrs. Lapidus.

Once arrangements were made to provide legal status for Jake and Esther to stay in Mexico, Menashe offered to customize the two back rooms of Soledad 3 into a "mother-in-law" apartment to house Malkah and Joseph, their parents. To do so, he would buy the property he had been renting and charge the siblings a share of the construction costs as well as rent. With Ben's help, Menashe could also expand his leather goods establishment and put Ruth, the youngest sister, and her husband, Rich Silver, in charge of manufacturing handbags, giving them a portion of the profits.

Thus in 1934, the extended Gesheft family was reunited once again. In typical Gesheft fashion, by 1935, they had banded together to gain a foothold but never bonded in affection. Sibling rivalries were too ingrained, and jealousy and envy too rampant to allow them to overcome the obstacles families have to work out. Money—particularly as a symbol of achievement—was the central source of hostilities and shifting allegiances among the clan.

Ben cautioned Leah and Mario, "Don't be like my family. You love and look out for each other. Of all the people in the world, your own blood you should be able to trust!"

5.

El Centro

Built over a series of lagoons, Mexico City's downtown area sank several centimeters over every decade, and flooded during the rainy season.

During the dry season, honking horns blared as impatient bus drivers vented their frustration at the traffic jams formed in El Centro. Buses and a few cars vied for the right-of-way against hand-pushed carts carrying produce or chickens, hand-me-downs, or milk jugs. But when the rains came in the summer, only canoes traversed the streets, and pedestrians needed to get into waist-deep currents to cross the streets. Public Works spent much of Leah's and Mario's growing-up years trying to funnel out the rivers that downtown streets became during the rainy season. Sewers overflowed and traffic, such as it was, floated down the flooded streets of El Centro.

The air was clearer during the rainy months—no smelly diesel bus engines spewing up black grit, no pungent gasoline fumes coughed up by old jalopies in sad need of tune-ups. From May to September, the poor made an extra peso or two carrying those who could pay perched on their back, legs straddling the human burro's neck. A smirk on the carrier's face insinuated a vicarious sexual thrill as he fondled the trapped female "passenger's" legs.

For years, Goittie made it a point to warn out-of-town visitors to stay away from the downtown streets of Mexico City during the rainy season, telling of her first experience with the "summer Venice."

She took Leah shopping, and they had to wait out the afternoon storm inside the store. Once the rain let up, they tried to walk the few blocks home and realized crossing the streets would be impossible.

"I just couldn't believe it! To get across, I would need to swim! What was I going to do? No one told me to expect being swooped up by a burly local wearing a huge *sombrero* who weaved between canoes to carry me across the strong current to the other side. He didn't say a word as he came up to us, braving the water. I stood at the edge of the sidewalk, holding Leah's hand, wondering what to do, when the man wrenched my hand away and put a howling Leah astride the shoulders of a youngster who was standing next to him in the water. I screamed for the police, thinking Leah was being kidnapped! But the man kept pointing to his neck, and people around me signaled me to mount him."

After two years of summer flooding, Goittie insisted they move from the big house in Portales. Ben, Goittie, Leah, and Mario moved to a tiny apartment in Colonia Alamos, an area a bit less industrial, where the flooding was sporadic. Moving out of El Centro meant moving up. The factory was installed in a warehouse in Santa Cruz. Living in quarters separate from the business was another indication of a rise in fortunes. Paying rent on both residential and factory premises signaled the first step into the middle class. And that required a car to get to and from work; having their own transportation was further proof that the Geshefts had arrived.

By the time Ninotchka, Ben and Goittie's third child, came along in 1937, the family hired a live-in maid and moved into a more elegant area to the northeast of the city where it never flooded. The neighborhood was called *Hipódromo*, after the horseshoe the streets formed surrounding <u>Parque</u> <u>México</u>, the park around which most upwardly mobile Jewish families moved as their finances improved. Here, no matter how much the rain came down, the water never rose.

Ninotchka only had fleeting memories of the three flights of stairs up dusky corridors, bicycles stacked on the landings under the staircase at the large apartment building at Avenida de los Campeones #20. But she remembered the taste of lime scratched out from the wall around her crib well. "There's something wrong with this baby," Goittie often cried. "She's picking holes in the wall again!"

Even though the Geshefts moved out of that apartment when Ninotchka was three years old, she remembered the difficulty of undoing the knots of the bows that tied the silk mittens on her little fists. And mimicking Goittie, Ninotchka constantly screwed her face up and admonished herself out loud: "Stop it! Don't DO that!"

Next they moved to a *privada* on Tamaulipas Street, a two-story townhouse apartment built around the periphery of a long courtyard with four little apartments on each side and two apartments at the back. A towering iron railing with a gate enclosed the front part of the rectangle.

In that courtyard, Ninotchka learned to tricycle and played hopscotch with the local kids on the one-foot by one-foot squares of red tiles, while Ben and Goittie were at work and Leah and Mario were at school. Estela, the maid, kept an eye on the children through the bars of the living room window as she ran the vacuum cleaner on the ground floor. The children playing in the courtyard caught a glimpse of the pink and white checkered pattern on her uniform as she methodically tracked back and forth over the carpet.

When Estela cleaned upstairs, she could watch them from Gottie and Ben's bedroom on the second floor. Looking out, she smiled, seeing how well her son Victor was accepted by Ninotchka and the others. "This is a good family to serve, a good place for us to be. Please God, let it go on until he grows up," Estela whispered, thanking and praying in the same breath. And when she hung the laundry out to dry, Estela called out to the children, *Ey, chavos!* just to let them know she had an unobstructed view of their antics even from the roof.

The front door of the townhouse opened onto a hallway with the stairs on the left and a half wall to the living room on the right. Under the staircase, a closet-like space held a toilet and a washbasin. Still, it <u>was</u> a "second bathroom" and thus a step up in elegance in the family's living quarters.

Further along the corridor was the kitchen. Its back door opened onto an outside patio with a built-in concrete washboard and washtub and from which arose a circular iron staircase. That type of staircase is called *caracol,* the word for snail. Its name was either determined by its shape—or alluded to the painstaking slowness needed to climb it. This was the only access to the clothesline on the roof and the servants' quarters.

One curve of the spiral staircase swerved up outside the windowsill of Leah's bedroom on the second floor. Ninotchka would often sneak into the room and climb out the window onto the *caracol.* Holding onto the railing with both hands, her eyes closed to avoid looking down, her heartbeat battering inside her ears, her breath coming in spurts, her top wet with sweat, Ninotchka inched up to Estela's room.

A symbiotic nexus existed between children and their nannies in Mexico. Servants were present at every instance, within earshot, aware and contributing to the family dynamics. Yet, they were never quite thought of as family. Considered inferiors to be kept in their place, and yet, they certainly weren't strangers. They partook intimately in the family's joys and sorrows. And they were far from slaves. They could always quit; and they certainly did so if they felt disrespected. Goittie constantly reminded the three kids that they were to "treat the servants right" or they would leave. A responsible adult at home was indispensable as Ben and Goittie worked full-time, so a trusted maid quitting caused major upheaval.

"Now I have to find another one," Goittie frowned. "And I'll have to spend time training all over again," she said, rolling her eyes. "And the new maid's faults may be even more annoying."

Beyond housework, cooking, and caring for the youngsters, a maid's error served as a plausible excuse. Ben's pretext for not returning his sisters' calls was often, "The maid doesn't know how to write, so she forgets to tell me you called."

Some nannies were certainly the loving caregivers who kissed boo-boos away. As much of the day was spent under their care, they also meted out rewards and punishment. They minimized whatever transgressions the children committed and often kept the reports from Goittie to shield them from further punishment. And because they lived with the family—often for consecutive generations—they took pride in the children's accomplishments and shared their upset when they were troubled.

Ninotchka had recurring nightmares about going up the staircase, stepping on those rickety strips of iron interspersed with emptiness, held together by a thick pole in the center, and developed qualms about walking on anything that wasn't solid, like steps without backing or any type of grating where you could see what was below. She didn't understand what the reward was that impelled her to brave the climb on those rungs purveyors of terrors, until years later when Leah told her the story of how Victor, Estela's son, had been conceived.

"Estela was desperate to find a partner, mostly because she wanted a baby. She was already pretty old," Leah said, "when she paid one of the workers at the factory to 'do her the favor.' Her pregnancy caused a terrible upset among the grown-ups, but Mario and Leah thought it was cool that Estela and Goittie grew big and nursed babies together. Mother weaned you within six months while Estela followed her native tradition and continued nursing Victor for years."

The dreaded expeditions to the servants' quarters had indeed had a compelling motivation. Ninotchka sneaked up there to suckle at Estela's breast.

Estela felt very sorry for Ninotchka, seeing her at the metal door of her room on the roof, pale with fear from the climb. "Come here, little one…poor little one…so little and no *chi chi*," she cooed as she cradled Ninotchka against her enormous bosom and moved to unbutton the top of her uniform. Ninotchka nuzzled at the pink and white squares of Estela's uniform. "You can have *chi chi* up here, but it's our secret! You hear? Just

Ninotchka and Nana know…nobody else …or NO MORE *chi chi*. OK?"

Ninotchka had no problem keeping the suckling sessions a secret. Like the princesses in the stories she loved, she was royalty trapped among commoners and thus merited a wet nurse like other princesses. Her notions of majesty were given further support as Goittie and Ben shopped to buy a house. Ninotchka overheard the realtor describing a large and luxurious one as a "castle." *We're moving because a princess needs a castle to live in.*

GOITTIE'S CASTLE

7he mansion at Avenida de los Campeones #37 was the first—and only— house Ben and Goittie ever owned. In spite of their now large creditworthiness, Goittie still refused to purchase anything she couldn't pay for in cash, so they bought it outright—no loan, no mortgage. Buying "in installments," as she called it, was another of Goittie's no-nos.

Goittie was pregnant again, so the family needed more space. And now that they had the cash to purchase a house outright, Ben wanted to buy an impressive structure that would attest to his escalating position in society. They were shown multiple houses, but Ben liked this one in particular. When Goittie asked what it was about this property that made him select it, he pointed to the Star of David soldered on an outside gate. "This one was meant for Jews. People like us…" Ben replied.

Goittie liked it because it had enough bedrooms for each child to have their own. "A room of one's own is the final gift of freedom. Cherish an opportunity that having money provides to which many children will never have access."

Because of its imposing size, friends and family dubbed the house *Goittie's Castle*. Ninotchka corrected all and sundry, "No, it's *mine*, Princess Ninotchka's Castle."

The Castle framed different periods in the family's life. Each space morphed as family needs changed. It had a warm terrace for the baby to take naps in, a vantage point for a six-year-old to watch goings-on below, a patio for a cantankerous 11-year-old to learn to bike and skate, and a window to the street for a teenager to be courted with serenades.

It was the quintessential model of the Mexican colonial style. The three-story house was sequestered by a six-foot high brick and stucco fence with bars. The bars and fence were topped with menacing metal arrow-like points, a threat to all who would consider climbing in—or out! Because *The Castle's* gardens faced north, ever-threadbare grass covered the ground between the gate and front door, and only a monumental Jacaranda tree flourished in it. When they first moved there, Ninotchka sat for hours on end in the crook of its bottom two branches, daydreaming and spying on the passersby. Its branches were low enough for a six-year-old to climb, while high enough for her to look out over the railing and watch the parade below while remaining hidden from view.

From that perch, "Nini" watched the ongoing show between the two sides of the street, on the *camellón,* a walkway of reddish soil tamped down by horse, dog, and human steps. On either side of this pedestrian lane, large trees provided shelter and food to flocks of yellowthroats, robins, and sparrows. Grasses grew sparingly under the trees and discouraged anyone from sitting down, but the wrought iron benches offered a welcome respite from weariness or the heat. The benches also provided a discreet meeting place. Ninotchka could see people's flailing hands in an apparently heated discussion at one bench and a couple at another bench with their arms around each other in an embrace.

The maids hated the Jacaranda tree, as the cluster of bluebells that formed each bloom continually dropped off. Stepping on the flowers stained the cement walk leading to the house. Goittie had the maids scrub until the stains on the cement came off. To save elbow grease, the maids were out three times a day (and more when it was windy or it had rained) sweeping up the droppings before they were squished.

Ninotchka loved those blooms—their cerulean blue, her favorite color, their pungent scent a little heady. The bell-shaped flowers had a hole at the base where they were attached to the cluster. Ninotchka would string the campanules together to make necklaces hand bracelets to adorn herself and those she wanted to please.

Here, Ninotchka also concocted multiple schemes to improve the world. The fixes began with herself. If she asked Goittie to bring her a girdle from their summer trip to the United States, she'd become slim. Maybe if she hung from the branches more often, she'd build up strength and be treated like a boy. Then she'd go out into the world and make her way in it, instead of having to get married and ask some fool of a husband's permission to do anything outside the home. Maybe if she read more books, she would know everything and never have to ask questions that might make her look stupid. If she watched intently, maybe she could figure out how it was that the birds always seemed happy.

Inside, the house also followed Mexican Colonial architecture style with the Grand Hall, a large rectangular expanse, its vaulted ceiling shared by the second floor. At one corner of the hall, a circular stairway of solid red granite slabs with a wrought iron railing crowned with red cedar polished to a satiny shine, led upstairs.

The Grand Hall's terracotta tile floor was covered with an enormous Persian rug to be rolled up and put in the garage when the kids became teenagers, and Leah was to throw her much-talked-about parties. The love seats, sofa, and other occasional chairs were pushed against the walls to make room for dancing and provide the wallflowers with a place to perch and watch.

Much as Goittie disliked entertaining, she preferred that the teenagers congregate at *The Castle*. "Then I can keep an eye on you all and make sure everything is on the up and up," Goittie announced.

Ninotchka wondered what the "down-and-down" would be. But Goittie's pronouncements were delivered as commandments, and one didn't ask that kind of question. So she tried to figure out what it was by spying on the elder siblings' get-togethers. Lying flat on the corridor in front of her bedroom in her pajamas, she could peer through the elaborate railing and watch the teenagers below apparently having a great time in the Grand

Hall. It was a terrific venue for parties, and Goittie was generous with the refreshments. No alcohol, of course, but wonderful eats and soft drinks.

To the right of the entrance door off the Great Hall was the entrance to the study. It was the only room on the first floor that had a door, which Goittie kept closed while she sat for hours on end doing the accounts or writing letters. Through the front window, she could look out into the garden and monitor the comings and goings into the house.

The adolescents' nemesis—a wood quarter grandfather mantel clock—sat on the fake fireplace's mantelpiece. Goittie admired it because it kept "razor-sharp time," chiming on the quarter, the half, and the hour, then bonging the number of hours. Thus, even if she had gone to bed, she kept tabs on the time by counting the bongs. Curfews were strict, and the punishment for transgression severe. Five minutes of tardiness could mean a whole weekend of being grounded. Punctuality was another of Goittie's requirements and in her moral scale, tardiness was akin to rudeness and a lack of integrity.

Across from the study, against the left-hand wall of the Grand Hall stood an upright piano. Above it hung a signed oil portrait depicting a small, wrinkled old lady in close-up, a bandana covering her hair and a few bedraggled gladioli in her arms. It was the only original painting Goittie ever purchased and displayed. When anyone questioned her sudden interest in "real" art, she responded curtly, "She reminds me of my mother, and I like gladioli." She did. Every week the vases in the living room and grand hallway were filled with peach-colored gladioli alternating with tuberous blossoms that provided an intoxicating scent.

Archways spanned the side walls to form the entrance to the formal dining hall on one side and the living room on the other. The stately dining room was only used to entertain guests—

dinner for Ben and Goittie's card-playing friends or a birthday or engagement party. Furnished in massive early colonial furniture that combined Rococo European with musty Country Mexican, it featured a table that seated 18 guests; two matching elaborately-etched sideboards, and a large armoire distributed along the walls. The sideboards held the elegant china, cutlery, and flatware used for the special occasions. The mammoth armoire was split in half by a drawer, which held napkins, napkin rings, decks of cards, and small scoring pads and pencils. The upper half housed fancy crystal glasses that tinkled harmoniously when pinged, while the bottom half of the armoire contained all kinds of prohibited goodies—liquor and chocolates and the scrumptious biscotti and large round tins of imported dried figs and halvah from the Piggly Wiggly market. Locked doors protected the delectable treats.

Ninotchka soon discovered that the drawer could be pulled all the way out. When her arms grew long enough, she was able to reach in and grab some of the square milk chocolates studded with walnuts, wrapped in gold foil paper that were her favorites.

"I'll just eat this one—no more," Ninotchka promised herself as she triumphantly fished one out. "This is the last one. I won't ever do this again!"

She struggled with her weight until puberty and developed a lifelong allergy to chocolate—convinced it was a consequence of the pleasure she derived from getting away with two things Goittie prohibited: eating sweets between meals and stealing.

The formal living room was where the adults retreated for a little privacy, as it was difficult to see into it from the upstairs corridor. Here, Ben sat in an overstuffed armchair to read *El Universal* on Sundays. The radio—which Ninotchka found mesmerizing—occupied the farthermost corner. She was often seen next to the four-foot high, wooden artifact listening to the wonderfully resonant pitch of the music, or the voices that spoke through slats covered with a loosely woven cloth, shot through with metallic threads.

Ninotchka was an avid follower of the "Fairy Godmother" who hosted a story-telling program on weekday afternoons from 5:00 p.m. to 6:00 p.m. Being a six-year-old, she thoroughly enjoyed the fairytale, but what captivated her most was the Fairy Godmother's reading of the mail at the end of the program. Children wrote asking for magical favors from her fairy wand ("Please make my dog well" or "Please make Mommy stop cooking spinach.") The Fairy Godmother selected excerpts to read out loud and announced the writer's name. To hear her name announced over the airwaves was an achievement Ninotchka coveted obsessively.

With her rudimentary printing skills, she labored for days to put together a letter. She didn't have a favor to request—all Ninotchka really wanted was to hear her name spoken over the radio. From the moment she deposited her note in the mailbox, she thought of nothing else. She waited anxiously each afternoon for the time when the Fairy Godmother came on.

Today, Ninotchka curled up on the couch in the living room and faced the huge radio. She mentally hurried up the telling of the story, ears perked up and breath held, awaiting the important part of the broadcast. Ninotchka just knew—knew for certain—that *today* was the day the Fairy Godmother would read her note. When the letters were finally read, disappointment that hers wasn't included cast a pall on her spirits until the following afternoon.

One afternoon, as the finale music began, Mario stomped into the living room. Looking straight through Ninotchka as if she were a pillow on the couch, he walked up to the radio and switched the station to the baseball game between the Mexico City Devils and the Veracruz Tigers, his favorite team.

"Don't do that, she's about to say my name!" Ninotchka screeched at her brother.

Mario gave her a long, piercing look of disgust and flew at her to pin her down on the couch. When she squirmed to pry loose, screaming and bellowing, he pulled out one of the seat cushions, placed it over Ninotchka's face, and sat down on it, immobilizing her with his full weight. Ninotchka went quiet.

Coming in to look for Ninotchka, the maid asked, "Where's your sister? It's time for her bath."

Hearing the muffled noises, Adriana realized what Mario had been up to and had a difficult time shoving him off Ninotchka, She managed to pry a sobbing Ninotchka from under him. When Goittie and Ben came home from work a couple of hours later, they were met by a howling Ninotchka sitting on the bottom rung of the stairs with Adriana standing over her.

"I hurt inside," Ninotchka wailed, "Mario killed me."

"What did that devil do to my *kukla*?" Ben asked as he picked her up and held her close. It was just what Ninotchka needed to launch into a retelling with grandiose detail, punctuated by hiccups and sobs.

"When did this happen?" Goittie asked Adriana.

"Probably during Fairy Godmother time," Adriana replied.

"Why that was hours ago…" said Goittie turning to Ninotchka. "Why are you crying now?"

"Because you and Papa weren't here then…and because now I won't ever hear my name on the radio." Ninotchka wailed, sobbing, "*Never*, ever!"

On the second floor of *The Castle*, the bedrooms and bathrooms were distributed around the corridor. The new baby, Liliana, and the nanny hired to care for her were assigned a bedroom that faced south. Next to it was Ninotchka's room which faced the neighbors to the West. The two bedrooms that faced north had large windows and a view of the street. Leah got the rose bedroom, ideal for the next-in-line marriageable *señorita* to see and hear the serenades the prospective *novios* might bring.

As Goittie apportioned the bedrooms, Nini pointed out, "Yours is a better place to watch what happens on the street, couldn't I have it?"

Goittie said curtly, "That is the master bedroom. Master bedrooms are for the master, the *señor and señora.*"

Goittie turned what had been the sewing alcove within the Master bedroom into a large walk-in closet where she liked to "fix the rags." She had a sewing machine that was so tiny it looked like a toy, but it featured the "<u>Singer</u>" brand name on the side and could really stitch. Goittie created a system to make each cotton item "earn its keep," as she called it. First, it was an item to be worn—pajamas, underwear, blouses; the kids would pass the items down as they grew out of them, and the next sibling grew into them. When the garments tore or became worn, they became cleaning rags. Goittie methodically tore the fabric and sewed the edges back to prevent the rags from unraveling.

One rainy morning when Goittie and Leah stayed home to nurse colds, Leah took advantage of a rare opportunity to be alone with her mother and sat watching Goittie sew. The sound of the rain pelting the windows seemed to encourage reminiscences, and with no others vying for her attention, Goittie allowed herself to recount old memories. Answering Leah's questions about her childhood and growing up experiences, Goittie chatted about her dreams and hopes and how different life had become from what she expected.

"Your father gave me this sewing machine for our first anniversary," Goittie mused, her cocked head, closed eyes, and a shadow of a smile betrayed the pleasure the memory brought her.

"There wasn't much spare money in those days, so I would make your clothes. I wasn't much of a seamstress, but your aunt was accomplished with needle and thread and taught me a lot," Goittie said.

"So in those days, you all spoke to each other?" Leah asked. It was well-known that the family had split into factions, but we never knew why they stopped talking to each other.

Leah built her reputation as the depository of knowledge of prior events in the Gesheft's early history on what she learned during that rainy day conversation.

From the second floor, the stairway curved back up towards Mario's suite of rooms on the third floor. It had three large, elongated windows that provided light to the stairwell. The openings replicated triple lancet windows in medieval castles and churches, which Goittie had always admired in her history books.

The stair landing on the third floor was a vestibule with two doors leading from it. One was the door to the bedroom, and the other opened onto a terrace that covered the expanse of the second floor below. This terrace was where Mario entertained his female visitors in private *al fresco tete-a-tetes*. Ninotchka often sat on her bed listening to the scraping sounds on the ceiling when Mario had guests. *I wonder what they're up to?*

Ninotchka tended to make friends among girls older than she, teenagers whom she got along with in most matters except that they "Yuck! Liked boys!" If Mario paid attention to them, to Ninotchka's great upset, the girlfriends lost all interest in her. Once, Goittie found her slumped against the locked door of Mario's bedroom where she had cried herself to sleep.

"Esther is my best friend, and she came to play with me," Ninotchka explained when Goittie asked what she was doing there. "But Mario invited her to watch cartoons on his new 8mm projector. I could have watched too...I like cartoons... but they slammed the door shut in my face and locked it. No matter how much I knocked and begged to be allowed in, they ignored me."

Mario didn't get along much with his older sister either. He taunted Leah night and day, playing on her feelings and delighting in her reaction, whether of annoyance or embarrassment. Once, ridiculing her for the key she wore on a chain around her neck, he bet Leah he could guess and then publicize the name of the boy she pined for.

"You really think that stupid key can keep me from reading about your sissy crushes in your diary?" Mario jeered. "If I want to, I'll go on the rooftop and tell the whole u-n-i-verse whom you lo-o-o-ve! Better give me some moolah to keep quiet, or I will, I will!"

Fingering the key that never left her neck, Leah felt her secrets were safe and pretended she hadn't heard him. One evening at the dinner table, Mario feigned to read aloud a passage from an assigned novel for school as he disemboweled her 14-year-old's deepest, most embarrassing desires to the entire family. Leah found the diary vandalized; Mario had cut the leather strip that fit the teeth of the lock into their slot.

Mario was also cruel to insects. He made cages to house the flies he trapped, so as to watch them impotently beat about, trying to escape their prison. He stuck straight pins through sliced bottle cork rounds to make the bars for the cage. The last pin was not inserted until he had caught a fly in mid-air with his swooping hand and put it into the cage. To Ninotchka's disgust, he'd sometimes press too hard into his fist and squish the fly in his hand.

At times, Mario justified his barbarism by calling it an "investigation." When there were enough corks to fish out of the trash and he had the patience to make several cages, he experimented with the sounds the flies made as they tried to escape. He caged one fly with wings; another was stripped of one wing and a third left without wings, then he listened attentively to see if he could hear a symphony of buzzes.

However, Ninotchka was no angel, either. She had a particularly favorite game: to sit on the edge of the sidewalk, armed with pebbles, and throw them at passing cars, just to watch the drivers' startled reactions. Most would brake in surprise and look out the window to see what caused the *ping* on the metal. Ninotchka pulled a nonchalant expression and stared with childlike interest, holding her peals of laughter until the cars drove off. Having played this game many afternoons on her own, Ninotchka decided to initiate her cousin Lulu in this most pleasurable of dangerous pastimes.

The girls were at it for a while that day, giggling with delight at the changing look on the driver's face: first surprise, then upset, and finally resignation as they failed to discern the source of the ping. Ninotchka showed Lulu how to time her thrust carefully, waiting until there was only one car passing by so that those behind it wouldn't see the culprits in action. But on one of the throws, they threw too large a pebble and hit the back window of their target solidly, splintering the glass. The girls dashed home and hid behind Adriana's skirt when the driver rang the doorbell, but there was no avoiding the consequences. When Goittie was informed what happened, she required Ninotchka to pay back the cost of the broken window with her weekly movie allowance.

"You'll stay home from the movies for a month of Sundays," Goittie admonished. To Ninotchka, "a month of Sundays" sounded like forever.

When Leah got married and moved out in 1946, Ninotchka, now the next marriageable *señorita*, was promoted into the rose room. Although at nine years old, she was still too young to be interested in beaux or serenades, she delighted in the street view the window afforded. She could look down at the neighborhood as it stretched to wake up: the chauffeur washing the car, the garbage truck driver walking up and down the street and clanging a large bell to announce his arrival, the maids running out with garbage pails to empty them into the maw of the waiting garbage truck.

From that window, Ninotchka also had a bird's eye view of the old lady's living room in the apartment building next door to *The Castle*. She spent hours watching the interaction between the woman and the couple of people who visited her. People-watching fascinated Ninotchka; she made deductions about who they were, and how they were related and concocted scenarios about how they lived their lives. She was always discreet, so her targets had no idea they were being watched.

Shortly after Ninotchka moved into the rose room, the old woman was murdered. The news photographers' flashes alerted Ninotchka to the excitement and she learned what had happened from the rumors flying around the neighborhood. Although she hadn't witnessed the murder, she knew who visited at the time the woman was killed. As soon as Goittie got home, Ninotchka told her they had to go next door to tell the police.

"We'll do no such thing, Ninotchka," Goittie sputtered, "snooping through windows is not what a well-brought-up child does…you should mind your own business. Other people's lives are not your business. Nor is accusing people of murder!"

Ninotchka was adamant. "Ma, I *know* who murdered her," she informed Goittie. "I watched from my window…she was yelling at one of her nephews who sometimes comes to see her. He had a knife in his hand. And then there were the flashes and I ran down to see what was going on, and the ambulance came and took her away in a little cart all wrapped up in a white bundle and the maids said she was dead. Killed with a knife!"

"You do go on, Ninotchka," Goittie answered. "You imagine all kinds of things and now it's a scene from a murder mystery play! I'll move you back to your old room if you keep making things up. This is not child's play!"

Not wanting to lose the upgrade in her sleeping arrangements, Ninotchka didn't mention the murder case again but kept her ears open for tidbits from the maids' underground rumor mill. They changed the subject every time she asked about the case, in fear of Goittie's edict to never again speak about what happened next door. Ninotchka was devastated that Goittie had said she "made things up." She knew that her mother hated lying and that she said God took away from liars what they loved most. What Ninotchka loved most was being Goittie's favorite. She *had* to prove to her mother that she hadn't made anything up and that she wasn't a liar!

Ninotchka often heard Ben point to an item in the newspaper as proof of something he said. It seemed that if it was in the paper, it was the truth.

"Daddy, how do you find what you are looking for?" she asked, pointing to *El Universal* in his hands. Ben was delighted that his little girl showed an interest in the news, the source of much of his pleasure in life since his first acquaintance with dailies in Rumania.

"It depends on what you're looking for. If it's news of the world, it's in this part of the paper called a 'section,'" Ben answered.

"No, I want news of this neighborhood," Ninotchka said.

"Well, if there's anything that's worth reporting from the area, it'll be in this one—the local section," Ben said as he handed it to her.

Ninotchka scanned the local section of *El Universal* every day for news of the investigation into *The Castle's* neighbor's death. When the newspaper reported who murdered the old lady, she'd be able to point to it and Goittie would know she told the truth. Ninotchka imagined the conversation with her mother as she brought her the newspaper and pointed out where it said the old lady had been murdered by her nephew.

"See, ma, I told you the truth, but you wouldn't believe me!"

"The truth about what, Nini? You do go on and on about things…what did you find in the newspaper that validates whatever you were going on about at the time?"

"About the old lady next door, ma, remember? I kept telling you we should let the police know I recognize the murderer." Ninotchka was so excited that she jumped up and down. "See, it says right here they found him and he will be put in jail." In Nini's mind, she could see Goittie gulping as she read the paper then turning to her and embracing her.

"You told the truth," Goittie would smile. "Good for you. But little girls shouldn't get mixed up in adult concerns. Let the police do their job and don't get involved."

But still, Ninotchka would feel vindicated and continue being her mother's favorite, and Goittie would be ever so proud when she learned that Ninotchka went looking on her own and now knew how to find what was most important to her mother: the truth.

The Geshefts moved into *Goittie's Castle* in April of 1942, just as news of the possible escalation of U.S. involvement in the war in Europe was uppermost in everyone's mind. As ever, Ben and Goittie's diametrically opposed personalities tinted their perception and influenced their responses accordingly.

Goittie worried, mostly about the possibility of Ben being called up for military service. They repeatedly discussed whether they needed to return to the U.S. Finally, at Goittie's insistence, they consulted with an attorney who worked at the U.S. Department of Justice to advise them. He informed Ben and Goittie that military registration to take part in the draft lottery was still voluntary, and citizens who were longtime residents abroad had not yet been required to return stateside. So the Geshefts decided to continue living in Mexico until Ben was required to register. Still, Goittie was concerned that their friends and customers might consider them unpatriotic Americans.

Ben was excited. As long as he didn't have to fight *in* the war, he looked forward to the business opportunities he was certain would come as a *result* of the war. Years ago, the war he prayed for as a youngster arrived in his village to rid him of his brother, favorably altering his circumstances, and he now looked forward to what this new war might have in store for him.

AT LONG LAST

Mexico City

*F*rom 1940 to 1942, Ben traveled to the United States several times a year to purchase raw material to manufacture the cutlery. The material—called scrap metal—came from smelting down decommissioned ships' hulls and railroad cars and was sold to the highest bidder at auction. He became a well-known figure among the wheelers and dealers who attended the auctions in the shipyards of North Carolina and railroad yards in Texas. With his innate conviviality and blustering, expansive personality, Ben made many friends among other business owners who manufactured goods from scrap metal.

At the auctions, everyone expressed concern about the scarcity of raw materials.

"If the U.S. does enter the war, I'm afraid laws will be passed restricting metal for use exclusively for the war effort," said the buyer from U.S. Steel.

"That'll put us all out of business," Ben added, groaning at the thought.

"This is the U.S.! We're a capitalist society, no way they're going to shutter manufacturing down," exclaimed the representative from Bethlehem Steel.

On December 5, 1942, President Roosevelt ended voluntary registration; now, Ben would be breaking the law if he didn't register at the American Embassy. Fortunately, that presidential order also set the conscription cut-off age at 38. Ben was 42, so the chance that his registration would be called up was, for the moment, eliminated. And no one could accuse him of having left the States to avoid the draft, as he had lived abroad for years before the war started. But Goittie worried: *would Ben, the pacifist, be looked at by their clients and friends as Ben, the cowardly Jew, a gringo draft resister?*

After the attack on Pearl Harbor, they feared Ben would somehow be drafted—despite his age—if he crossed the border, so it was decided that Goittie would travel to purchase the raw material. Although the war hadn't reached American shores, its effects were felt at every turn within the U.S. transportation system. Schedules went haywire as trains were canceled, bus seats were commandeered to accommodate soldiers, and local transportation became spotty at best, given the scarcity of gasoline.

Those trips were exhausting and accommodations were particularly uncomfortable for women. In a strongly patriarchal society, females traveling on their own—above all for business—were still an oddity.

With Goittie away at the auctions in the States, Ben paced and glowered while he kept the factory running. He missed going on those buying trips. He liked spending time around other buyers and was sure he could have extracted more concessions or a better price from the sellers. His greatest regret was that the window of opportunity was closing; the way the war was going, all metal would soon be requisitioned by the military. Fear gnawed at him—how could they continue to stay in business if they had no raw material from which to manufacture product?

In late 1944, a form letter arrived from the U.S. Embassy warning that citizens living abroad in non-aligned countries would no longer be under the protection of the U.S. government. It recommended that all U.S. citizens return home as soon as possible to ensure their safety. If naturalized citizens stayed abroad, the government didn't want to use its limited resources to protect them, so unless they returned, they ran the risk of losing their citizenship.

Ben and Goittie sat long into the night, first listening to the world news and then discussing their options. "What happens if we lose our citizenship?" Goittie asked. "Will we become *apátridas*—citizens without a country? Think of the many people we know sitting around waiting for Mexican citizenship... and it's practically impossible to get now."

"Surely they can't expect us to return to the old country?" Ben sputtered. "We need to ask a lawyer."

They debated what they ought to do when a letter *requiring*, not *recommending*, their return arrived, as it surely would. Given the news from Europe, the U.S. government would undoubtedly soon give naturalized U.S. citizens a firm deadline to leave Mexico; the Geshefts would then be forced to either comply or forfeit the right to go back.

Every evening after dinner, once Leah had gone up to her room, Ben and Goittie said goodnight to Ninotchka and the baby before the nanny took them to bed. The parents then sat down in the formal living room, one on each side of the cherry wood radio cabinet, to listen to news from the battlefronts. Sonorous male voices boomed out from behind the woven gold metallic cloth, interspersed with crackling sounds that they imagined might well be the sound of artillery.

While they listened to the darkening news from the European front and the recent reports of the Japanese campaign, Ben and Goittie's anguish grew. It was imperative that they decide whether to return to the States.

"Aren't you afraid of going to fight?" Goittie asked.

"And you? Aren't you worried about losing our American citizenship?" Ben said. "That's what'll happen if we don't go back. And yet, going back…even if I can manage to find some way to stay out of combat…"

Ben stopped abruptly.

Ben couldn't even verbalize the thought of once again being an employee, going back to the days of clocking in. He was loathe to face giving up his privileged position as a successful entrepreneur. It wasn't about the money, he'd never been interested in being rich; now that he had a large business enterprise, a showcase house, a car, and the funds to support that lifestyle, he had nothing he wanted to spend on. Although, it felt good to donate large sums to Jewish charitable organizations, the Jewish schools, and the Jewish old folks home; he liked supporting those less well-to-do and it increased his standing in the community. *It might help to be thought of as 'gospodin.'*

Returning to the U.S. meant having to take orders either from a superior in the Army or a supervisor in a job. He clearly remembered when he had sworn *I will never again work for anyone else.*

And much as Goittie anticipated a return to America, she feared with increasing certainty that to remain a U.S. citizen, Ben would have to go to war. The dream of returning to a less ostentatious life, of reliving the closeness to the days when they were first married, of weekends of having a good time with their friends, would have to be put off until after the War ended.

There were other considerations as well: their oldest daughter, Leah, had been dating Daniel for several years, and they were talking about eventually marrying, even though Daniel was years away from being able to support her. If Ben and Goittie were forced to go back to the States, Leah would surely balk at leaving!

"It's not going well for the Jews in Europe," Ben lamented as he turned the radio off.

"It doesn't ever go well for Jews anywhere," Goittie sighed, thinking of her mother and sisters. She hadn't heard from them since she'd left the *shtetl*, more than two decades before. Goittie assumed they had perished in Stalin's Russia during the *pogroms.*

"At least the Geshefts were among the lucky ones to get out to safety. We didn't have any family left for the Nazis to turn into soap. And it has gone pretty well for us right here!" Ben said, gesturing to their surroundings.

"But, are Jews safe here?" Goittie's worried tone made Ninotchka's stomach flutter as she eavesdropped from her upstairs listening post. And her father's words reminded her of the bar of soap her cousin Lulu's mother kept on the mantelpiece in their living room, so they'd never forget. Ninotchka wondered whose body was burned for the soap she washed with.

"Certainly safer than at the front," Ben answered.

"We have to decide," Goittie said. "Putting this off doesn't do any good; we need to get on with it!" But still, they couldn't make up their minds, so Goittie called it a night with her ritual phrase, "Let's sleep on it."

The Mexican lawyer they consulted advised them they'd have no trouble obtaining Mexican citizenship should they apply for it, so Ben and Goittie decided not to decide. They did not reply to the warning letter and allowed their U.S. citizenship to be revoked. They were granted Mexican citizenship very quickly as they had resided in the country for a long time, were important investors, and had four children born in the country.

Becoming Mexican citizens brought an unforeseen benefit: they were now foreigners in the U.S. As *aliens*, the Geshefts were able to lawfully purchase scrap metal that hadn't been declared strategic war materiel to export to Mexico, a non-aligned country. Scrap metal could not be sold to American firms unless it had been declared unusable for the war effort. Now, Ben traveled to the States as a Mexican, making regular appearances at the periodic shipyard and railroad yard auctions. He discovered that he was able to bid for the raw material for export at lower prices as there were fewer dealers to compete against. *Government regulations sometimes just don't go as planned...*

Then, it occurred to Ben that, being a foreigner, he was not prohibited from reselling the material itself. *Why, I could make a fortune by marking up the scrap metal and selling it to manufacturers in the U.S.* He contracted for twice the scrap metal required to keep the cutlery production going smoothly and shipped half of it to Mexico. The other half was sold to the dealers he had previously bid against, who clamored and paid top price for the material they were barred by the Export Control Act from buying directly.

By the time the War ended, Ben was the principal provider of raw material to the largest manufacturer of reinforcing bars for construction in the U.S. Bethlehem Steel simply bought the contract of the scrap metal Ben purchased and paid him a 10% overage. No shipping, no production line, no fuss! Ben rubbed his hands together: he was making enormous profits without having to invest any capital, man-hours, or payroll to put the material through the entire production-through-delivery cycle.

Extremely satisfied with his ingenuity and flush with income, Ben wanted his achievements admired; he needed to visually display his success to society in general and his hated brother Menashe in particular. He couldn't imagine more tangible evidence of having progressed on the road towards great wealth than parking a brand new sleek, black Cadillac outside his mansion. So he put in the order for one and hoped the wait for it wouldn't be very long—when it arrived, it would be the perfect match to the elegance of the *Castle*. In the meantime, he insisted Goittie hire more maids so that the elegance and cleanliness of both automobile and mansion could be maintained. After all, a castle requires multiple servants for proper upkeep!

Goittie had a different response to the change in their circumstances. A rise in economic status was not something to be flaunted. *Money doesn't change who you are…even if he becomes a millionaire he'll never be anything more than an uneducated Jew who was lucky.* But she went ahead and hired more help. She employed a chambermaid to clean the house and do the washing and hired a full-time nanny to take care of baby Liliana, who was now a toddler. Feeding the family members plus cooking for the additional servants became a full-day enterprise, so she hired a live-in cook.

But Goittie was a little ashamed that Ben had motives and aspirations so alien to hers. She never approved of Ben's purchase of luxury transportation and referred to his Cadillac as the "beloved cart."

"Look, look," Goittie said to Ben's siblings, pointing to a diminutive "beetle" Volkswagen which had just begun production in Mexico. "That's what Ben's 'beloved cart' looks like."

"But doesn't he drive a Cadillac?" Jake asked. "That's a… that's not a luxury auto; it's the people's car, the cheapest auto one can buy. Surely Ben wouldn't buy a German car, would he? "

"Oh, I think his car looks just like that. I guess he must have paid more to call it a Cadillac and American, which I'm sure you know he can well afford. Yes, yes, that looks just like his 'beloved cart,'" Goittie smirked.

Goittie refused to learn to drive but soon employed a man to help with heavy cleaning chores and drive her to work or to run her errands and the kids to school. Having a chauffeur increased Ninotchka's sense of entitlement.

After the war, most steel reinforcement bars produced in the U.S. were shipped across the Atlantic for the reconstruction of war-torn Europe. At the same time, Mexico was experiencing an explosion in population growth, which required building multiple low-income housing projects by the Mexican government. Anticipating an increase in demand for rebar—the backbone of all those government construction projects—Ben decided to build a steel mill to produce the steel rods in Mexico. His contacts with steel manufacturers in the U.S. would provide advice on the best way to do so.

"What do you think, Goittie, isn't it a terrific idea?"

"It's a terrible idea. You need to get enmeshed in a new business like you need a hole in the head. Why do you want to make yourself crazy?"

"It's such a wonderful opportunity—the need for rebar is already enormous and no one else is manufacturing it—it has to be imported. We could end the importation the way we stopped imports of cutlery when we first came. We'll be responsible for much of the building going on. We can become multi-millionaires."

"What would you do with more money? Why do you need more than you already have?"

"I'll just do some research into what it will take, then we can talk about it again," Ben said. *I'd better drop the subject now. If I find out it's doable, I'll have to talk her into it.*

Goittie opposed the project for many reasons. She always counted on and made plans for their return to the United States one day, and now that the War was over—thankfully—she thought it was time to do so. She recalled the years they'd spent in New York with the fondness people reserve for the carefree days of childhood.

"Remember when we first came here after the stock market crash," Goittie asked, "and we agreed that Mexico was to be only an interlude?"

"You weren't so crazy about our life back in New York," Ben reminded her, "we couldn't go out without having to ask for favors. Don't you love having in-house babysitters?"

"I don't like living in a fishbowl where the servants can see and hear everything that goes on. I liked the days when New York was our oyster, and our private life was private, instead of being lived among the servants, silent but observant critics of the disparity between the economic classes. They're waiting to start a revolution to overthrow their bondage, and all of a sudden, I find myself on the side of the oppressors!"

After Trotsky's murder in 1940, Goittie severed all communist connections and even stopped considering herself a socialist, but she still believed having more than enough money was detrimental to one's moral health and a bad example to one's children. Creating another factory was lusting after wealth, and how were they ever to go back to the simple life they'd had in New York if Ben kept accumulating businesses? She dreamed of a return to the days when they lived on a salary, had no servants, and Ben dried the dishes she washed. That was Goittie's version of a simple life of *togetherness*.

Now that he was so successful, Ben yearned to be more than an entrepreneur. Cubiertos Gesheft was lucrative, but it did not symbolize true power. It was just a first step that provided the funds to realize his childhood dream—to be addressed as *gospodin* or its equivalent wherever he ended up living. Cutlery was a minor product; he wanted to manufacture what would build the country's infrastructure; to be awarded the respect that came from producing the steel underpinning of the offices, apartments, and public buildings that sprang up in the post-war economy; to become a prominent businessman who merits respect; to wield the power that a valuable contribution to his adopted country would accord; to have *Gospodin* before his name.

Although Goittie always managed to have her decisions honored, she couldn't risk her authority being challenged. So she was careful about where to dig in her heels and picked only those instances where she felt likely to prevail. Meddling with Ben's ambition was a risky proposition, so she trod carefully, trying first to dissuade him with reasoned arguments as Ben was no match for her logical thinking.

"*Say you-who!*" Goittie began. "How many suits can you wear at the same time?" When Goittie called him "*You-who*" Ben sensed trouble; it was as if she had removed his individuality and addressed him as a non-entity.

"Do you need to go into yet *another* business?" she asked rhetorically. She knew what the answer was. It was her way of signaling disagreement, hoping not to have to prohibit the project outright.

"It's a golden opportunity; we have access to the process and are first in line for raw material. The Mexican government has offered to close down the borders for any product not currently manufactured in Mexico. We'll be exclusive providers to a single client with enormous demand, plus tax advantages and interest-free loans to set up the factory," Ben ticked off the business reasons he hoped Goittie's mindset would accept as sound.

"All of that is still in the future, and I refuse even to consider the business aspect until we thrash out the bottom line; why do we need another business, golden though it may be?" Goittie retorted, escalating to the next step, moving into the territory of values, where Ben floundered in a sea of relativism and she felt secure. Where values were concerned, Goittie knew exactly what to do: she simply did *what was right.*

Ben didn't know how to express his need to continually increase his control over life's circumstances. It was the same need that got him out from under his brother Menashe's thumb, drove him to immigrate, first to Rumania, then to the U.S., and finally to Mexico, creating more and more sources of income. But because he couldn't come up with a rational explanation to justify his decision to establish a new steel foundry in Mexico, his stubbornness flared up. So he turned to the *because I say so—* with which adults often shelter themselves when they've run out of convincing, deliberative strategies.

Thus, whether to establish a steel factory or not became a tug-of-war, a tussle between two strong-willed individuals that degenerated at first into not speaking to each other and eventually into threats, the very foundation of their marriage being called into question. Both Goittie and Ben felt the outcome would establish a precedent; whoever lost out would be forced to adhere to the decision. This struggle would redefine "who had the last say."

Ninotchka listened intently to the raised voices in the continual arguments. For years, she eavesdropped on their discussions, lying flat on her habitual listening post: the cold red granite slab in the corridor outside her bedroom door. But now the voices sounded different, there was a new tone, even scarier than the ones that wafted up during wartime. Now Goittie's voice was raised in anger, not trembling with concern as it had been then, and her mother repeatedly said "I" or "me" instead of "we" or "us." Her parents were entrenched on opposite sides of whatever was going on, and Ninotchka realized it must be serious because Goittie was making increasingly severe threats.

"I will not have it. As you know, *adversity makes you human, prosperity makes you monstrous*," Goittie hissed, quoting another favorite aphorism.

Ninotchka's heart skipped a beat and then beat faster, as if making up for having stopped. Her mother was using other people's words—when she used others' words, it was a sign that the final battle line was being drawn.

"Are you saying I'm a monster?" Ben retorted, raising his voice. "What are you talking about?"

"Shush, don't talk so loud, you'll wake the kids," Goittie said. "I'm saying building another factory is looking for trouble. I'm saying I don't approve of it."

Ben clutched his face. "What can I do to have you give the idea a chance? I want you on my side, not fighting me. You know how much I have always wanted to be secure and independent."

"I am on your side, that's why I don't want you starting a steel mill, particularly when you are already secure and independent. Tell me what you're missing that a steel mill will provide, other than more worries and starting with a new business all over again, worrying about financing and sales and more profits. I won't let you start a new business!"

"You won't *let* me? I've always gone along with what you say because you are brilliant and you are my wife, but I don't need your permission. At least think about the plans I've laid out and see if you can change your opposition."

"If you continue with these plans, I will divorce you," was Goittie's culminating dictum.

Divorce was a terrible word. Although Ninotchka wasn't sure what it meant for her, she knew Goittie would keep her word if her father went ahead with his plan. Surely Ben wouldn't cross Goittie once she had expressed the threat; establishing another factory was non-negotiable. All four children felt an impending sense of doom as Goittie stopped addressing Ben directly and applied the ice treatment.

For months, the entire household seemed to hold its breath. Everyone tiptoed around in an environment where the atmosphere twanged with silent tension, waiting to see who would back down. Even baby Liliana seemed to sense the upset, adding her constant howling to the palpable frustration in the house. *What would Ben decide to do? Would Goittie really divorce him if he went ahead with his plans?* Surely, Goittie would have the last word and no new steel mill would come to be.

The impasse continued, but remained simmering in the background, as daily life went on and other issues needed to be addressed. Leah and Mario were now teenagers and Goittie often found occasion to repeat her adage: *little children ruin your nights, grown children ruin your life.*

As Mario grew older, his schemes and practical jokes to harass Leah and Ninotchka became more and more dangerous. "I've had it with the incessant torture you inflict upon your sisters," Goittie announced when she returned from the hospital with baby Liliana in a cast. Mario had incited the toddler to emulate him and slide down the banister from the second to the first floor. Liliana slipped off and broke both legs in the fall. "I warned you…if you didn't stop your rash and thoughtless tricks, we would come to a point where the only solution would be to send you away."

Goittie worried that Mario behaved like a consummate bully, picking on his sisters because they were weaker than he. Of course, she couldn't take action without consulting Ben and was forced to give up the ice treatment to discuss the best way to discipline Mario.

Ben was delighted that the storm seemed to be over and Goittie was speaking to him again. He concurred with her plan to exile Mario. "With all these girls in the house, it's best he be only among boys. And military school should teach him discipline."

As Mario had not yet gone through the growth spurt that 14-year-olds typically have at that age, Goittie thought being among older boys would put him at the receiving end of bullying and perhaps help him see the victim's point of view. He was enrolled at Virginia Military Academy in Lexington.

"Maybe I'll get to use guns," Mario relished his banishment. "It'll be *vunderbar* to be away from girls altogether. This house reeks of female—even the dog is a bitch." Mario was not to come home again—except for summers or special occasions—for the next nine years.

The inhabitants of the *Castle* felt a collective sense of relief as the emotional atmosphere relaxed; Ben and Goittie's communications were back to usual, and with Mario gone, there was little infighting among the girls. Ben stopped talking about the steel mill. And there was no more talk of divorce. Goittie and Ben had new family issues to deal with.

Leah and her boyfriend Daniel had become *novios* when they met at the Jewish winter camp in Veracruz four years earlier. *Novios* literally means *bride and groom* and signifies a couple's betrothal: an announcement to the world that a couple planned to marry as soon as it was feasible. It was the equivalent of the 1960s ritual of becoming "engaged to be engaged," two steps away from marriage itself.

From the moment they paired up, Leah and Dan behaved like husband and wife in all but the marriage bed. By now, Leah was 18—a ripe old age, according to the tenets of the post-war Mexican Jewish community—past which time unmarried young women stood on the verge of spinsterhood. Daniel was only 20 years old and still in school; it would be another decade before he became a doctor and could support a wife. Goittie feared that if the *novios* were forced to wait that long to consummate their union, Leah might lose her maidenhead before marriage.

Daniel's capacity to earn a living was pushed back one more year into the future when he pulled a *black ball* in the military draft lottery. He'd have to take a year off from school for the compulsory military training. A married man was exempted from the training, so circumstances converged, prompting the wisdom of setting an early wedding date for the lovebirds.

Daniel's parents were summarily invited to dinner at the Castle so they could meet Ben and Goittie and discuss options for their children's future as a couple.

The lead-up to a wedding resembled a preset ballet piece, with ancestrally designed choreography, where each point and counterpoint step was cued and followed until the dance was completed. Daniel's ancestors were also Ashkenazi Jews from the Russian Pale, although they migrated one generation earlier than the Geshefts and arrived in Mexico via Vienna instead of New York. Still, they all danced to the same music.

The bond between two sets of Jewish parents of children who intended to marry was another peculiarity of Jewish customs, forged from an intricate set of relationships so foreign to non-Jews that it had no counterpart word in the English language. *Mekhutonim,* which was what the relationship was called, could be loosely defined as "in-laws who may feel free to take liberties restricted to members of the inner family circle." Although in-laws were treated with the apparent inclusiveness reserved for friends, they were often disparaged as acquaintances who "pretended to familiarity." In reality, their bond resembled corporate board members; they were engaged in an enterprise that could aptly be named Grandchildren, Inc.

During the dinner at The Castle, the new enterprise reached an executive decision. Daniel would forgo his medical studies and, in the tradition of Ashkenazi Jews, go to work at the bride's family business to ensure sufficient income to start and support a family. Once the items of the dowry—who would pay for the wedding, the newlyweds' honeymoon, and abode—had been discussed, haggled, and agreed upon, plans were made to hold the wedding the following year.

Goittie's personality was not conducive to thriving in such a relationship; she was studiously reclusive. Mary, her long-ago roommate, was the only person she ever confided in, and that stopped once they both married. The expectation of intimacy from the groom's mother was exactly why Goittie abhorred the in-law familiarity. She felt she acquired another set of siblings who had to be made privy to what was going on within the family. What Goittie considered private now needed to be shared with those not bound by nuclear family loyalty. So every attempt Daniel's family made to increase their connection was rebuffed by Goittie, in the same way she had managed to keep her distance from Ben's family.

Yet Goittie was careful to follow the prescribed steps in the pre-nuptial dance. The next round in the pre-wedding festivities was a dinner offered by the groom's parents at *their* home. The following month, they sat around a small dining room table discussing how Daniel would be incorporated into the Gesheft's family business.

"Will Daniel be working at the new steel mill?" The groom's father asked after the coffee and cake had been served and the servants dismissed.

"I...we...haven't really decided where we'll put him," Ben stuttered, his face a flaming red. "I'm not...it's not certain... we aren't really sure when the steel mill will be up and running." And to change the touchy, unresolved subject, he turned to Daniel and said, "We'll have Goittie give you a tour of the cutlery factory on Monday."

"What new steel mill, Ben?" Goittie queried, her face a thunderbolt.

Her tone dripped acid and silenced the room. After a long interval, everyone attempted to bridge over the palpable tension with small talk about the meal and the upcoming weather. Clearly, the evening needed to be cut short and everyone seemed relieved when Ben reminded Leah it was a school night and they'd better say their goodnights.

Goittie didn't say a word until they were home. Once inside The Castle, she turned to Ben and, almost hissing, said, "Over my dead body, there'll be a steel mill."

In a quiet whisper, with a frog in his throat that sounded almost like a sob, Ben said. "It's too late. I've closed the deal!"

"I will never step a foot in that factory. I will train Daniel and by the time of Leah's wedding, he will be ready to take my place at Cubiertos Gesheft," Goittie announced.

Ben accomplished the unthinkable: he hadn't buckled under Goittie's opposition and bought the smelting furnace and purchased land past the northern exit of Mexico City, where he could buy in hectares what meters cost within the city.

Laminadora Gesheft, the only steel mill in the country, was established and began production in 1951. The Mexican government closed the borders to imported rebar, so Ben's factory produced the only steel rods for sale in Mexico. He had, in effect, managed to corner the supply of steel rebar for the construction market, and he won the power struggle against Goittie. Divorce was never mentioned again, but after Daniel and Leah married, Goittie became a full-time housewife and mother. She never stepped inside the premises of Laminadora Gesheft, and refused to acknowledge its existence.

It had taken 30 years, but Binyamin/Ben finally achieved his destiny: to become a powerful mogul. As a child, circumstances helped him break the hierarchy of birth order to become the breadwinner, even though he was the youngest male in the family. The intensity of his drive for success, three migrations—from Russia to Rumania to the U.S. to Mexico—and years of hard work allowed him to amass enough power to merit the title of respect he had yearned for. As a youngster, he dreamed of one day having people place *Gospodin*—the title accorded to respected members of society in the old country—before his name. The equivalent of *Gospodin* in Mexico was *Don*, originally the acronym for **De Origen Noble**, signifying "of noble origin."

At Laminadora Gesheft, the staff and foremen addressed Ben as "*Don* Benito," which was music to Ben's ears. He felt the honorary title in Spanish rounded out the real meaning of his name in Spanish: one who is blessed.

Glossary

YIDDISH	MEANING
Adonai	our Lord
beseider	agreed
bobe maises	old wives' tales
boychik	little boy
chai	tea
challahs	braided loaves of yeast-leavened bread
cheder	school
cholent	stew
dumbkof	dumbbell
gefilte	stuffed
gelt	money
goldeneh mazal	golden luck

YIDDISH	MEANING
Goldeneh Medina	Golden Country
gospodah	Russian title of respect
goy	non-Jewish
greenhorn	one who is unfamiliar with the ways of a place or group.
groschen	cents
gutte neshumah	kind-hearted soul
guverniya	territorial division of Imperial Russia
hausfrau	housewife
heshboiness	accounts
iungatsh	brat
kadish	prayer after the death of a close relative
kishkah	intestines
kopeks	bills
kukla	doll
kvetching	complaining
laideggaier	lazy good-for-nothing
lantzmen	fellow Jews who come from the same district or town
lei	Rumanian currency
mamzer	bastard
mein liebe	my love
meshugaz	crazy idea
mincha	afternoon service

YIDDISH	MEANING
minyan	ten adults - number required for religious services
mitzvah	worthy deed
pecorlich	type of pastry
pogroms	officially encouraged massacre or persecution of a minority group
Shabbos, Shabbat	Sabbath
shiksele	non-Jewish young woman
shivah	seven-day period of formal mourning
shul	temple
Tatte	father
undzere shtetl	our village
vunderbar	wonderful
yokel	rustic; a bumpkin.
zeide	grandfather
zeijl	brains

Acknowledgments

So many family and writing group members, friends, mentors, and readers have contributed to the completion of this long-delayed project that it would take several pages to list you by name. You know who you are: A heartfelt "thanks" to each one of you for your indispensable support.

A special acknowledgment for their assistance in creating the maps to Tina Engels, Carla Itzkowich and Jon Golding.

Author bio

Norma Armon is an immigrant, as were her parents and grand-parents. She vividly recreates the experience of otherness and the quest for integration while continuing to live within the values of the culture of origin. This is the first novel of a planned trilogy. Norma Armon was born in Mexico and has lived in the U.S. since 1977.

9 781952 281716